MOVING ON

"Why are you putting yourself through this?"

"Because . . . because I came here to set things straight between Buck and me, to tell him what I thought of him, and to expose him to the town for the man he was—a womanizer, an adulterer, a man who ruined lives without ever looking back. I needed to do that to move on."

"And the way he is now, you can't do it."

"No."

"You're only torturing yourself, Honor. Nothing is going to get better if you stay here. It'll only get worse."

"You can't be sure of that."

"I'm sure."

"So you want me to run away. You want me to leave before I do what I came here to do."

"I want you to stay clear of the trouble you're heading for."

"I won't run."

"Don't be a fool, Honor!"

"Better to be a fool than a coward!"

His hands grasped her shoulders as Jace said, "Listen to me! I know what I'm talking about. I know how things can be twisted into tragedy. You're heading for more heartache."

Wrenching herself free, Honor said, "You're not the man I thought you were. I thought there was some part of you that felt what I felt. I thought you understood, but I was wrong."

TEXAS GLORY

ELAINE BARBIERI

LEISURE BOOKS NEW YORK CITY

To my husband, Ben,
my greatest supporter, my best friend,
and my "other half" who makes me whole.
What would I do without you?

A LEISURE BOOK®

September 2004

Published by

Dorchester Publishing Co., Inc.
200 Madison Avenue
New York, NY 10016

ISBN 0-8439-5408-6

The name "Leisure Books" and the stylized "L" with design are trademarks of Dorchester Publishing Co., Inc.

Printed in the United States of America.

Visit us on the web at www.dorchesterpub.com.

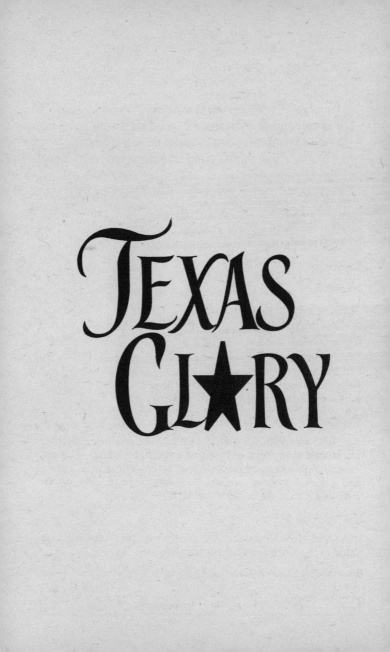

Prologue

Marston, Texas, 1869

The darkness of night enveloped Honor Gannon's bedroom in shadow. Uncertain what had awakened her, she sat up abruptly in bed. At the sound of a footstep, she demanded, "Who's there?"

She gasped with terror at the sight of a figure moving rapidly toward her. Her feet had barely touched the floor when the weight of a heavy male body knocked her backwards against the bed, pinning her there with its weight. Struggling to break free of the rough hands that tore at her nightdress, she scratched and pounded, kicked and gouged her attacker. She was fighting furiously when she heard him mutter, "I'll teach you . . ."

Struck an unexpected blow, Honor felt consciousness dim. The acrid taste of blood filled her mouth as the man slurred, "That's right, lie back . . . because I've got something for you that you'll never forget."

Her strength returning in a sudden burst of fury, Honor kicked the fellow with all her might. His howling response was still echoing in the silent room when she scrambled toward her dresser. Breathless, she turned back toward him with gun in hand.

Her assailant took a lunging step toward her and she rasped, "Stop where you are!"

He hesitated, then took another step.

Her gun aimed directly at the bulge below his belt, Honor responded, "All right, come on if that's what you want. I'm a good shot, but I won't kill you. I'll just make you wish you were dead."

Honor felt his uncertainty. She watched him step back, swaying unsteadily as he said, "Hold your horses." She glimpsed his sneer as he continued, "I only sneaked in here because everybody in town was laying bets on who'd be the first fella to take you. Well, it ain't going to be me, and I don't give a damn. You ain't worth the price I'd have to pay. I'm leavin'."

The drunken cowpoke's words cut deep as he turned away from her abruptly and staggered to the window, then slipped out clumsily into the darkness.

An icy rage enveloped Honor as she stared at the open window. She fought to control her shuddering as she pulled her torn nightdress closed over her breasts. She had faced that degenerate's kind of thinking all her life. Before her mother died, she had defied it. She had told herself she was smart, had a quick mind, and was capable of supporting herself without a man's help just as her mother had done. She had convinced herself that adversity had made her stronger and wiser than most girls her age, and that those attributes allowed her to rise above the painful innuendos.

But her mother was dead now, and everything had changed.

Honor walked to the window and locked it tight despite the heat of the night. She then returned to the dresser, lit the lamp there, and drew open the bottom drawer. She removed a carefully bound pack of letters, revealing letters she had found lying in a drawer beside an old diary after her dear mother died a few months earlier. The letters had been written by her mother over a period of years to the man who had fathered her only child. Those letters her mother had never mailed.

Honor clutched the packet, a familiar ache twisting tight inside her. Despite her mother's protests, Honor had always suspected she was illegitimate. Unfortunately, so did everyone else in the small Texas town they called home. The resulting problems had multiplied as she grew older. They had finally culminated in the attack she had barely escaped minutes earlier.

Unable to stop herself, Honor sat back on the bed and opened the first letter, then the second. She read them all again, one by one, as she had many times before. The familiar words of her mother's anguish echoed through her, stirring a deep, responsive distress as the story unfolded.

Betty Gannon had been married to a much older man whom she admired and respected, yet she was unable to stop herself from falling in love with the handsome, sympathetic husband of her closest friend. At a moment of great emotional stress after her husband's death, Betty had succumbed to her feelings and shared an afternoon of loving intimacy with her friend's husband.

Ashamed of her actions afterwards, Betty was unable to face her friend. When she discovered she was pregnant, she was distraught. Panicking, she sold her ranch, paid off the longstanding debts, and left town. She traveled as far as her limited remaining funds allowed, and found work in Marston, Texas. Using her maiden name, she raised Honor while continuing to love the same undeserving man until the day she died.

Honor's hand clenched unconsciously tight, crumpling her mother's final letter as a tear slipped down her cheek. Her mother had been too deeply in love to realize that the man she loved had merely used her, as he had doubtless used many women before her. That fact was borne out in Honor's mind by the man's easy dismissal of his infidelity once his carnal interest was sated; by his lack of interest in the reason for Betty's unexpected departure from town; and by his total, irresponsible disregard for Betty, proven when he made no attempt to ascertain where she had gone or how she had fared.

Neither had it missed Honor's notice that the fellow had given no thought at all to the possible consequences of the day that had impacted so heavily on Betty's life. The reason was simple enough to figure out. Since his life had continued on without repercussions, he could not have cared less. With those realities had come Honor's certainty that her mother was neither the first nor the last vulnerable woman he had used in the same way.

The terrifying attack she had just thwarted still fresh in her mind, Honor made a decision. The man responsible for the lifelong stigma her mother and she had suffered had escaped unscathed for too long.

Honor raised her chin with cold determination. It was time this man faced the living, breathing consequence of his actions.

Yes, it was time for her to meet . . . *Buck Star.*

Chapter One

It wasn't much of a town.

Honor stepped down from the afternoon stage and perused the main street of Lowell, Texas. The sun was bright and hot as she looked around her, coldly assessing the false-fronted stores lining the unpaved thoroughfare. She saw a general store, hotel, barbershop, livery stable, and several other nondescript commercial establishments, the largest being the saloon at the end of the street. There was little difference between this and the countless other Texas towns she had traveled through on her way to Lowell.

Honor briefly scrutinized the few pedestrians walking the boardwalk between the stores. She tried to imagine her mother walking those same boards—young, newly married, without the weight of silent guilt that had so heavily burdened her. Failing in that effort, she looked at the inevitable traffic of shoppers, occasional horsemen, wagons, and jaunty buckboards moving down the street.

"Ma'am . . ." Honor turned toward the stagecoach driver as he appeared beside her with her suitcase in hand. The gray-haired, heavily mustached fellow continued, "I figure you might like me to carry this case somewhere for you—unless you're waiting for somebody to meet you, that is."

Honor smiled. Pete Sloan was a crusty old fellow who obviously had been shocked to see her traveling alone. He had advised her two disreputable-looking fellow passengers in no uncertain terms that he was "looking out for her." Pete's outspoken concern had been a new experience in her lifetime of raised eyebrows and sly innuendos.

Touched by his manner, she replied, "Thanks, but that won't be necessary. The hotel's only a few steps away."

"The hotel . . ." Pete shook his head. His gravelly tone dropped a note softer. "If you don't mind my saying, that ain't no place for a respectable young woman like you. This town gets a lot of drummers and out-of-work wranglers staying at the hotel when they pass through. Them fellas seeing a pretty young thing like you alone there . . . well . . ." He flushed, but forced himself to continue, ". . . they just might get the wrong idea."

A pretty young thing . . .

Strangely, Honor had never thought of herself that way. She had never been "young" in the normal sense of the word. And pretty? Maybe. She had her mother's thick, tawny-colored hair, even features, and hazel eyes. She'd always thought her mother was truly beautiful when she smiled, but she didn't believe her own smile matched the rare brilliance of her mother's.

But, yes, she was a "respectable young woman," despite the shadow of illegitimacy that had hung over her all her life. She could not help wondering, however, if Pete would change his opinion when the reason she had come to Lowell became public knowledge.

Pete continued, "I'm thinking you might be better off talking to Sophie Trevor to see if she has a room in her boardinghouse for you. She runs a real nice place. It's the first house around the corner. You'd be safer there."

"Thank you, Pete." Honor took her case from his hand. "You're a nice fella. I hope we meet again."

Pete's polite tip of the hat tightened Honor's throat as she started in the direction he had indicated. His warning to her two fellow passengers had been well noted by them. They had all but ignored her for the duration of the trip, but their conversation had been more informative than she had ever expected it could be.

With a tightening of her lips, Honor recalled the moment the men's conversation had turned to the Texas Star ranch. She had come immediately alert at the mention of the ranch name—a name she had read over and again in her mother's letters. Owned by the handsome, appealing Buck Star—the man her mother had loved—the Texas Star had also been the most successful ranch in that part of Texas; yet according to her fellow passengers, the ranch had recently come upon bad times. A series of natural disasters and a rash of rustling in the area had evidently affected it even more adversely than other nearby ranches. To hear the two fellows tell it, the ranch was now debt-ridden to the point that half the hands had left, and the Texas Star's future was dangerously threatened.

Gripping the handle of her bag more tightly, Honor recalled the moment when Buck Star's new wife was mentioned. The revelation that her mother's best friend, Emma Star, had died years earlier was somehow devastating. Yet she had not been surprised to learn that shortly afterwards—within a few months—Buck had married Celeste DuClair, a widow young enough to be his daughter. The deed had evidently estranged him from his two young sons.

Even more disturbing, however, was the talk of Buck's almost slavishly faithful devotion to his fashionable young wife from New Orleans—a fidelity he had extended neither to the mother of his legitimate children nor to Betty Gannon, who had borne his child in dishonor. Honor's longing for justice had intensified as the two fellows had spoken of Buck's "dancing to Celeste's tune," of his laughable subservience to her wishes, regardless of its effect on others, as she "wrapped him around her dainty little finger" with no apparent effort.

Her dark thoughts interrupted by the sound of loud shouting across the main street, Honor slowed her steps and scrutinized the two men confronting each other there. The one doing the shouting had obviously spent more time at the saloon than was wise, while the other was restraining his anger with obvious difficulty.

The first man continued accusingly, "You killed him is what you did! He was a better fella than you'll ever be, but this town is letting you get away with it!"

Honor's heart skipped a beat. An altercation seemed inevitable. A fistfight was never pleasant, but if either of the men attempted to draw the guns holstered on their hips . . .

The second man, a big fellow with sun-streaked hair and a rock-hard demeanor, warned in a deep voice that traveled clearly on the suddenly silent street, "You're drunk, Boyd, and you're treading on dangerous ground. Get out of my way while you still have the chance."

"Is that a threat?" the drunk sneered. "What are you going to do—shoot me like you shot Jack Grate? Oh, wait a minute." The drunk's smirk darkened. "It wasn't you who killed Jack, was it? It was that wife of yours who done the job. She—"

Honor gasped as the big man's fist snapped out in a blur of movement that sent the drunk sprawling. His face flushed with wrath, the big fellow then walked out into the street where his opponent had fallen, stared down at him for long moments, then grated through clenched teeth, "Can you hear me, Boyd?"

The big man waited. When there was no response, he grasped the drunk's shirt and jerked him to a seated position. Holding him upright, he said, "I asked you a question."

The drunk nodded weakly.

The big man continued, "I'm going to ignore what

you said just now because you're drunk, but I'm warning you—if you ever mention my wife's name again, those'll be the last words you ever speak. Do I make myself clear?"

The drunk mumbled a response.

The big man demanded, "What did you say?"

The drunk gulped. "I said I heard you."

Releasing the drunk so abruptly that he fell flat on his back, the big man started across the street. Honor was unable to move as he walked in her direction. Her gaze fixed on him, she watched as he stepped up onto the boardwalk and turned toward the hitching rail a few feet away. She remained motionless when a matronly woman emerged from a storefront unexpectedly and rushed toward him. Honor saw the anxiety in the older woman's face as she said, "Are you all right, Cal?"

"I'm fine."

"Roddy Boyd's a drunk and a trouble-maker. He'll never be anything else. Just ignore him."

"I took care of it, Doc." Honor saw the warmth that flashed briefly in the big man's honey-colored gaze as he added, "Don't worry about it."

"But—"

"Like you said, Boyd's a drunk. When he sobers up, he'll turn tail and run as far and as fast as his pocket will take him."

"I suppose you're right."

"I am." The big man glanced back briefly at the drunk as the fellow staggered shakily to his feet and started down the street. Then tipping his hat at the concerned woman, he said, "I'm going home. Pru's waiting for me."

The older woman was watching the big fellow ride off when a passing cowpoke stopped beside her and snickered, "Cal sure set that Roddy Boyd straight enough. Boyd won't be shooting off his mouth again too soon." When the woman didn't respond, the cowpoke sobered and said, "Don't you worry, Doc. Nothin's going to happen to him. There aren't too many people in town who are going to forget what Cal Star did for us."

Cal Star.

The cowpoke continued talking, but his voice faded from Honor's mind.

She was incredulous. She hadn't been prepared for this. She wasn't ready.

But the truth was, the big man was . . . *her brother.*

Chapter Two

"What did you say your business in town was?"

Honor had followed Pete's advice. She had walked around the corner and arrived at Sophie Trevor's boardinghouse minutes earlier, but she had not gotten the reception she had expected. The middle-aged woman was still staring at her with eyes as keen as an owl's while awaiting her reply. It occurred to Honor that the woman actually *resembled* an owl with her stiff posture, rounded shoulders, and unsmiling demeanor dominated by large eyes and dark brows.

Numbed by the street scene she had witnessed and her unorthodox introduction to Cal Star minutes earlier, Honor was unintimidated by Sophie's manner as she responded, "I didn't say. I said I needed a place to stay, and Pete Sloan recommended your boardinghouse. But if you don't have a room—"

Undeterred, the older woman replied, "This is a respectable house. I need to know if the persons I let my rooms out to are respectable."

"I'm respectable."

"And I need to know you'll be able to pay for your room and board. I ask for a week in advance."

"I have the money."

Sophie studied her a moment longer, then offered, "Do you want to see the room?"

"That isn't necessary. It's either a room here or at the hotel. Pete said the hotel might be a mistake, so it looks like I don't have much choice." She asked flatly, "Do you want the money now?"

"Real direct kind of person, aren't you?" Surprising her, Sophie smiled, transforming her disapproving expression into welcome as she continued, "I figure that's good. This way there won't be any misunderstandings between us." She pointed to a sign on the wall and said, "One week in advance to be paid now; breakfast at six; dinner at six. If you don't make the meals on time, you go hungry."

"That's fine with me."

Waiting until the sum had been counted out into her hand and Honor had been shown her room, Sophie asked, "Will you be looking for work here?"

"Work?"

"I'm thinking you're accustomed to taking care of yourself. I know what that's like, you know, so if you're looking for a way to support yourself, I'll ask around town to see who's needing some help."

Honor was taken aback by the woman's turn-around in attitude. She hadn't come to Lowell with the thought of staying. Rather, she had expected her visit to be brief. Yet with Sophie waiting for her reply, she said, "I thought I'd look around town first . . . but if you could make some inquiries for me, that would be good."

Grateful when the door closed behind the older woman, Honor scrutinized the room. Spare but pleasant furnishings, clean bed linens, and a view of the street. What more could she ask?

Honor glanced out the window at the main street bathed in the warm glow of midday. The answer to that was simple. What she needed now was to find the right time and place to face down Buck Star.

He hadn't eaten yet that day, but it wasn't the first time he'd gone hungry.

Jace Rule rode slowly in the unrelenting afternoon sun. He glanced up at the clear Texas sky and realized it was almost noon. He'd been riding for hours in the diverse hill-country terrain of harsh granite outcrops, sunny pastures, and meandering riverbeds without any sign of a town coming into view. He looked down at his mount as the plodding bay continued moving steadily along the trail. He had used up the last of his money and supplies the previous day. He had accepted the horse in lieu of payment for his first job after being released from prison with only the clothes on his back and a few dollars in his pocket. He had figured it would be a good bargain when the rancher first suggested it, and he'd worked damned hard to earn his payment. When he was done, the fellow had presented him with the sorry mount he was now riding, and had told him to move on.

Jace patted the gelding's neck. Actually, old Whistler and he made a good pair. Both of them had traveled a hard road, had suffered greatly, and were coping as best they could.

As if in response to his thoughts, Whistler suddenly snapped up his head and increased his pace. Jace was not surprised when a tree-shaded stream became visible in the distance. He dismounted at the stream's edge minutes later and watched as the horse waded in ankle deep and began drinking.

The simple pleasures of life . . .

Jace's jaw hardened. He remembered a time when he had taken the simple pleasures of life for granted—simple pleasures that included working his own ranch and waking up in the morning in a soft bed with his beautiful Peg lying beside him.

Memory returned Jace with a paralyzing jolt to the image of Peg lying sprawled on that soft bed in their ranch house, her clothing torn from her body and blood draining from the gash in her head as her eyes stared lifelessly upward.

Dead.

No!

Disbelief. Agonizing grief.

Why . . . how . . . *who*?

He remembered seeing it then—a riding glove on the floor where it had lain almost hidden by the disarrayed bedclothes. Monogrammed and made of the finest leather, it had been unmistakable. It belonged to Winston Coburn, the spoiled young heir to the Coburn banking fortune who had recently arrived in town from back East. Supposedly visiting on business at his father's bank, he had immediately left no doubt in anyone's mind where his true interest lay.

Jace had tortured himself:

He should've realized what Coburn had in mind the first time the lecherous bastard looked at Peg!

He should've warned Coburn to keep his distance.

He should've protected Peg!

He should've . . . could've . . . would've . . .

Those regrets had been racing through his mind when he had tied up his horse in front of the bank and walked directly to the office Coburn occupied.

The next few moments were etched so clearly in his memory that Jace knew he would never forget them:

Jace pushed the door open, and Coburn stood up behind the desk without speaking a word. Coburn's matching riding glove was lying on the desk in front of him in glaring confirmation of his guilt. Then Coburn suddenly pulled a gun from a drawer and fired at Jace point-blank.

The burst of pain that struck Jace's chest with Coburn's bullet was almost simultaneous with the shot Jace fired in return.

Memory grew cloudy at that point. Jace remembered the startled look on Coburn's face as Coburn fell, then the sensation of the hard wooden floor against his own back . . . his struggle to breathe . . . the sound of running feet and excited voices. All blurred in his mind, except for a moment of utmost clarity when he turned his head and glimpsed Coburn lying motionless on the floor behind the desk, when he knew instinctively that Coburn would never open his eyes again.

Jace forced back the harsh memories, filled his canteen from the river, then walked the few steps to a nearby tree. Seated, he quenched his thirst, then turned at a sound beside him. A pecan had fallen to the ground. He looked up. The heavily laden tree was beginning to drop the first fruit of the season.

Succumbing to impulse, he picked up the nut, cracked it open, and popped it into his mouth. It tasted better than he remembered a pecan ever could. He scooped up the pecans lying nearby and had begun eating his first meal of the day when a violent thrashing in a nearby thicket was followed by the sound of a cow bawling.

Reacting instinctively, Jace stood up and approached the clamor cautiously. He halted when he sighted the cause of the animal's bawling.

Wolves . . . three of them surrounding a cow and her newborn calf.

Jace drew his gun and fired warning shots into the air, and the wolves took off running.

The panicked cow was still frantically urging her newborn to its feet when Jace heard movement in the brush behind him. He turned with gun raised toward the horseman who broke out unexpectedly into the open.

The rider jerked his mount to a halt. His pale, lined face was composed in a hard frown as he snapped, "Don't point that gun at me unless you intend to use it, boy!"

Boy.

"Did you hear me?"

"I heard you."

Jace holstered his gun, and the horseman dismounted. "That wily cow got away from me. I figured

she was ready to drop that calf, so I came after her."
He shook his head. "Time was when one cow more or
less on this spread didn't mean nothin', but now . . ."

The old man looked at Jace, his pale eyes pinning
him. "Drove off some wolves, did you?"

Jace nodded.

"Why didn't you shoot them? Them animals are
nothing but trouble."

The old man waited for a reply that was not forth-
coming, allowing Jace a few moments for further
scrutiny. The old fellow looked sickly, but his voice
was strong. "You took a chance, you know. Those
wolves could've turned on you."

"I wouldn't have let that happen."

"What are you doing on my land anyway?"

"Your land?" Momentarily doubting the authentic-
ity of the man's claim, Jace studied him more closely.
The old fellow's frame was emaciated, he had dark
circles under his eyes, and his hands were unsteady,
but his gaze was direct and sure. It was his land, all
right, but Jace had been run off more spreads than
he could count of late. Another one didn't faze him.
He responded, "I'm just traveling through."

"Traveling pretty light, aren't you? Looks to me like
you could stand a good meal, too." The old man
glanced at Whistler. "Your horseflesh isn't much to
speak of either."

"He takes me where I want to go."

"Where's that?"

"Where's what?"

"Where you want to go."

The old man had something on his mind. Not one

for beating around the bush, Jace asked, "You got something you want to say?"

The fellow assessed him a moment longer, then said unexpectedly, "I got a big spread here, but I'm short of help. We had a problem with rustlers that set us back, but that problem's been taken care of. I expect things to start looking up soon. I figure it might be a good time to hire some wranglers."

"So?"

"So I'm guessing you're no stranger to ranch work and could probably use a job and a place to set yourself down for a while."

A warning note sounded in Jace's mind. He replied cautiously, "I'm a stranger, but you're offering me a job when you could probably find all the help you need in the nearest town."

"None of the fellas around here will work for the wages I can afford to pay."

"And you think I will."

"If looks can tell."

Jace returned the man's pointed stare, then said bluntly, "I won't work for board only, if that's what you're thinking."

The old fellow raised his brow.

"I'm not *that* hungry."

The old fellow considered Jace's reply, then said, "All right, here's my proposition. You work for board, and at the end of the month, if things go right, I'll pay you what you're worth."

"No, thanks."

The old man almost smiled. "Heard that one before, have you?"

Jace did not need to reply.

"I'll pay you board and half what I pay my other men for the first month—until I see how things work out."

"Half."

"That's right."

"And after the first month?"

The old man's gaze hardened. "I don't make guarantees. Is it a deal or not?"

Jace's stomach growled. Hell, who was he kidding? He wasn't in a position to dicker.

"It's a deal."

The old man nodded and asked as he extended his hand, "What's your name?"

Accepting his hand, Jace replied, "Jace Rule."

"All right, Rule. In case you didn't know it, this is Texas Star land you're on. My name is Buck Star."

"Buck, sometimes I just don't understand you!"

Celeste glanced toward the kitchen where she had left Madalane frowning at the newly hired cowpoke, who was eating hungrily at the table. In his usual manner, Buck had gruffly ordered Madalane to set something out for the stranger. Celeste knew her faithful nanny and servant resented Buck's attitude, and she knew she would hear about it later. She also knew it wasn't time for Buck's "sickness" to resurface yet.

Celeste drew her husband into the privacy of their bedroom, then continued with a wide, incredulous gaze of practiced innocence, "Why did you do this? You don't even know this man, and you know as well as I do that we can't afford to pay another ranch hand."

"That situation is temporary, darling. Now that the rustlers have been caught—"

"They haven't *all* been caught!"

Celeste was breathless. She hadn't been prepared for this. She had worked long and hard to get Buck to the point where he wouldn't make a move on the ranch without discussing it with her first. That situation had facilitated her passing of information to Derek and his gang, and she knew the success the rustlers had enjoyed in the area could be attributed directly to her. She had gloried in that realization until Cal Star came back to Lowell. It did not sit well with her that Buck's long-estranged son had unexpectedly returned to town and just as unexpectedly whittled the rustlers' number down from six to one. Her only consolation was that Buck still refused to accept Cal.

She was still uncertain if she was glad that of all the rustlers, only Derek remained alive. Her heated sexual affair with Derek too often stimulated a side of herself she did not choose to acknowledge—a side as dissolute as Derek himself—yet it was her greatest weapon against her revulsion each time her doting, impotent husband touched her. It had allowed her to maintain her facade of loving wife and retain the control over Buck that continued to keep Cal and his father apart.

Now this unexpected hiring of a new ranch hand! She had shrewdly driven off most of Buck's hands, leaving him with only three wranglers too stubborn to quit. She had consoled herself that those three were also reaching their limit. She had been sure the time was fast approaching when Buck would be left with only her standing beside him. She had been certain he would no longer resist her then, and would change his will to read any way she wanted it.

Victory—revenge against Buck Star—had been so clearly in sight.

Disguising her anger with tears, Celeste whispered hoarsely, "Buck, you know how I worry about you and the ranch. I don't want you to overextend yourself."

"You don't have to concern yourself about that. I know a bargain when I see one."

"What do you mean?"

"I'm saying I know an experienced cowhand when I see one. Rule has the look. I saw it the moment I laid eyes on him, but he's down on his luck and hungry. He was ready to take just about anything he was offered."

"But you can't be sure—"

"Like I said, I know a good cowman when I see one."

"Buck—"

"You'll have to trust me on this, Celeste." His voice grew conciliatory as Celeste allowed another tear to trail down her cheek. "Don't worry, darlin'. I can fire Rule as fast as I hired him if he doesn't work out. But he will. I'm sure of it. And things are going to pick up, too. I know I don't look it, but I'm starting to beat this sickness of mine. I can feel the strength coming back into my limbs day by day. I'm going to restore the Texas Star to what it was before I got sick and before everything started going wrong. Then I'll show everybody in town who counted me out that I'm not beaten yet."

Celeste stared at Buck's intent expression. She knew he was right. He *was* feeling better—and she didn't like it. She had been so clever. Derek and his men had been bringing the Texas Star to ruin with their rustling, while Madalane and her black-magic potions had been destroying Buck's health a step at a time.

Celeste's plan had been working so well. She'd had no problem entering Buck's life. She had arrived in town after the deaths of his wife and daughter. All too familiar with his weakness for young women, she had easily captivated him with her sensual charm. They were married within months. Cal had left the ranch before she came, and she had played the part of the loyal, adoring wife while convincing Buck to send off his rebellious younger son, Taylor, as well. It had not been difficult to keep Buck so intimately involved with his "new, loving wife" that he was soon isolated from his friends, too.

Madalane's part in Celeste's plan had functioned just as seamlessly. The ageless Negress had used her skill with herbs and poisons native to the islands to foster Buck's illness—an illness for which Doc Maggie could find neither a name nor a cure. As Celeste had anticipated, Buck's illness had guaranteed her his undying gratitude for her devotion, while gradually reducing him to a pathetic shadow of the man he had once been.

But she paid the price of her success each time

Buck took her into his bony embrace. She detested him, and were she not so dedicated to her vengeance—

"You're the only one who never lost faith in me, darlin'." Celeste's thoughts snapped back to the present as Buck gathered her against his scrawny body with unexpected ardor. She knew instinctively what was coming next when he whispered, "You won't be sorry, and I won't forget it . . . ever."

Her mind raging in protest, Celeste murmured sweet encouragements as Buck slipped her bodice off her shoulders. She screeched in silent revulsion as Buck's lips followed a familiar, intimate path.

Yes, she'd make Buck pay dearly for every moment she had been forced to endure his touch.

And then, rejoicing, she'd watch him die.

Silent and unseen, Madalane listened at the door of the bedroom that had gone suddenly quiet. She heard the soft mumblings that occasionally broke the stillness within, distinctive sounds that needed no explanation. Her handsome face drew into tight lines and her dark eyes narrowed as she ground her teeth in fury. The itinerant cowhand that Buck had just hired was in the kitchen finishing up the last of the food Buck had ordered her to set out. She had seen Celeste draw Buck into their bedroom, where she had known Celeste would adamantly voice her protest. The result of Celeste's effort was now only too apparent.

Madalane silently raged. Buck Star had caused the death of her dear, beautiful Jeanette—Celeste's mother—years earlier when he had callously discarded Jeanette after their brief affair. With that act, he had destroyed Jeanette and ruined the life of her young daughter. Dedicated to vengeance, Madalane had remained with Celeste, sharing the dissolute lifestyle they had been forced to live for years afterwards. With every day that Celeste and she had suffered want, and with every man that Celeste had intimately satisfied in order to finally restore them to the life they had known, Buck Star had earned the misery he now suffered.

Madalane shuddered with growing wrath. The unexpected return of Cal Star had severely damaged their plans, but she was avowed that nothing and no one would interfere with their revenge or the glorious future Celeste and she had planned. When they returned to New Orleans, wealthy and victorious, they would—

Madalane's head snapped up at the sound of a kitchen chair scraping against the floor. The newly hired wrangler had finished eating and was getting up. A few steps, and he would see her listening outside Celeste's bedroom door.

Madalane turned and rushed hastily back to the kitchen, her irritation growing. She didn't like the looks of that Jace Rule. He appeared to be down on his luck, but his present circumstances had in no way humbled him, and his astute scrutiny left her uneasy. She needed no further complications to the plans Celeste and she had set into motion. She would not allow a vagrant cowhand the opportunity to—

Madalane gasped as the hallway rug slipped out

from underneath her feet. She cried out in pain when she hit the floor with a thud that was simultaneous with the harsh crack of breaking bone. Writhing in agony, the angle of her twisted leg clearly declaring the result of her fall, Madalane looked up moments later to see the vagrant cowhand standing over her . . . to see Buck and Celeste emerging from their room still adjusting their clothing.

Teeth clenched with pain, Madalane let out a low wail of raging frustration.

Chapter Three

Honor walked briskly down Lowell's sunny main street, enjoying the early morning sun. She glanced around at the gradually escalating traffic of the day. She saw two horsemen riding into view at the far end of the rutted thoroughfare; glimpsed a milk wagon turning a corner; saw a woman sweeping the walk in front of a storefront; watched a concerned husband help his heavily pregnant wife down from a buggy. She frowned at the inevitable idlers gathered on a corner, then allowed her gaze to linger on three children who had emerged from a doorway with schoolbooks in hand. A smile tugged at her lips as a determined mongrel dog followed at the children's heels, ignoring commands to "go home."

It was all so normal . . . such a tranquil way to start a day that Honor sensed would be anything but serene for her.

She breathed deeply, her disquiet growing. She had not slept well, despite the comfort of Sophie

ELAINE BARBIERI

Trevor's boardinghouse bed. Nor had she had any appetite despite the appeal of the ample breakfast Sophie had set out for her guests. She had thwarted all attempts to be drawn into conversation by a bearded wrangler named Wyatt Stone who had introduced himself at the breakfast table, and had purposely left before the other guests appeared. Honor was a woman with a mission that allowed no distractions.

Her mother's pitiful regrets, written to the undeserving man she had so desperately loved, droned again through Honor's mind as they had during the sleepless night just past.

It was my fault, I know that now. My silent love for you must have been visible in my eyes in those moments of grief after William died. You just wanted to comfort me. It was I who allowed the situation to slip out of control. I want you to know that I understand why you showed no interest in me afterwards, why you went your way as if you had forgotten I existed.

I hope you'll forgive me for my transgression, and for my hasty departure from Lowell without saying goodbye to either you or Emma. The truth is, I could not look my dear friend in the eye while knowing my own shame and the guilt I had fostered on you. Nor did I want my weakness to endanger your beautiful life with Emma and the children.

I know how much Emma loves you, my dearest Buck, and how much you love her. But, selfishly, I hope you will keep buried somewhere deep in your heart the knowledge that I will always love you, too.

Words steeped in torment . . . words of undying love.

There had been no mention of Honor in her mother's letters. Nor had there been a hint of recrimination for the handsome, heartless man who was her father—the man who had not even considered the possibility of Honor's existence.

Honor had decided she would waste no time before confronting Buck Star. She would obtain directions to the Texas Star at the mercantile store, rent a horse at the livery stable, and face her father at last. As for Cal Star, the brother she had never known . . .

Honor forced that thought from her mind and concentrated on the mission ahead of her. She had lost weight since her mother's death. The simple split skirt, white shirtwaist, and riding hat she presently wore were suitable for the ride out to the Texas Star, but the clothes hung loosely on her slender proportions. It had not missed her notice, either, that her extended journey and the past night's sleeplessness had made her skin pale and ringed her eyes with dark circles. She pushed back a wayward strand of tawny hair and raised her chin, knowing she did not look her best, and was annoyed that she even cared.

The two horsemen Honor had seen entering town diverted her from her thoughts as they dismounted at the mercantile store's hitching rail. The first rider was an old man who had seen better days. It occurred to her that the second, younger man appeared to have seen better days as well, but it wasn't their appearance that captured her attention. It was their expressions. Something was wrong.

As if in response to her thoughts, Doc Maggie, the

middle-aged woman she had seen with Cal Star the previous day, emerged from the storefront a few steps away.

As Honor drew closer, she heard Doc say, "You're sure?"

"There's no doubt about it. Her leg's broken." The old man continued, "I would've come out yesterday, but she wouldn't hear of it. My wife took her side, of course." Honor saw the flash of annoyance the old man sought to hide before continuing. "They both were sure she could take care of herself, but this morning was another story."

"That sounds like their way of thinking, all right." Doc belatedly acknowledged the silent younger man for the first time by saying, "Who's this you've got with you? I don't think I've seen him before."

The old man responded impatiently, "He's my new ranch hand."

"New ranch hand?"

"That's what I said."

Not intimidated by his tone, Doc responded, "He has a name, I assume."

"I don't figure this is the time for introductions."

"Oh? Well, I don't abide rudeness, Buck Star."

Buck Star.

Honor's thoughts stopped cold.

It couldn't be!

Honor released a gasping breath, then stepped back into the shadows of the store overhang. No . . . Buck Star was muscular, vibrantly masculine, with dark hair and "startlingly blue eyes." Even taking into

34

account the years in-between, this man couldn't be he!

Honor took another short step in retreat. This man's hair was gray and sparse, his features almost indistinguishable within the network of harsh lines and gaunt hollows that marked his face. His skin had a sickly pallor, and he was so thin as to be almost wizened, causing his clothes to hang limply on his emaciated frame. The only similarity this man bore to her mother's references to Buck Star lay in his blue eyes, which had somehow faded to a colorless hue without losing the "startling" impact of their stare.

Unable to catch her breath, Honor leaned against the storefront as Buck Star motioned to the man standing silently beside him and replied to the doctor, "All right, have it your way. His name's Jace Rule. I want to introduce him to the Bowers so he can charge supplies to the Texas Star account at the store. He'll stay behind to take care of some things for me while I ride back to the ranch with you."

Still indignant, Doc Maggie replied, "I don't need you to ride back with me, Buck."

"Yes, you do."

"I can take care of myself."

"Not the way things stand at the Texas Star right now, you can't."

Doc stilled and studied Buck's expression. "Things are that bad, huh?"

"I'd say."

Doc frowned, then turned to say, "Nice to meet you, Jace Rule. Everybody calls me Doc Maggie. Sorry

35

I don't have time to talk." She smiled briefly at the polite tip of Rule's hat, then started back toward her office.

Still frozen with incredulity, Honor watched as Buck Star and his new wrangler turned toward the mercantile.

"Buck Star's not going to get many takers for that job."

Agnes Bower, the stiff-faced matron behind the counter, looked at Jace speculatively, then glanced back at the list Buck had given her. She continued despite her husband's obvious efforts to restrain her, "You're new at the Texas Star, fella, but I'm telling you now, Celeste Star isn't very popular in this town. Neither is that servant of hers." Agnes's thin nose twitched before she added, "To tell you the truth, that Madalane woman sends a chill down my spine every time she comes in here."

"Agnes!"

Agnes responded to her husband's reprimand with a shrug. "Truth is truth. And I still think Celeste is the one who's standing between Buck and Cal . . . especially now that Cal and Pru—"

"Agnes . . ."

Agnes paused at the intensified warning in her husband's tone.

Jace studied the woman's expression. She didn't like her husband's interference. She was a gossip. She wanted Jace to prompt her so she could fill him in on the situation at the Texas Star in more detail, but he had no intention of accommodating her. He had

36

sensed that he'd stepped into a hornets' nest the moment he walked through the kitchen door of the Texas Star ranch house. He figured he'd seen just about everything in his thirty-two years of life, but he had been stunned when Buck introduced him to the beauteous Celeste. Blond, with silver-blue eyes and delicate features, she was probably the most beautiful woman he had ever seen, as well as being young enough to be Buck's daughter.

And she seemed to adore Buck.

Jace barely restrained the wry twist of his lips that that thought elicited. Somehow, he doubted it.

As for Madalane, he had felt the Negress's eyes burning into him the moment he entered the kitchen. He had told himself the situation there was none of his business, that his job at the Texas Star was only temporary, but he had known instinctively there was more to the Negress than met the eye.

Aware that the only thing he was sure of in his present situation was that Madalane was truly in pain after her fall, Jace broke the silence at the mercantile counter by saying, "That may be true, ma'am, but Buck's the boss at the Texas Star. I do what he says."

Frustrating her husband further, Agnes shook her head disapprovingly. "I suppose Celeste is too delicate to take over at the ranch while Madalane is off her feet."

"All I know is that Buck wants that order for supplies filled, and he wants me to make sure the word is passed that he's looking for somebody to take over the kitchen chores at the ranch as soon as possible."

"Well, *I* think—"

"You heard him, Agnes," Harvey Bower interrupted with firm determination. "This fellow needs to get that order filled now." Agnes darted her husband a cold glance, then said to Jace, "How long will Buck be needing someone in the kitchen?"

"I don't know that either, ma'am."

"So I guess someone is supposed to hire on at the Texas Star without any assurances at all about how long—"

"Agnes, that's enough!"

Agnes's lips tightened. "All right, I'll pass the word on."

The woman put her head down and went about her work as Jace replied, "Thank you, ma'am. I'll wait outside until you're done."

More relieved than he dared reveal, Jace walked out of the store, leaving the coldly irate Agnes Bower behind him. If he knew anything at all about the discourse between husband and wife, the two of them would discuss the matter of Agnes's gossiping in detail that evening. He was glad he wouldn't be there to hear it.

Jace straightened up, enjoying the sunlight as he emerged from the store. He unconsciously flexed his tight shoulder muscles and took a deep breath. Five years in prison had left their mark. The value he now placed on the warmth of a free Texas sun had never been greater.

Jace leaned his broad back against a porch post and tilted his hat down farther on his forehead. Cautiously relaxed, he surveyed the street while his thoughts wandered. The first few years in prison had been almost more than he could bear. Coburn had fired first. He had fired back in self-defense. He had told himself there was no way he should've gone to prison, that he should've been allowed to grieve for the woman he loved on his own ranch, in his own way. It had taken him a few years to admit the truth to himself, that even if Coburn hadn't fired the first shot, he probably would have shot him anyway.

Yet the truth was that Coburn did fire first.

The final truth, however, was that Coburn-family money had put him in that prison cell. His only consolation was that Walter Coburn, whose wealth and tolerance had allowed his son's perversions full range, hadn't been successful in getting Winston Coburn's killer hanged.

Jace had returned to the site of his ranch only briefly after being released. With a new family in residence, no sign remained that either he or his beautiful Peg had ever lived there.

Pain stabbed Jace's gut at the thought, but he forced it aside. He allowed few things to matter to him now. The sun on his back during the day, a decent place to sleep at night, three square meals in between—and his independence. That was all he needed.

Instinct, a sharp sense of being watched, turned Jace abruptly to scrutinize his immediate surroundings.

His gaze stopped on the woman looking at him from the shadows of the store overhang. She was tall for a woman, and she appeared to be young. Her riding clothes hung on her lean frame, and the broad brim of her leather riding hat obscured her features. What could not be missed, however, was the gun she wore on her hip and the intensity of her stare.

A shaft of sunlight touched the tawny hair the woman wore swept to the back of her neck as she started in his direction. Another few steps and he was able to see her even features, the sober line of her lips, and the clear hazel eyes fixed so keenly on him. There was something about the way she carried herself, as if she were set on her course and cared not a whit what anyone said about it.

She wanted something.

Startled by the stirring of an emotion inside him that he had believed long dead, Jace clamped his jaw tight.

Whoever she was, whatever she wanted, he didn't have to see the gun on her hip to know she was trouble—and he'd already had enough trouble to last a lifetime.

Whoever she was, whatever she wanted, he knew one thing for certain. The answer was *no*.

His name was Jace Rule, and he hadn't meant a word of that "thank you" he had spoken so politely to Agnes Bower after their conversation in the store. Honor was sure of it.

She had heard it all from where she stood outside the doorway of the mercantile. It hadn't been difficult, with Agnes talking boldly in a voice meant to carry. The problem had been hearing Rule's responses, as soft-spoken as they had been.

Yet Honor was certain the soft-spoken responses in

no way indicated fear or subservience on the tall cowboy's part. She had only to look at him to know that. Rule's gaze was too hard and keen, his expression too alert. She recognized that look as one she herself often wore. That look had been honed by adversity, and his responses reflected that caution. He was a man with no intention of becoming involved in what appeared to be the increasingly complex situation at the Texas Star—a situation with Buck Star at the center of it.

Still uncertain of her own intentions, Honor approached Rule steadily. His broad frame was thin but firmly muscled, conveying a power that could easily be underestimated.

She knew instinctively that underestimating Jace Rule would not be one of her failings.

Reaching his side at last, unaware that she had made a decision, Honor startled herself by saying, "I overheard you talking in the store. I'll take that job that's open at the Texas Star."

There was no sign of surprise in the dark-eyed stare Rule fixed on her. She felt its heat burning into her as she waited for his reply.

She *was* young, and prettier than Jace had believed at first glance. Thick brown eyelashes emphasized the unusual fluctuating color of her eyes as she faced him boldly. She made no pretense about having listened to his conversation with Agnes. He had the feeling there wasn't much pretense in her.

Jace asked unexpectedly, "What's on your mind, ma'am?"

"What do you mean?"

"If you heard the conversation I had with Agnes Bower just now, you know the situation at the Texas Star isn't exactly desirable."

"You work there, don't you?"

"Temporarily."

"Oh?"

"Besides, what I do or don't do is none of your business."

"What I do or don't do is none of your business either."

Jace replied gruffly, "Take my word for it, whatever you're running away from, the Texas Star isn't the place to hide."

"Does that mean you've already discarded it as a hiding place?"

"We're not talking about me. I'm not the person asking for a job at the Texas Star."

"And you're not the person who'll make the decision whether or not to hire me." Green sparks in the young woman's eyes betrayed her growing irritation when she said, "Look, I'm going back to the ranch with you whether you like it or not. If Buck Star hires me—"

"Then his wife will probably fire you."

"She didn't fire *you*."

"I'm not a pretty young woman."

"*Neither am I.*"

Jace chose not to reply.

"Mr. Rule . . ." Agnes Bower's call turned Jace toward the doorway. He noted the way Agnes looked at the young woman and him before she continued,

42

"I've finished filling the Texas Star order. You can take it whenever you're ready to leave."

"I'm ready now," Jace replied flatly.

Agnes walked back into the store and the young woman said, "I'll get a horse. It'll only take me a few minutes."

"I said, I'm leaving now."

"Have it your way, but I'll be right behind you." The young woman turned toward the livery stable, then looked back coldly to add, "By the way, my name is Honor Gannon. Don't bother to introduce yourself. I know your name. It's Jace Rule." With an acid-sweet smile, she added, "I overheard that, too."

Jace watched with a frown as Honor Gannon walked briskly down the boardwalk. He noted the tilt of her head, her purposeful step, and the sway of her slim hips as she made rapid strides toward the livery stable. He felt again a warning tug in his groin.

There was no doubt about it. Honor Gannon, of the tawny hair and fiery eyes, was trouble—and he couldn't escape the feeling that he was somehow headed right for the middle of it.

No.

He'd be damned if he'd let that happen.

His face was pleasant enough. It was too bad his personality didn't match.

Honor unconsciously assessed Jace Rule further as she rode beside him toward the Texas Star ranch. Strong brows over dark eyes, angular features, and full lips—average. But those thickly lashed eyes that appeared to miss very little were definitely not aver-

43

age. An old jagged scar on his chin caught her eye. She unconsciously wondered how he had gotten it— and how many scars the other fella wore because of it. She scanned his tall, broad-shouldered physique, noting that her first assessment had been accurate. He appeared to have missed a few meals somewhere along the way, but that deprivation in no way affected the quiet strength of his demeanor.

In any case, Jace Rule had been true to his word. He had turned back toward the Texas Star as soon as the supplies were secured onto his saddle. She supposed she'd never know if he had been surprised or had been expecting her to catch up when she finally reined her mount beside him on the trail. She doubted the job at the Texas Star would last long enough for her to find out. Buck Star appeared to be an irascible old man who wasn't easy to take. She hadn't realized until she had seen him, however, that she needed to have one question finally answered:

Why had her mother's love for him lasted a lifetime?

Frowning, Honor brushed perspiration from her brow. She broke the silence with Jace Rule by asking abruptly, "How much longer until we reach the Texas Star?"

"Not much."

"How well do you know Buck Star?"

"Not well."

Honor frowned. "You don't say much, do you?"

He did not reply.

All right, if that's the way he wanted it.

As silent as he, Honor glanced at Jace when his

horse began limping. She noted his concern as he drew the animal off the trail, dismounted, and secured the reins to a tree. Automatically following him, Honor reined back but remained mounted as Jace patted his horse's neck and spoke a few indiscernible words of encouragement before lifting the gelding's front hoof to inspect it. She saw his annoyance at the stone lodged in the horse's shoe. She watched as he dug a knife out of his saddlebag and began prying it loose.

The gelding started nervously and reared back, and Jace murmured a soft command.

Calmly drawing the gun at her hip, Honor leveled it coldly in the direction of man and horse. She saw surprise flash in Jace's eyes when he saw her gun aimed in his direction—the moment before she squeezed the trigger and fired.

Honor's gunshot shattered the silence of the sunny trail. Jace fell a few unsteady steps backwards, his heart pounding as he stared for silent moments at the rattler a few feet away that had been cut in half by Honor's single shot.

Still frowning, Jace looked back at Honor to see her holstering her gun. Her expression was cool and controlled. She appeared unaffected as she returned his gaze unblinkingly.

"That was a fine shot." Hardly aware that he had spoken the words aloud, Jace questioned gruffly, "How did you learn to handle a gun that way?"

"Does it matter?"

"I suppose not." He didn't know how she had

learned to shoot that way, but he had the feeling he knew why. She was a woman who had learned to take care of herself against odds that she didn't choose to discuss. He could understand that, but it didn't make him any less wary as he stated flatly, "I suppose I should thank you."

"Don't bother."

"Don't worry, I won't." Jace continued, "I figure you just did what comes naturally when you shot that rattler. So I'll just say you can expect me to do the same for you if the situation presents itself. I'll leave it at that—if it's all right with you."

Jace waited for Honor's hardly discernible nod before picking up his knife to resume prying the stone loose from Whistler's shoe.

Mounting a few minutes later, Jace turned his mount back onto the trail. Honor fell in beside him as he silently acknowledged that the incident with the rattlesnake had proved two things very clearly.

The first was that Honor Gannon was not a woman to be dismissed lightly.

The second was that he wouldn't be able to dismiss her lightly even if he tried.

Chapter Four

Alone in the silence of his opulent New York office, Walter Coburn opened the humidor that occupied the far corner of his massive mahogany desk and withdrew a cigar. He held it up to his nose to inhale its scent, then frowned when it failed to meet his expectations. But he wasn't truly surprised. So little met his expectations these days.

Walter lit the cigar, still frowning, then stood up abruptly and turned toward the windows behind him. He stared out into the sun-swept street below, at the nameless, faceless people who walked briskly past.

Nameless . . . faceless . . . because they were all *common*. They worked their mundane jobs and went about their mundane lives, wallowing in the muck of mediocrity while knowing little of the finer things that life had to offer—for which they would have little appreciation even if exposed—simply because of their supreme ignorance.

Walter unconsciously nodded. He had been born

poor, but he had never been ignorant. He had sworn to himself early on that he would not die poor. He had worked diligently toward that end. Using his pleasing appearance and glib tongue to great advantage as a young man, he had made the move that had finally guaranteed his future. With almost shameless ease, he'd convinced his employer's homely daughter that he loved her. Seducing her then was no problem, and with his daughter two months pregnant, his employer had had no choice but to provide a lavish wedding that would establish the beaming couple socially.

Unfortunately, Walter's bride did not survive the birth of their son, and it was then that he was faced with a decision that would affect the rest of his life. His grieving father-in-law died unexpectedly, but not accidentally, a year later, leaving the company assets under Walter's control.

Comfortable in his new role, he had assumed management of the family business, Cunningham Industries, with a show of humility that did not interfere with the questionable business practices he employed to triple the company assets within five years. The fact that he became known as the "shark of manufacturing" did not bother him. His lawyers were paid well to protect his interests.

He had been secure in his financial status and proud of his son, who, fortunately, bore no resemblance to his plain mother. Walter had been determined to lavish on Winston all the luxuries he had been denied as a child, and the boy had pleased him by growing into manhood handsome, intelligent, and worldly. It had not bothered Walter that he indulged Winston to excess, because Winston was all he had ever dreamed his son could be. And if the scope of Winston's sexual deviancies had sometimes startled even Walter, he had had no objection as long as his lawyers saw to it that his son never suffered publicly because of them.

Walter shrugged his well-tailored shoulders, then discarded his cigar with disgust. He stroked his fine gray mustache as he resumed his observance of the street. As for himself, he had maintained his comely appearance into middle age. He only needed to look in the mirror to see that, although streaked with gray, his hair was still thick enough to tempt a woman's fingers, and that his even features had weathered the years well. Although his height was average, his body had maintained its muscular form, was well proportioned and free of fat. Most important of all, his sexual appetite and potency had almost matched that of his virile son.

Yes, he had had it all—wealth, women, social prominence, and a son who had wanted nothing more than to follow in his father's footsteps.

He had made only one mistake.

That mistake had cost his son his life.

Winston's sexual involvement with a local debutante had started the deadly debacle into motion. The vociferous outrage of the debutante's politically prominent father had caused Walter to suggest to his son that he take a trip out West until the furor died down, with the excuse of examining the records of a bank recently annexed into the family empire.

The unforeseeable and unimaginable had followed. Walter still could not envision how Winston could have been driven to such sexual excesses with an ordinary rancher's wife that he had left her dead in her own home!

It didn't matter to him that Winston had killed the woman. Nor did it matter to him that Winston had shot first when the woman's cowboy husband came to avenge his wife's death. It only mattered to him that the husband had survived and Winston had not.

Enraged when the cowboy's common image flashed across his mind, Walter cursed aloud.

Five years later, and his pain at losing his dear son was still acute.

Five years later, and his determination to achieve vengeance was stronger than ever.

Five years later . . . and the time had finally come when he would see Jace Rule *dead*.

Walter Coburn turned at a knock on his office door and smiled as a well-dressed gentleman was ushered into the room. He scrutinized the man briefly from head to toe. The fellow was wearing a suitcoat, hat, and trousers that were the epitome of fashion; his shoulder-length, curly red hair was stylishly cut; and the modest beard he sported was well trimmed. His features were unremarkable, except—

Walter's scrutiny jerked to a halt. Yes, the man's features were unremarkable, except for eyes that were a dull brown so cold and lifeless that they sent a chill down his spine.

Walter inquired, "You are Mr. Bellamy, I presume?"

"That's my name."

A flush of satisfaction suffused Walter at the sound of Bellamy's Western accent, and he said, "You come highly recommended to me. I sent for you because I was assured you can easily handle the task I'm hiring you for and there will be no confusion about what I want you to do."

"I don't make mistakes."

"In that case, let me make my demands very clear, Mr. Bellamy. I want you to go back to Texas where you came from. A man named Jace Rule was recently released from Huntsville Prison. He killed my son, and I want you to kill him."

"No problem."

Suspicious of Bellamy's quick acquiescence, Walter snapped, "What, no questions? You don't know anything about this man. You don't even know where he is, which is something I can't tell you because I don't know exactly where he is either."

"Let *me* make something clear, mister." Bellamy's expression hardened at Walter's verbal assault. "Don't let this outfit I'm wearin' fool you. I dress the part wherever I am, but I ain't no dandy. And I don't need to know where this fella, Jace Rule, is now neither. You just told me where he started out from— Huntsville Prison—and that's all I need to know. There ain't nobody better at tracking than me . . . and there ain't nobody better at killing what I'm tracking."

"I don't want you to just *kill* him!"

Bellamy frowned. "What do you want, then?"

"I want you to make him suffer . . . like he's made me suffer since my son's death. I want him to yearn for all the years ahead that will be stolen from him, just as he stole them from my son. I want to make sure he dies a thousand times before you put the bullet into him that finally ends his misery. And just before you kill him, I want you to tell him *I* hired you to end his life, just as he ended my son's."

"I told you—no problem."

"Let me finish! This is the most important part." Walter paused, then said, "I want proof that he's dead."

"What do you want me to do, bring you ears?" Bellamy gave a harsh laugh. "I'll bring you anything you want if the price is right."

"Bring me positive proof that you killed him, plus a full report of the torment he suffered, and you can write your own ticket."

"Meanin'?"

"Set your price, and I'll pay it. Half now, and half as soon as you walk back through my door with your proof."

His cold gaze intent, Bellamy responded, "You just made yourself a deal."

Walter shook the hand Bellamy extended toward him. His heart pounding as he accompanied the fellow into the outer office, he instructed his secretary gruffly, "Write Mr. Bellamy a check for the amount he specifies."

Walter turned back to his office without another glance. He closed the door behind him, then walked to the window to stare down at the street below.

It wouldn't be much longer now.

* * *

"Who's this?" Buck Star glanced at Honor, who stood across from him in the ranch-house kitchen. He looked at the small traveling bag in Jace's hand, then asked bluntly, "What's she doing here?"

Honor struggled to maintain control of her emotions. Outwardly, she had forced herself to appear coldly unaffected by the incident with the rattler on the trail, but the realization that Jace Rule's life had depended on a single twitch of her trigger finger had left her shaken. Now she was only a few feet away from her father, the man who had destroyed her mother's promising life in a single afternoon, the man who had left her to struggle through a miserable existence filled with shame.

In reply to Buck's question, Jace said, "Her name is Honor Gannon. She's here about taking the job you're looking to fill."

"Is that right?" Buck directed his attention toward Honor more keenly, and she withheld a gasp at the impact of his gaze. When she did not immediately respond, he said, "I asked you a question, girl."

Angry heat flushed Honor's face as she snapped back sharply, "My name's not 'girl.' And, yes, I came here about the job."

Buck's penetrating gaze perused her more closely, and Honor's heart beat a rapid tattoo in her chest. He said abruptly, "You're too young for the job. I need a big woman, somebody older who can handle hard work."

"What kind of work do you have here that you think I can't handle?" Honor challenged. "You said you wanted somebody to work in the kitchen, and I'm more than capable of doing that. I've been doing it for years. I can cook and bake, and I'm a good hand at smoking meats and other miscellaneous chores. I clean up well after myself, too."

"Is that right?"

"Yes, that's right." Her composure rapidly returning, Honor continued, "I arrived in town yesterday. Sophie Trevor said she'd keep an eye out for a job for me, but this one sounded too good to pass up."

"Too good to pass up, huh?" Buck gave a caustic snort. "What brought you to Lowell anyway? This town doesn't have much to offer a young woman like you."

"That's my business."

Ignoring her response despite his raised brows, Buck said, "The work's only temporary. You'd be out of a job again when our housekeeper's leg is healed."

"I know. I heard you talking to Doc Maggie."

"There's no tellin' how long that'll take."

"I heard that, too."

"You got a good ear for overhearing things, don't you?"

"When it serves my purpose."

"You don't mind speaking your mind either."

"Not when I need to."

Buck scrutinized her more closely. He glanced at the gun on her hip. "You know how to use that thing?"

"I can use it if I need to."

Honor heard Jace move behind her, but he did not speak, and she was glad. She needed no interference in the first conversation she had ever had with her father.

Buck studied her a few, tense seconds longer before he glanced at the clock on the kitchen mantel and said, "It's early enough—we'll try you out today. If you can handle the work here, you're hired."

"Wait a minute." Honor's gaze narrowed. "You didn't say how much you'd pay me."

"Oh, yeah. Room and board."

Jace made another restless move behind her before she responded, "And?"

"And a weekly salary that suits your efforts."

"Not good enough."

"What sounds fair to you?"

"Five dollars a week, plus room and board."

Buck considered her statement for a moment, then nodded. "Start cooking. We'll see if you're as good as you say you are."

A sound in the hallway preceded the entrance of a young woman into the kitchen, and Honor was stunned breathless at the sight of her. Beautiful . . . blond . . . *young*, but obviously distressed. She could be no one but the new wife.

The young woman's tone confirmed Honor's assumption when she said tightly, "What's this all about, Buck, dear? Who is this woman?"

"Celeste, darlin', this here's Honor Gannon. She came to take on the kitchen work until Madalane is up on her feet again."

Honor felt the subtle animosity in Celeste's gaze as she swept her from head to toe, then turned back to her husband to say with a cloying smile, "I don't think so, dear. We need an older, more experienced woman."

Obviously eager to gain his wife's approval, Buck replied gently, "We don't have too much to choose from in Lowell, darlin', and we need help now. You're too busy with Madalane to take care of things in the kitchen, and the fellas will be coming back from the range expecting supper in a little while. We don't have nothing to lose by giving her a try."

"Madalane will be well soon."

"Not as soon as you think. Doc Maggie says bones take time to heal, especially when somebody's not so young anymore."

"Oh, what does she know!"

Buck frowned at Celeste's sharp response, and that brief flash of insight into Celeste's character recalled to Honor's mind the brief meeting she and Jace had had with Doc Maggie on the trail. The way the older woman had rolled her eyes and wished her luck when Jace explained she was seeking a job at the ranch had said it all.

Noting Buck's frown, Celeste said, "I'm sorry. I guess I shouldn't have said that, but Madalane is in pain, and Doc Maggie wasn't any real help. Besides, where will we put this woman? She can't have Madalane's room, and she certainly can't sleep in the bunkhouse."

"The storage room will do fine for a while. We have an old bunk in there, and we can fix the room up to be suitable if things work out."

Celeste moved a step closer to Buck. Honor's stomach twisted as Celeste looked up into his eyes and said more softly, "I don't think they will."

If Buck Star hires me—
Then his wife will probably fire you.

Jace's prophetic response resounded in Honor's mind in the brief silence that followed. Behind her, she heard Jace clear his throat, and she knew he was remembering, too. She was about to turn away when Buck took his wife by the shoulders and said, "You don't realize it now, but you need help here, darlin'. I don't want you exhausting yourself by trying to keep up with everything that'll need to be done. I told this young woman we'd give her a chance. I don't expect to go back on my word."

Honor saw the telltale twitch of Celeste's smooth cheek before she whispered apologetically, "You're right, Buck, of course. You're always right." She looked down at the cup in her hand. "I only came out here to get Madalane a cup of water. She's suffering so badly."

"Yes, dear, I know." Buck's gaze lingered lovingly on Celeste's slender figure as she filled the cup and walked back down the hallway toward Madalane's room. Then he looked back at Honor and said, "Celeste will come around."

Honor barely withheld the response that sprang to her lips. The man was blind to his wife's manipulation! It was obvious Celeste didn't want her there, and that wouldn't change.

Honor was still biting her tongue when Buck turned to Jace and said, "Show her where the smokehouse is. I'll leave it to you to set up the storage room and get her what she needs. It's too late for you to go out and help the fellas with the fencing now anyways."

Looking back at Honor, Buck warned, "You'll have to prove yourself here, girl."

"My name's Honor."

Buck turned away without a reply, and Honor seethed.

She'd have to prove herself, would she?

Honor looked at Jace and growled, "You heard the boss. Let's get started."

They were on the way back from the smokehouse with supplies in hand when Jace broke his silence by saying abruptly, "It won't last, you know."

"What won't last?"

"Your job here. The boss's wife doesn't want him to hire you, and it looks to me like she gets what she wants."

"Maybe."

"I wouldn't get my hopes up."

"I'm not in the mood for advice."

"You're setting yourself up for a disappointment."

"That's my business."

"Look, Honor—"

Honor pulled open the kitchen door and said tightly, "Just put those things on the table. I've got work to do."

The setting sun shone through the window as Jace sat at the bunkhouse table, fork in hand. His plate was almost empty, and he was already looking for more. It occurred to him that Honor was making him eat his words, and he'd be damned if he wasn't enjoying every bite.

Jace glanced at the men seated around him. Randy, probably the oldest of the hands by a few years, was eating heartily. He had told Jace the previous day that he had been at the Texas Star since its inception, but he was still lean and fit and showed few signs of age.

Mitch was bigger and grayer. He was as steady a man as Jace had ever met, and he hadn't stopped eating since he sat down at the table.

Big John's name said it all. The burly wrangler stood eye-to-eye with Jace but outweighed him by at least sixty pounds of man and muscle. No, he wouldn't like to come up against Big John in a fight, but there was little chance of that. Jace had never met a fella who was so even-tempered. Or so hungry.

Jace's thoughts sobered. His association with these men was limited, but he knew instinctively that with loyal hands like these three backing Buck up on the ranch, there was nothing that couldn't be accomplished on the Texas Star. He had gotten the impression that Celeste was responsible for Buck's present shortage of help, and if he was any judge, there was no love lost between her and the hands remaining. He wondered if Buck knew the true worth of these fellas. The thought nudged that if he had had hands like these on his ranch years ago, things might've been different. Peg might still be—

"Pass them potatoes, will you, Jace?"

Jerked back to the present by Big John's request, Jace handed him the bowl.

"Damn! It's almost empty!"

"What did you expect?" Randy swallowed a mouthful and continued, "It's your third helping. There is a bottom to that bowl, you know."

His disappointment almost comical, Big John responded with a sheepish smile. "Truth is, I ain't had a meal this good on the ranch in a dog's age. That little gal sure knows how to cook."

"Her name's Honor," Mitch commented. "And I've got the feeling cooking ain't all that 'little gal' is good at."

Jace turned sharply at Mitch's remark, then relaxed as Mitch added, "I saw her ride in here today. She sure knows how to handle a horse, and I'm thinking she doesn't wear that gun on her hip for the fun of it."

"What's a pretty young thing like that doing taking a job cooking in a hornets' nest like this one?" Randy shook his head. "Seems to me she should be married and toting a baby or two on her hip. If I was a few years younger . . ."

"Age never stopped the boss."

Turning to Mitch's baiting with a raised brow, Randy said, "But I've got more sense than the boss has." He frowned. "Is there any more ham on that plate?"

"All gone."

"Damn."

A smile tugged at Jace's lips. Honeyed ham as tender as he had ever tasted it, mashed potatoes that were creamy and thick, corn that tasted too sweet to have been stored, biscuits as light as a cloud, and gravy that was smooth and fine. Honor had delivered it all to the bunkhouse in plates and bowls that were steaming and filled to the brim. She had proved herself, all right, and he had a feeling that, unlike him, Celeste didn't much like the taste of her own words.

"How long do you think it'll be before Celeste gets rid of that little gal?"

Big John's sober question momentarily froze all movement at the table. Shrugging, Mitch said, "She probably won't last the week. She's a bit too pretty and young for Celeste's tastes."

Big John looked at Jace and said, "Sorry to say, I'm thinking you won't last too long here either. Celeste is in the business of driving off the boss's help, not having him take on anybody new."

Jace frowned. "Why would she do that?"

"Because she's got the devil in her."

"All right, that's enough!" Randy pushed his chair back from the table with a warning glance that halted further conversation. "We're done eating, and I figure that young woman is looking for these empty plates."

"I'll take them back," Jace heard himself say. "I have to fix some things in the storage room for her anyway."

"Well, well . . . the new girl and the new hand seem to be getting along real fine."

Big John snickered at Mitch's comment.

Randy cleared his throat.

Jace picked up the plates and left without a response.

They could never be more wrong.

* * *

"I won't stand for it." Her voice a low hiss, Celeste stood beside Madalane's bed, rigid with ire as she rasped, "I won't have that Honor woman in my kitchen *or* in my house! Buck hired her the minute he finished eating. He told her he'd send somebody back to town for the rest of her things in the morning, and the witch barely acknowledged what he said."

The Negress's dark eyes were dulled with pain. Hair usually worn in a gaily colored turban was tangled across her pillow in disarray, and her ageless features were strained as she asked, "Is this new woman as beautiful as you?"

"Not hardly," Celeste responded haughtily. "But Buck looks at her strangely. He ignores her arrogance. He tolerates it in a way he would never tolerate it from anyone else. It worries me."

"Your husband will tire of her ways."

"I don't want to *wait* for him to tire. Don't you understand? I'm tired of waiting. I want him dead! I want his family destroyed. I want his precious Texas Star ground into the dust until there's nothing left of it, and you're no help to me in accomplishing it the way you are now!"

Madalane stared at Celeste, her brow drawn into a frown that was part anger and part pain. She had always known her dear Celeste was a spoiled child—a spoiled child who had suffered deprivation and want throughout her youth because of the man who was now her husband; who had been forced to use her beauty and her body to lift herself from the New Orleans gutters; who was now dedicated, as was she, to the vengeance sworn on her mother's deathbed—but she was a spoiled child nonetheless. That fact had never been more evident than at this moment when Celeste so easily dismissed Madalane's pain and saw only her own.

Madalane whispered, "Shattered bones take time to heal."

"You sound just like Doc Maggie and I won't stand for it! Use your potions . . . your brews. They've never failed you before."

"You ask too much."

"No, I don't! I want that woman out of my house, do you hear?" Celeste trembled with rage. "Everything was going so well. The rustling had destroyed Buck's finances and fattened my bank account, most of his ranch hands had left, and your potions had all but destroyed his health. Then Cal came back. Now Derek is the only man left of his entire gang, Cal is the town hero, and Buck is recuperating."

"Your husband is not recuperating. We have just taken a cautious pause in administering my potions. He will never regain what my herbs have taken away from him."

"I'm a better judge of that than you, and I tell you he is recuperating."

"No."

"Yes!" Celeste shivered. "He didn't *fail* when he made love to me yesterday. I was forced to endure his wretched, aged member deep inside me while I moaned and gasped with pretended ecstasy."

"That is impossible!"

Her eyes bright with ire, Celeste demanded, "Do you doubt my word?"

"No, but—"

Celeste's jaw tensed. "I *order* you to get well, Madalane."

Madalane briefly closed her eyes. She had not taken any of the weak drugs for pain that Doc Maggie had left for her. She preferred the more powerful powder she kept among the bottles secreted in her dresser drawer. She would have Celeste get it for her later, when the sleep it induced would not be broken.

Madalane looked up into Celeste's exquisite, raging countenance. She had seen Celeste reach this level of agitation only a few times before, and the sight frightened her. Celeste was furious and desperate to reverse the recent trend of ill fortune that had beset her. There was no certainty what she would do if the situation remained unchanged, and if Celeste made an unwise move now, her sweet Jeanette might never be fully avenged.

Madalane whispered, "You are not alone in your distress, Celeste. I curse the misstep that brought me to this pass—not because of *my* pain, but because of *yours.*" Madalane continued, "But I have the medicines that will numb both your pain and mine until I may again stand beside you."

"What medicines?"

"Bring me my bag from the bottom drawer." Madalane did not miss Celeste's momentary hesitation before complying.

Perspiration beading her forehead and upper lip, Madalane pushed herself to a seated position and withdrew a bottle from the bag Celeste placed on the bed. Holding up the bottle, she said, "This powder is your salvation, Celeste. Give it to your husband tonight, just a pinch—no more—and all signs of his 'recuperation' will disappear."

The small smile that played at Celeste's lips caused Madalane to caution, "Remember, you must be careful! The dose I have indicated will return the symptoms of your husband's illness, but more than that would end his life."

"I'll be careful." Celeste's smile slowly broadened. "I don't want him dead until his signature on his will assures me that he has turned his back on his family forever. When he's too weak to protest, I'll get rid of the girl, too."

"Remember what I said, Celeste. Only a pinch."

"I heard you!"

The bottle clenched tightly in her hand, Celeste left the room and pulled the door closed behind her.

Silent, Madalane leaned back against the pillow, her brow knit with concern. Celeste was not responsible when in a temper, and she had placed a powerfully dangerous tool in her hands.

Madalane grimaced as her leg throbbed more strongly. She would need to repeat her warning tomorrow, when Celeste was more rational. Until then, she consoled herself that with a little more patience, she would be back on her feet to assure that her dear Jeanette would be avenged at last.

"You made a pecan pie?"

Buck's question echoed in the silence of the kitchen as Honor turned toward him. Before starting to cook, she had changed from her riding clothes to

65

a simple blue cotton dress that had served her well in the past. The worn frock lent a fragile quality to Honor's appearance that she would have abhorred, but she gave little thought to her looks as she replied, "Is that so unusual? You have plenty of pecans in the root cellar."

Buck did not reply. Frowning, he looked back at the table where the pie lay cooling, and she was confused. The supper she had prepared had earned her Buck's approval and a place in the Texas Star kitchen. She had believed, however, that if the meal didn't accomplish her purpose, the pie, with its golden crust and tantalizing aroma, would.

If Buck had had any interest in getting to know her, she would have explained that her cooking talent had been acquired during difficult years spent while her mother washed the town's laundry with only minimal payment and sly innuendo in return. She would have told him that during that time she had discovered a hundred different ways to stretch a piece of salt pork into a meal, while considering anything that couldn't be grown in her mother's small garden a delicacy. She would have continued that she had learned to make pies only through the kindness of an old woman who had taken pity on her mother and her; and if she thought he had any interest at all, she would've told him she had no idea what she was doing working in the kitchen of the man she had learned to despise.

Honor looked at the haggard old man standing in front of her. But this wasn't the handsome, virile fellow of her mother's letters; the man her mother had loved all her life. This was—

"Cut it."

"What?"

"You made the pie to be eaten, didn't you?"

"Yes, but—" Honor frowned. "I intended to bring it to you at the dining-room table in a few minutes."

"Cut it here."

Complying, Honor watched as Buck lifted the first forkful of pie to his mouth. He savored, then swallowed it without a smile. He put the fork back down on the plate.

Something was wrong.

Buck said abruptly, "You said you could cook, and you proved you can. You said you could bake, and you proved you can do that, too." He said flatly, "Don't make any more pecan pies."

Honor took a backward step. "What's wrong with it?"

Buck's face paled. "Take it to the boys in the bunkhouse. It won't last long there."

With that, Buck strode toward the outer door. He looked back to say, "We eat breakfast at four and supper at six. I expect to have meals on the table when I get there."

Jace waited in the shadows of the ranch-house porch until Buck disappeared into the barn. He was strangely disturbed by the exchange he had overheard between Buck and Honor, but for the life of him, he didn't know why.

Jace stepped up to the kitchen door, nudged it open with his shoulder, and walked inside. Honor's back was to him. When she turned around to face him, her eyes were suspiciously bright, and she was frowning.

"I brought the dishes back."

"I would've come to get them."

"I had to fix the leg on your bunk anyway."

"It's all right. It'll hold."

"I'll fix it."

"No." She took a breath. "Thank you for bringing back the dishes. You can put them in the bucket over there."

Jace's jaw ticked as he complied. It occurred to him that Honor looked startlingly young in the faded blue dress hanging loosely on her slender frame, with her carelessly upswept hair in ragged wisps around her face, and her shoulders uncharacteristically slumped as if the weight of the world rested on them. He saw the weary hand she raised to her brow and the twitch of her lips that belied the cool, unaffected expression she strove so hard to maintain, and his stomach twisted tight. Heated emotions lay behind her facade. He knew, because he had used a similar defense when prison life became too difficult to bear. He was still adept at the practice.

Angered by her distress, Jace said abruptly, "I told you what your reception here would be. You shouldn't be surprised by it."

"Do you always enjoy saying I told you so?"

"You should get out, leave this ranch before you end up with more trouble than you can handle."

Honor's gaze jumped back to his face. "What makes you think I'd be in trouble if I stayed?"

"Isn't it obvious?"

"No."

Jace took an involuntary step, his voice dropping a note softer. "Celeste doesn't want you here, Honor. She has the boss wrapped around her little finger, and she'll get you out one way or another."

"She has no reason to want to get rid of me. I'm needed here."

"That doesn't make any difference to her."

"I'm not leaving until I'm ready."

"Why?" Jace took another step, unsure why he persisted. "Something's wrong here. You know it, and I know it. Buck is twisted into knots over something, and his wife is pulling the strings. It's not going to get better for you."

"But it's all right for *you* to stay."

"I don't have much choice."

"And I do?"

"You have more choice than I do right now."

"Why?"

"Why what?"

"Why don't you have a choice?"

Jace's jaw tightened. "That's my business."

"Right."

Jace persevered, "Look, I'm not trying to tell you what to do—"

"You're not, huh?"

"Dammit, listen to me, will you?" Jace grasped Honor's shoulders and said, "I'm no stranger to trouble, and I've got a good eye for it. Even if I didn't, it's plain to see that the last thing Celeste wants is an-other woman in her kitchen—another *young* woman. I didn't see much of that servant of hers before she got hurt, but I saw enough. Right or wrong, that woman backs her up in everything she does."

"So?"

"So you don't stand a chance!"

Jace felt the shudder that shook Honor. He saw a flash of distress cross her face before her jaw stiff-ened and she said, "Take your hands off me."

Jace dropped his hands back to his sides.

Honor continued flatly, "For your information, I'm no stranger to trouble either."

"So why stay here when you'll only get more?"

Honor did not reply. Jace thought he saw a tear glisten in her eye before she turned toward the bucket, then said over her shoulder, "You heard what Buck said—take the pie to the bunkhouse. Hopefully, the men will enjoy it."

That was it. She was done talking. Well, that was all right with him.

Jace picked up the pie and turned toward the door.

"Tell the boys breakfast will be ready at four."

"Yes, *ma'am.*"

Jace strode across the darkened yard cursing under his breath. He halted abruptly when he reached the bunkhouse. Why did he let a hardheaded twit who thought she was too smart to listen to good advice get under his skin?

The obvious answer to that question caused Jace to make a soft, frustrated sound. All right, her shoulders had been soft and warm under his palms when he had gripped them in anger, and the scent of her hair had reminded him of spring rain, but it was the almost indiscernible wobble of her lips before she turned away from him that had caused a painful twisting somewhere in his gut. His certainty that her emotionless facade would be sorely tested if she remained would allow him no peace.

Jace took a mental step backwards. What was the matter with him? Why was he allowing himself to get involved in the mess Honor had walked into? She had made it plain that her problems were her own. Big John had stated just as clearly that Honor would probably be gone before the week was out.

Jace pushed open the bunkhouse door.

As far as he was concerned, it couldn't be soon enough.

Chapter Five

Honor glanced out at the morning sky through the kitchen window. Dawn had barely penetrated the dark cover of night when she had knocked on the bunkhouse door and told the men breakfast was ready. She recalled the startled look on Randy's face when she told them to come to the kitchen to eat. When he hesitated, she had stated flatly that she had no intention of transporting food back and forth from the kitchen when there was plenty of room at the kitchen table for the men to sit.

She had then returned to the house, where the dining-room table was set for Celeste and Buck to take their breakfast in privacy and the kitchen table was set for the hands. She had waited with bated breath for the explosion to follow.

It hadn't happened.

Tense and silent, Honor now served the men their breakfast—eggs, sliced ham from the previous night, biscuits and gravy, and coffee dark and strong. She heard the men's whispered comments and felt Jace's sober stare. She smiled briefly when Randy complimented her cooking. The hands' expressions announced Celeste's entrance into the kitchen before she heard the woman's light step. Honor was determined not to betray the agitated pounding of her heart when she turned toward Celeste's disapproving glance.

Deliberately ignoring her, Celeste addressed Randy, her voice emotionless as she said, "My husband suffered a relapse of some sort last night. He says he wants you to continue working on the fencing in the north pasture after you send somebody for Doc Maggie."

"Mitch will go for Doc right away."

Mitch's chair scraped back in response as Celeste turned back toward the hallway and Randy said, "If you need any help, ma'am—"

"I don't need help."

"If the boss wants me to—"

"I already told you what Buck wants you to do." Celeste's gaze was cold. "Nothing more needs to be said."

Honor heard herself ask, "Can I get him something—broth or tea?"

Celeste turned on her sharply. "I don't want you in my husband's room, do you understand? I'll take him whatever he needs."

Uncertain of Celeste's reasoning, Honor pressed, "What about your servant? Do you want me to bring her breakfast?"

"Leave Madalane's breakfast on the stove. I'll take it to her."

Celeste glanced out at the ranch yard as Mitch prepared to leave. Without comment, she turned and disappeared into the hallway.

Breaking the silence following Celeste's departure, Big John whispered, "I figured things were going too well to last. The boss was feeling real good, too."

"Yeah—too good."

Hearing Randy's softly voiced comment, Honor asked, "What do you mean? What's wrong with him?"

"Nobody knows. Doc Maggie's been trying to figure it out since the day the boss took sick." Randy's expression tightened. "And we sure ain't going to get any information out of the boss's wife."

Big John stood up with a scowl. "Let's get going. We can't do nothing here and we've got work to do."

Her stomach knotting tight, Honor watched as the men started toward the door. Randy turned back to instruct, "Not you, Jace. Stay here, just in case. You can ride out and join us if Doc Maggie says it's safe to leave."

If Doc Maggie says it's safe to leave.

Honor glanced toward the hallway, then back at Randy, but the lean cowpoke was already walking out the door.

Honor looked back at the empty hallway, her face blanched of color and her stance unsteady.

Jace started toward her instinctively and asked, "Are you all right?"

75

He saw Honor swallow, then swallow again before she responded, "I'm fine."

"You don't look fine."

Ignoring his comment, she rasped, "What do you think Randy meant by that?"

"By what?"

"That you should stay behind, 'just in case.'"

"In case the boss's wife needs some help."

"Oh."

"What did you think he meant?"

"Nothing."

Nothing.

Jace said abruptly, "Sit down before you fall down."

"I'm fine." Honor turned back toward the stove, but she was trembling, and Jace heard himself ask, "What's wrong, Honor?"

"I told you, nothing."

Turning her to face him, Jace searched Honor's stricken expression with concern. The sight of her distress stirred a disturbing agitation inside him as he whispered, "All right, so you don't want to tell me what's bothering you. I can understand that." He continued resolutely, "But whatever's bothering you, it isn't going to get any better here. Can't you understand that? You'd do yourself a favor if you'd go back to town with Doc Maggie when she's done taking care of the boss."

"Celeste wants to get rid of me." Honor shook her head. "I'm not going to let her do it."

"Why do you care, anyway?"

Honor responded hotly, "Because I've been pushed as far as I'm going to be pushed in my life, and I'm not going to do anything or go anywhere that I don't want to anymore."

"Honor . . ." Jace's voice dropped a note softer, "Believe me, I know how you feel, but maybe this isn't the time or place for you to take that stand."

Honor started to reply, then halted. Her expression hardened. "This isn't your affair."

"I just wanted to—"

"Leave me alone, please."

Jace's hands dropped back to his sides. "I'll be in the barn if you need me."

Doc Maggie leaned over the bed where Buck lay. He was as white as a ghost, cold perspiration marked his brow, and his breathing was shallow. She had listened to his heart and to his lungs and had checked his circulation, but she was at a loss as to what had caused the relapse of his strange malady. She felt Celeste's annoying presence close behind her, and she turned to ask sharply, "What happened last night to start this thing all over again?"

Celeste's face was pale and her eyes red-rimmed. She replied shakily, "Nothing happened. Buck was fine when he went to bed, but he woke up retching and gasping for breath. It frightened me."

Doc barely controlled the tight twist of her lips that Celeste's recitation elicited. It was no longer strange to her that Mitch should arrive to summon her to Buck's bedside, describing Celeste's reaction to Buck's illness as cold and uncaring, only to arrive and discover that although Celeste was meticulously dressed with not a hair out of place, she was devastated. The occasional tear Celeste now shed was so becoming to her faultless countenance that it made Doc want to spit.

There was no doubt in her mind that Celeste was a supreme actress—and Buck was a fool. But Buck was a very sick fool, and Doc was frustrated and upset that she was unable to help him.

Doc Maggie's full face was soberly composed as she whispered, "Do you feel any better, Buck?"

"A little." He gasped for breath. "I thought I was getting better. Just yesterday—" He halted and glanced at Celeste, then said, "I just thought I was."

Doc could imagine.

Celeste took Buck's hand. She gripped it tightly, her expression adoring, and Doc ground her teeth tightly shut. She couldn't stand much more of this. She said, "It looks to me like Buck's stomach distress has calmed down for the moment. Let's hope last night was just a bad case of indigestion." She smiled at Buck encouragingly. "We have no reason to believe this illness will continue, you know. You've been free of these symptoms for a while."

"Yeah . . ." Buck glanced at Celeste, then back at Doc again. Alert to Buck's silent signal, Doc said tentatively, "How did Madalane do last night, Celeste?"

"Fine, I suppose. I haven't been able to spend too much time with her this morning."

"Maybe you should look in on her. There might be something I can do for her before I leave."

Celeste's expression stiffened. "I'm sure she's fine."

"I'd rather you checked. I know Madalane has her own ways, but I wouldn't want to leave without seeing her if she has any problems."

Celeste's tone became haughty. "I called you here to take care of Buck, Doctor, not to check on Madalane."

"Maybe you should do what Doc says, dear," Buck interjected weakly. "I don't want Madalane to suffer because of me."

"All right." Celeste looked down at Buck and forced a smile. "But I'll be right back."

Waiting only until Celeste had closed the door behind her, Doc prompted, "How do you really feel, Buck?"

"Real bad, Doc. My stomach's on fire and my head is reeling. It came over me in a rush last night—all that upchucking and the rest. Celeste was so upset—"

"I suppose she was."

"She didn't know what to do. That's why I wanted to talk to you alone. I'm worried about her."

"You're worried about *her*."

"With me and Madalane sick, it's going to be too much for her."

"You got yourself some help in the kitchen, didn't you? I saw that young woman out there. She seems to have everything under control. She can help with your care."

"Celeste will never let her in here."

"Why?"

Buck smiled weakly. "She's kinda possessive. She doesn't want anybody to take care of me but herself."

"She accepted Madalane's help."

"That's different. Madalane's been with her all her life. She's family."

"Oh, that's what she is."

"Doc—"

"All right. So what do you want me to do?"

"I want you to tell me if I'm going to get better."

Doc paused, her throat suddenly tight. She hadn't expected this. Buck, damn him, was an old friend! He was looking at her with that penetrating stare of his that demanded the truth from her. There was only one thing she could say.

"Maybe not." There, she had said it. Doc continued levelly, "I told you, I've never seen anything like this, Buck. If you'd only go back East to see a specialist—"

"No."

"You're so damned stubborn!"

"Maybe, but I ain't going back East to die in some hospital among strangers."

"Who said you'd die there?"

"Forget it, Doc."

"You *will* die if this thing continues and you refuse to let another doctor look at you. I've done all I can for you. There isn't much else I can do."

Buck blinked.

"I'm sorry, Buck."

"It's just that it's so hard on Celeste."

Doc's patience snapped. "I'd be more worried about myself if I were you, but since you're worried about overworking your young wife, why don't you come back to town to stay with me for a while? I'll be able to get a better handle on what's ailing you if I'm around you all the time, and it'll take the pressure off Celeste until Madalane's better."

Buck's response was forestalled as Celeste responded from the doorway, "No, I won't have it!" She rushed to the bed and grasped Buck's hand. Her face suitably strained, she whispered into Buck's pallid countenance, "You wouldn't do that to me, would you, Buck? You wouldn't leave me?" A single tear trailed down her cheek as she rasped, "I . . . I couldn't stand being separated from you."

"Don't cry, Celeste, darlin'."

Buck was still consoling Celeste weakly when Doc Maggie took a backward step, then turned to the door with disgust.

Yes, Celeste was the consummate actress . . . and Buck was more than a fool.

Snatching up her bag, Doc walked out the doorway toward Madalane's room. She grimaced as she neared the door. It occurred to her that there were times when that Hippocratic oath she had taken was a real pain in the neck.

"Doc?"

Doc looked up at the slender figure clothed in a baggy blue dress in the entrance to the kitchen. If she remembered correctly, the young woman's name was Honor Gannon. Doc unconsciously shook her head. The poor girl had gotten more than she had bargained for when she took this job.

It appeared to Doc as she approached that Honor's face was unnaturally pale and her voice unsteady as she asked, "How's Buck? The . . . the ranch hands were worried."

"The truth?" Doc shrugged. "I don't know. His sickness has me puzzled. I can't really say how it'll go from here."

"But he's not going to . . . I mean, he's not—"

"Dying?" Doc shrugged again. "I couldn't tell you. He's damned sick, that's for sure, but he rallied once before. He could do it again, I suppose. I just don't know how much more of this his heart can take."

"Is there anything I can do for him?"

"You mean, is there anything Celeste will *let* you do for him?" Doc glanced over her shoulder at Buck's bedroom doorway and frowned. "I suppose that wasn't too wise to say, under the circumstances, but it's the truth. There's not too much she'll let you do for Buck, so there's no use worrying about it."

"I'm not worried. I . . . I just wanted to help."

Doc stared at the girl's ashen face. There was something about her . . .

"*Doctor!*"

Doc looked back at the sound of Madalane's call. The damned woman had ears like a cat!

"*I would like to see you now, Doctor.*"

Damn that Hippocratic oath!

Frustrated, Doc said, "I have to see to my other patient." She paused to scrutinize Honor a moment longer before adding, "Don't worry about anything that's happening here. Just do your job. That's all anybody can ask of you."

"*Doctor . . .*"

Doc turned toward Madalane's room, her frown tightening.

* * *

No, this couldn't be the way it would all end. She couldn't have come all the way to Lowell just to have her father die before anything was settled between them!

The close confines of the kitchen felt overwhelming, and Honor rushed into the ranch yard to get some fresh air. She closed her eyes against the tears that threatened.

What was the matter with her? She had come to Lowell to meet a man she despised, not to shed tears because he was ill. He wasn't worth her tears, anyway. He hadn't given a thought to her mother, much less shed a tear for her when she was dying.

Yet . . .

Honor raised a weary hand to her forehead. Nothing was the way she had expected. She needed to take a step back and assess the situation more clearly. She needed time.

The sound of approaching hoofbeats raised Honor's head. A rider was coming into sight in the distance. Unwilling to be found so disheveled and shaky, she faded back out of sight beside the ranch-house porch.

The rider drew closer, and Honor gasped. She recognized the man's broad stature and sun-streaked hair at first glance. He reined up at the hitching rail, and she was about to step into sight when the door of the house slammed open and Celeste walked onto the porch.

Her beautiful face flushed with wrath, Celeste demanded, "What are you doing here, Cal?"

Honor saw the restraint Cal employed as he responded, "I was told in town that Mitch came to get Doc this morning because my father had a relapse. I heard it's pretty bad. I wanted—"

"I don't care what you wanted. Your father made it plain to you that he doesn't want you here."

"He's my father, Celeste. If he's sick, I want to see him."

"He doesn't want to see you. He'll never forgive you for your sister's death."

"Bonnie's dead. Whether it was my fault or not, it's all in the past."

"Is it? You'll never convince your father of that."

"I want to see him."

"Buck is ill . . . very ill. He's too weak to argue with you again. If you really care about him, you'll leave now, before he realizes you're here."

"I want to see him, Celeste."

Honor took another backward step when Doc Maggie's buxom figure appeared behind Celeste on the porch. Surprising Honor, Doc Maggie interrupted to say, "I just checked on your father, Cal. He's sleeping." Doc glanced at Celeste's flushed face and said reluctantly, "Celeste is right. Your father's too weak right now for any excitement."

Cal's chest was heaving with emotion, and Honor's heart ached at the sight of him. The lump in her throat tightened when he said, "I just wanted to talk to him for a few minutes, Doc."

"Not now."

"Not now. Not ever." Celeste ordered, "Get out! You're a hero in Lowell where those poor fools are too stupid to see the person you really are, Cal Star, but here at the Texas Star we're not so ignorant. Your father remembers what you did, and so do I. He doesn't need you around here. I'll take care of him the way I've always taken care of him. You can be sure of that. So get out, and don't come back!"

Her throat choking tight, Honor watched as Cal glanced again at Doc Maggie, then turned his horse and started back down the trail.

Ignoring the sharp exchange between Celeste and Doc that followed, Honor hurried toward the barn. She gasped as Jace stepped into sight with her livery-stable horse saddled. She said, "I need him . . . now."

Jace handed her the reins. He did not speak as Honor pulled herself up into the saddle and spurred the animal into motion.

Swinging out behind the barn, Honor merged onto the main trail in sight of Cal as he rode steadily back toward town. He reined back and turned his mount toward her as she approached at a gallop. Honor slid her mount to a halt beside him, her expression tremulous as she faced her brother fully for the first time.

"Are you looking for me?" Cal's eyes were the color of honey. She supposed he had been a handsome child, because he was a handsome man. She supposed that those eyes could burn with warmth, but they were presently cold as he waited for her reply.

"Yes, I am." Honor's throat was so tight that she could hardly speak. What could she say? *Hello, Cal, I'm the sister you've never known, and you're the brother I never knew existed. I wish I knew you. I wish we could be friends. I wish—*

She said, "I wanted to talk to you."

Cal studied her more closely. "Who are you?"

He was truly handsome in a totally masculine way. He bore no resemblance to Buck or to her, but Honor was strangely proud as she replied, "I . . . my name is Honor Gannon. Buck hired me to work in the Texas Star kitchen until Celeste's servant recuperates." She continued in a rush, "I heard what happened back there at the house, and I just want to say I'm sorry. I know how you must feel to be kept from seeing your father when he's sick . . . not to be allowed to be a part of your own family." She blinked back the heat of tears as she continued, "I can't say I really understand what's going on at the Texas Star, but I want you to know I'll do whatever I can to watch over your father for you while I'm there."

Cal looked at her strangely. "I don't understand."

Honor managed a smile. "It's simple enough. Celeste has no right to keep you from your father if you want to talk to him."

"Honor . . ." Cal said simply, "I appreciate your concern, but the truth is, my father doesn't want to talk to me."

"He's making a mistake."

Cal did not respond.

"He should be proud to have a son like you."

Cal searched her face more intently. "Do . . . do I know you from somewhere?"

"No, but I've seen this happen before. It's just the people involved who are different."

"I suppose."

Honor took an unsteady breath. "I just wanted to tell you I'll do my best for . . . for your father and you." Cal maintained his silence, and Honor managed a smile. "That's all I've got to say."

Honor was about to turn her mount back toward the ranch when Cal leaned over to grip her hand. His gaze direct, he said unexpectedly, "Thanks, Honor. For what it's worth, I appreciate what you said."

The lump in her throat made speech impossible, but Honor nodded. She did not look back as she spurred her horse toward the ranch.

Jace stepped into sight as she drew her mount to a halt at the barn minutes later. Not waiting for her to dismount, he swung her down from the saddle. His expression was tight as he said, "Celeste is looking for you. Doc wants to talk to you before she leaves. I told her I'd send you back to the house as soon as I found you."

Feeling she ought to explain herself, she said, "I went—"

"I know where you went."

When she did not reply, Jace said unexpectedly, "Do you love him?"

Honor went momentarily still. Cal . . . her brother.

A rush of warmth filled her. Yes, she supposed she did.

Appearing to read her response in her eyes, Jace urged coldly, "You'd better hurry up if you want to keep your job."

That thought resounding in her mind, Honor walked quickly back to the house.

She turned toward the barn before entering, to see Jace leading her mount toward Doc's buggy. She realized she hadn't thanked him—for being there, and for . . . caring.

Jace led Honor's mount across the ranch yard, but his mind was far from the task at hand. He had seen the look in Honor's eyes when she rode out after Cal Star.

He hadn't expected it, but he had realized at a glance that she loved the big cowboy.

Jace swallowed the lump in his throat that the thought evoked. He remembered a time when he was no stranger to love. Peg had made his life worthwhile, but when she was gone, she had taken all his love with her.

The image of a thin woman in a baggy blue dress returned to mind, and Jace felt a familiar twinge in the pit of his stomach. He was uncertain how he had allowed himself to get involved in Honor's difficulties. The incident with the rattler aside, he had been drawn to her from the first, but for the life of him, he couldn't understand why. Aside from a purely male reaction to her that he had sought to deny, he supposed her stubborn arrogance had intrigued him; yet it was the fleeting vulnerability and need he had glimpsed in her eyes, so contrary to the image she sought to present, that lingered in his mind. She had struck a chord in him that somehow bound him to her. He wanted—

Jace struck the unfinished thought from his mind. The hard truth was, he had made a mistake. He had been right in sensing Honor's need, but it wasn't *him*

Honor needed. He knew now that it wasn't an accident that she had come to the Texas Star.

Jace tied Honor's horse up behind Doc's buggy as Randy had instructed before leaving, then returned to the barn to saddle up old Whistler. The rest of the hands were waiting for him in the north pasture, and he had no intention of remaining at the house any longer than necessary. Honor had probably found Celeste and Doc Maggie waiting for her when she walked into the kitchen. The exchange between Celeste and Doc on the porch after Cal left had been fiery. He supposed they had a lot to say to her.

Honor had chosen a hard way to go.

The knot inside Jace tightened.

He hoped Cal Star was worth it.

"I'll arrange to have a wheelchair made in town." Doc Maggie's full face was still stained with angry color as she glanced at Celeste, then turned back to Honor, continuing, "Celeste tells me that Madalane must be mobile. I feel it's a mistake for Madalane to attempt to do too much too soon, but Celeste insists, and Madalane agrees. John Sickle is a handy carpenter. He can make anything if the price is right, and Celeste assures me *any* price will be right."

Doc Maggie paused briefly, her small nose twitching revealingly. "I have convinced Celeste that until Madalane is able to help her with Buck's care, you must be allowed to assist with his needs."

Surprised at Doc's statement, Honor glanced at Celeste. Celeste's lips were tight. The clash between Doc and her that had begun on the porch after Cal left had obviously escalated; and if Honor was any judge, Doc had agreed to arrange for the wheelchair *on her terms*.

Doc continued, "I'll be back tomorrow to check on Buck and Madalane, and to make sure things are working out as we agreed—isn't that right, Celeste?"

Celeste nodded. "My only concern is that Buck should have the best care possible."

"I know that, Celeste." Doc Maggie's smile was stiff. "I feel that way, too. That's why I wanted to make sure Honor would be allowed to take over when you wearied."

Celeste's response was frigid as she said, "It appears we have everything settled, so I'll say goodbye, Doctor. I'm going back to Buck. He gets upset if I'm not there when he opens his eyes."

Doc's smile became a grimace when Celeste turned toward the door. When Celeste disappeared from sight, Doc said, "I'd appreciate it if you'd walk back to my buggy with me, Honor." Waiting only until they had cleared the doorway, Doc hissed a stream of profanities that snapped Honor's eyes wide.

Doc noted Honor's reaction and said, "I forgot. You don't know me well, but if you did, you'd know swearing is the way I get rid of frustration. Unfortunately, it's sometimes the only relief I get."

Keeping her eyes straight ahead, Doc said, "I have no doubt Celeste is watching us from the window, so I'll make this brief. Buck is a dear friend, but he's proof of the adage that there's no fool like an old fool.

"You probably heard what Celeste said to Cal," she continued. "To my mind, it's her fault that Buck is holding on to his anger and still blames Cal for his sister's death, even though we all know it was an accident. To put it bluntly, I don't like Celeste, and I don't trust her. I feel the same way about that woman servant of hers. I don't know how you happened to get stuck in the middle of all this, but you're here now, and this is fair warning. Watch out. Celeste won't hesitate to step on you if you get in her way."

Doc Maggie scrutinized Honor's reaction to her statement, then said, "Fortunately, if the talk in town is correct, you're not the type to let anybody get away with anything. That could work to your benefit, but it could also work against you here. All I can tell you for sure is that, despite what Celeste tried to say, you're needed here—even though I can't imagine why you'd want to have any part of this mess."

"Did all that talk about me in town say anything about my being stubborn, Doc?"

"It sure did."

"And about my knowing what I want to do, and doing it?"

"That, too."

"Well, that says it all."

"The only question remaining is, why?"

"I don't know." Honor shrugged. "I suppose I don't like Celeste either."

Doc gave a short laugh, then climbed into her buggy. She glanced to the rear where Jace had tied up Honor's livery-stable horse and said, "I suppose I'll be returning your horse for you. I'll also have Sophie pack up the rest of your things at the boardinghouse and I'll bring them out to you tomorrow." Looking down at Honor with the reins in hand, she said, "I need to say that I appreciate your being here, Honor. Buck may be a fool, but Emma and he . . . well, I've known him for a long time. I want to do right by him."

I've known him for a long time.

As Doc Maggie's buggy moved briskly down the trail, Honor wished she could say the same.

Celeste sat silently beside Buck's bed, her expression fixed. His breathing was uneven and his face was gray.

Just a pinch . . .

She remembered the pinch of Madalane's powder that she had added to Buck's coffee before they retired. She smiled, remembering she had then added a little more. The bastard, with his knobby, seeking hands and scrawny body, hadn't had the strength to touch her after that.

She had been *so concerned*, of course, when Buck was taken violently ill shortly afterwards. She had cleaned up after him and reassured him that he would be fine, while enjoying every minute of his physical distress. Buck's gratitude, which he had expressed between bouts of retching, had silently amused her.

It still did.

Buck moved restlessly in his sleep, and Celeste assessed him coldly. She doubted he could withstand another dose of Madalane's powder at the strength she had given him the previous evening. She needed to be careful. If he died before his will was changed, before she could make sure he removed Cal and his long-lost brother, Taylor, from it, the brilliant future she and Madalane had planned in New Orleans would be drastically curtailed.

Buck was a stubborn bastard, all right. While despising his sons for reasons she constantly reminded him of, and proclaiming his intense love for her, he continued to avoid any discussion of his will. She could not understand why he refused to make that last concession, but she was determined to change his mind. It was just a matter of time.

Her mind came back to the present at the sound of hoofbeats approaching the house. Celeste moved toward the bedroom window. She had heard the men depart earlier, and had heard Jace leave shortly after Doc Maggie. She had deliberately seen to it since marrying Buck that they would have few visitors at the Texas Star. She wondered who this could be.

Celeste looked out the window at the approaching horseman, and her heart jumped to a rapid pounding. Within moments, she had stepped out onto the porch. Annoyed to find Honor already standing there, she ordered brusquely, "Get back to work. I'll take care of this."

Celeste waited until the door had closed behind Honor before turning to look at the man on horseback. His features were heavy, his clothes sweat-stained, his boots covered with muck, and she could smell his unclean odor from a distance as he said, "Howdy, ma'am. I heard in town you was looking for help out here, and I rode out to see. I figure I'm as good a wrangler as there is in these parts, if you're looking to hire somebody."

"We're not." Celeste's response was cold despite the continued thudding of her heart. "I'm sorry, but you wasted your time riding out here. Goodbye."

"Ma'am . . ." The fellow's raspy voice turned her back toward him as she started toward the door. "I'm hoping I haven't *really* wasted my time . . . that you'll keep me in mind."

"Yes . . . of course." Celeste took a ragged breath. "Good day."

The sound of the fellow's mount departing echoed behind her as Celeste walked stiffly toward Madalane's room. Not bothering to knock, Celeste pushed the door open, then closed it firmly behind her. She walked to Madalane's bed, noting her servant's frown as Madalane asked, "What is wrong, Celeste?"

"He came *here.* I told him never to do that!"

Madalane mumbled softly under her breath, then said, "You must make sure he does not repeat that mistake. We have too much to lose."

"I know that. It isn't necessary for you to remind me." Agitation increased the pounding of Celeste's heart as she hissed, "Damn you, Madalane! Your carelessness has caused all kinds of complications. I should leave to meet with him. He's made it clear that he'll be waiting, yet I'm trapped here because I don't want that Honor woman going near Buck when I'm not around."

"You said the doctor gave your husband a powder to make him sleep."

"Yes."

"He is in a weakened condition. He should not awaken for hours. If you are wise, you will find a way to be back before he does."

"Buck should sleep—of course—but we both know my husband seldom does what's expected of him."

"You have no choice."

Her breast heaving, Celeste snapped, "My present dilemma is all your fault, Madalane. If you hadn't fallen—"

Celeste halted briefly at Madalane's glance, only to continue more hotly than before, "Don't look at me like that! Every word I've said is true. This debacle is all your fault, and because it is, I expect you to see to it that Honor doesn't go near Buck while I'm gone."

Madalane replied coldly, "I am injured. I will be unable to move easily until the wheelchair arrives."

"I won't listen to your excuses!"

Silent for a moment, aware of the danger of confronting Celeste when she was in her present state of agitation, Madalane responded, "You may depend on me, Celeste, as you always have."

"*As I always have . . .*" Celeste gave a contemptuous snort. "That may have been true before, but you have yet to prove that I may depend on you now."

Dismissing her silent servant with a hard glance, Celeste left the room. In the kitchen minutes later, she addressed Honor coldly.

"My husband is asleep. I need fresh air to clear my mind. I'm going out for a ride. I expect to be back before he awakens."

She did not wait for a reply.

Randy turned toward Jace as he approached the north pasture where they were working. It did not miss Jace's notice that Big John and Mitch dropped their work at the sight of him and were standing beside Randy when he reined up.

"Well, what did Doc say?" Randy asked as Jace dismounted.

"Not much," Jace responded. "I figure she's thinking it's just more of the same as far as the boss is concerned."

Big John and Mitch mumbled under their breath, but Randy pressed, "What about Honor? Seems to me Celeste would have something to say about her serving us our meals in the main house."

"She hasn't said anything . . . yet."

"Nothing, huh?" Randy shook his head. "That don't sound like her."

"I'm thinking she was too busy arguing with Doc about the way she ran off Cal Star when he came to see how his father was."

"So Cal showed up at the house and she ran him off." Randy's graying mustache twitched with irritation. "It's Celeste's fault that Buck's sticking to his guns the way he is, instead of using his head and seeing that Cal came back to Lowell to make peace. But the boss is too damned taken with that wife of his to listen, even now that there's a chance for all of them to be a family again, especially since Cal and Pru got married.

Married.

The word reverberated in Jace's stunned mind. He said, "Cal's married?"

"Right. There's only one thing that could make that fella happier, too, and that's to settle up with the past."

"The past."

"With his father and with his brother, Taylor." Randy shook his head. "But nobody's seen hide nor hair of Taylor since he graduated from that school back East where his pa put him in order to get rid of him after he married Celeste; and Celeste keeps feeding Buck's muleheadedness about what happened to Bonnie all them years ago."

Still numb from Randy's unexpected revelation, Jace nodded. Cal Star was married, yet Honor's expression had clearly revealed that she loved him.

Did she know?

Did she *care?*

Big John's voice jerked Jace back to the present as he commented, "Celeste ain't the type to let Doc get the best of her."

"Maybe not," Randy interjected, "but I'm thinking Doc might have the upper hand, with Madalane off her feet like she is."

"And with Honor in the kitchen." Mitch gave a short laugh. "I'm thinking that little lady ain't the type to take what Celeste hands out, either."

97

"There ain't much we can do about it either way, except do what Buck pays us for." His expression sober, Randy said, "It's time to get back to work."

Jace secured his horse and picked up a shovel as the men resumed their tasks.

His mind was reeling. It was going to be a long day.

Pushing her buggy to a furious pace when she was out of sight of the house, Celeste reined back beside the dilapidated cabin minutes later. She swung herself down, raised a hand to smooth her upswept coiffure, and entered the cabin boldly. The familiar odor of mildew and rancid filth met her nostrils as the door slammed shut behind her, enclosing her in the darkness of the airless cabin. She halted as a familiar voice said harshly, "It's about time you showed up!"

Celeste gasped as she was gripped tightly from behind. Derek's calloused hands moved mercilessly over her breasts before slipping down to grip her crotch possessively.

Celeste felt her lover's hot breath against her neck as he whispered, "Damn you, Celeste! I've been missing you. My body's been aching for what only you can do for it, and I ain't too happy with being kept waiting."

Despite herself, Celeste felt a heated surge of desire jump to life inside her. Images of erotic hours spent with Derek flashed across her mind. She fought her body's response to his strong body odor, the rough surroundings so unlike the boring cleanliness of her marriage bed, the deep shadows surrounding her that brought to mind those years spent learning to please her admirers in a New Orleans bordello—when she realized, perversely, that she was learning to please herself.

Celeste gasped as Derek turned her roughly to face him. His sweaty, unshaven countenance was flushed with lust. "You didn't even kiss me, darlin'," he grated.

Derek's thick lips covered hers and his tongue delved deep into her mouth. She struggled against the offensive taste of him as his wet lips moved over hers and he clawed at the neckline of her dress.

"Wait." Breathless, Celeste rasped, "Let me loosen my dress. I can't afford to return disheveled." Carefully slipping her bodice off her shoulders, Celeste gasped aloud as Derek's mouth closed over the crest of her breast. She moaned as he bit her sharply, then crushed him closer, offering her breasts to him freely.

Wild with her frenzied response to Derek's crude lovemaking, Celeste struggled to free herself of her clothes. Satisfied only when she was naked under Derek's lascivious touch, she then drew him with her to the stained cot they had used countless times before.

Celeste grunted when Derek drove himself inside her. She wrapped her legs around him and rode his frenetic thrusts with encouraging whispers. She opened her mouth under his kiss as he paused to savor the taste of her. She reveled in the animalistic scents and sounds that filled the cabin. She felt Derek's body swell inside her, then groaned aloud, joining him as his physical heat spilled hot and wet within her.

Lying naked and sweltering underneath Derek's still-clothed body, Celeste pushed him off her roughly. She heard his satisfied growl as he fell back against the cot beside her, and a familiar heat ignited anew inside her.

Celeste ordered softly, "Take off your clothes, Derek."

Her eyes now accustomed to the semidarkness, Celeste saw Derek turn toward her with a hard laugh. "What's the matter? Ain't you satisfied yet, darlin'?"

"I'm not your darlin', Derek, remember that. I'm your business partner and the woman who's going to end up making you rich—but I still want you to take off your clothes."

Watching as Derek raised himself to strip away his clothing, Celeste whispered, "I'm going to make you hunger for me like you never did before, Derek. I'm going to make you burn so hot that you'll never want to cross me. I'm going to make sure you understand I mean what I say when I tell you I don't want you *ever* showing up at the Texas Star ranch house again. And when I'm done, you and I are going to start making plans that'll put an end to the Texas Star forever."

Celeste's words drifted away as Derek's hairy, thickly muscled body was exposed to her at last. Her mouth went dry with sexual thirst at the sight of him, and excitement crawled up her spine. Hot, fast, and hard—Derek knew how she liked it.

Now it was her turn.

Climbing on top of him, she was titillated by the feel of Derek's sweaty body and the odor of his sexual exertion. Celeste lowered her mouth. Derek was already groaning when she bit him, hard. The taste of him, sound of him, smell of him pushing her over the edge of control, Celeste manipulated Derek's body with a voracious hunger. Her libidinous frenzy growing, she worked him harder until her lust exploded with a shout that earned her the full measure of Derek's wet, sticky reward.

Breathless atop him, Celeste looked down at her dissolute lover and smiled. Rolling to the cot beside him, she whispered into his ear, "You'll do anything I tell you to do, won't you, Derek?"

His breathing still uneven, Derek lazily opened his eyes.

"Say it. Tell me you'll wait for my signal about when to meet me here again. Tell me that while you're waiting, you'll amuse yourself however you want, but when I call, you'll come running to do whatever I ask. Tell me there's nothing you wouldn't do to please me. Tell me you'll come *begging* if you need to—because you know there's nothing I won't do to please you in return."

When Derek did not immediately respond, Celeste ran her tongue over his unshaven chin. The salty taste of his skin excited her anew, and she whispered, "Or do you want me to convince you a little more?"

She urged softly, "Answer me, Derek."

Derek turned unexpectedly toward her. He grasped her breasts and squeezed them hard, and she gasped. He dug his hands into her hair and pulled her head back painfully to cover her mouth with his wet lips. Sucking and biting her tender flesh, he rasped thickly, "I heard what you said, but we'll see who comes begging when I'm done."

Crude . . . rough . . . relentless. Celeste reveled in Derek's sexual assault.

Responding with a frenzy of her own, Celeste mumbled against the heat of him, "Yes, we'll see."

Her mind in a turmoil, her fingers working automatically as if of their own accord, Honor continued scraping the potatoes piled on the table in front of her. Celeste had left "to take a ride to clear her head" almost an hour earlier, and the house was silent.

Shaken from her meeting with Cal, Honor had stood motionless as the sound of Celeste's buggy faded from her hearing. She remembered Cal's expression when Celeste drove him away from the ranch without seeing his father. She recalled looking into his face minutes later, and feeling his pain as if it were her own. The promise she had made to him, that she'd look after his father for him, remained vivid in her mind. The thought had raised her gaze toward the hallway. She had started toward Buck's room when Madalane had summoned her.

She knew she would never forget the malice in the Negress's gaze when she entered her bedroom. Nor would she ever forget the warning in her tone when Madalane said, "You will stay away from the master's room while the mistress is gone. *I* will go to him if he calls."

When Honor had challenged Madalane's ability to

follow through on her words, Madalane had repeated venomously, "*I* will go to him if he calls."

She had returned to the silent kitchen with Madalane's warning ringing in her mind. Celeste and Madalane were suspicious of her intentions.

Honor closed her eyes and pressed her palm to her throbbing temple. A lifetime of friendlessness and innuendo had hardened her, but she had been unprepared for the assault on her emotions that her arrival on the Texas Star would bring.

Something is wrong here, Honor. Buck is twisted into knots over something, and his wife is pulling the strings.

Jace's assessing words.

Leave this ranch before you end up with more trouble than you can handle.

His sober advice.

Celeste is looking for you. I told her I'd send you back to the house as soon as I found you.

His warning.

Honor took a sudden determined breath. No, she didn't need Jace's assessment of the situation, his advice, or his warnings, especially when he had secrets of his own. And if she foolishly clung to the memory of the earnest look in his dark eyes and the warmth it had evoked, of the strength and determination she sensed lying below his unaffected exterior, she needed to shake off that dependence. She had come to the Texas Star with one purpose in mind, and she would not forget it.

A muffled sound interrupted Honor's thoughts, and she raised her head toward the hallway a few steps away. She tensed when she heard it again—Buck calling Celeste.

Her heart pounding, Honor entered the hallway, then halted abruptly in front of Madalane's door. She waited.

Silence.

Buck called again, and anger flushed Honor's face with heat. She pushed open Madalane's door to see the Negress sleeping, her mouth open, and the sound of her steady breathing loud in the silence.

Honor opened Buck's bedroom door and approached the bed.

Her steps slowed as she neared him. Her mind raged, *No, it isn't fair!* She didn't want to pity the poor, wasted shell of a man lying in the bed in front of her. She didn't want to watch his life drain gradually, painfully from his body. She wanted only to face, at last, the man responsible for making her mother live a lifetime of neglect.

But this wasn't that man.

"Honor." Surprise registered in Buck's heavy-lidded eyes when he saw her. He took an unsteady breath. "I wasn't expecting it to be you. Where's Celeste?"

Honor heard herself say, "Celeste went for a ride to clear her head."

"Oh, that's good." Buck nodded. "This has been hard on her. She's frantic, and doesn't know what to do." He paused for a shaky breath. "I'm thirsty."

Her inner trembling was not reflected in the steadiness of her hands as Honor filled Buck's cup from a pitcher on the nightstand, then raised him up to hold the cup to his lips. She watched his throat work laboriously as he sipped.

Appearing exhausted by the effort, Buck slipped back against the pillow and briefly closed his eyes. When he opened them again, he said with surprising harshness, "You weren't expecting this when you came here, were you?"

Honor tensed. "I wasn't expecting what?"

"To find yourself tending to a dying old man."

"You're not dying."

"Really?" Buck appeared pained. "I wish I could believe that. There are so many things . . ."

His voice trailed away, and Honor responded, "Doc said you rallied once before and you can do it again."

"She did?" Affection touched his tone. "That old woman doesn't know what she's talking about."

Honor responded instinctively, "I bet you wouldn't say that to her face."

Buck almost smiled. "I'd have to be a lot stronger than I am right now to try."

Suddenly at a loss, Honor said, "Is there anything I can get you? Some tea, maybe?"

"No."

"You're sure?"

"I'm going to sleep for a while."

Without her conscious intent, Honor adjusted the coverlet on Buck's bed. She snatched back her hands when he said, "Don't fuss. I'm all right."

As she started toward the door, she heard Buck say, "Don't tell Celeste you were in here. She'll feel bad if she knows I woke up while she was gone."

Honor went momentarily still. She drew the door

closed behind her with Doc Maggie's words resounding in her mind.

There's no fool like an old fool.

Harsh words that were painfully true.

Celeste reined up her buggy at the barn, then hastened toward the ranch house. She entered and looked sharply toward Honor Gannon when the young woman looked up from the table where she worked. Celeste swept her with a glance. It occurred to her that Honor might be pretty in a way if she weren't so thin, or perhaps if her clothes did not look as if they had been fashioned for a more robust frame. Her hair might be considered passably fair if it were more carefully coiffed; her eyes might be outstanding if they were not so cold; and her small features might even be pleasant if she ever chose to smile. But she was plain. All she had to recommend her—as far as a man was concerned—was her youth.

The thought of her husband's weakness for young women brought a frown to Celeste's face. She snapped, "Did my husband wake up while I was gone?"

Celeste noted the almost arrogant rise of the young woman's chin before she replied, "No."

"Am I to assume you went nowhere near his room?"

"Yes."

Still annoyed by the tenor of the young woman's responses, Celeste pushed open the door of Buck's room. Standing at his bedside, she looked down at him, stone-faced. He was a sorry sight—pale, emaciated, breathing with difficulty, but he had stopped vomiting. Yes, this had been a close call, but she had been angry. Fool that he was, Buck had never even sensed it.

Celeste stopped to check her appearance in the bedroom mirror on the way out of the room. Her hair was slightly askew, and her face a bit reddened from Derek's rough handling, but a brisk ride and time spent in tears over her husband's condition would have had the same result. As for her attire, she was always too cautious to have a concern there.

Celeste walked slowly to the doorway. She would use the bedroom chaise to sleep for a while, with the excuse that her husband was too ill for her to share his bed. The truth was, however, that the brush of Buck's paper-dry skin and bony frame repelled her.

Celeste's mind slipped back to the hour recently past and the press of Derek's thickly muscled body against hers. She had ridden him well, and she had proved her mastery over him. He would do anything she said. He had gasped those words with his own mouth as he had surrendered to her at last.

Celeste's temporary satisfaction slipped away. In the end, she had run out of time with Derek and had been unable to formulate plans for the future demise of the Texas Star. That annoyed her, but she needed time to work on Buck in any case. She would start tomorrow, and she'd be damned if she'd quit that pursuit until his will was changed.

Celeste paused at Madalane's bedroom door. Madalane's injury was a delay she hadn't anticipated, and Madalane would pay for the inconvenience she had caused.

Celeste did not bother to knock.

* * *

Madalane glanced up as her bedroom door opened abruptly. She had had a difficult afternoon. The barest necessities were difficult to accomplish with her leg splinted and the pain ever present. She dared not alleviate her pain with use of the powders Doc Maggie had left for fear of falling asleep and letting the activities of the household go by unnoticed. She had worked too long and too hard to risk complications now because of a strange woman in the house who was no more than common kitchen help.

Exhausted by her trials, Madalane had dozed briefly as the long afternoon stretched on. She had dreamed she had heard Celeste's husband calling, but she had awakened to silence and the realization that her concerns had only been reflected in her dreams. She had been relieved when she finally heard the sound of Celeste's return, but as she stared at her now, it was plain to see that Celeste's mood had not improved.

"Have you finished assessing my appearance, Madalane?" Celeste's question was harsh. She confirmed Madalane's reading of her mood by continuing, "Is my attire suitable enough not to stir the suspicions of my dear husband or the intruder now working in my kitchen, or must I make up a plausible excuse for the way I look?"

Madalane responded carefully, "I assume you accomplished your purpose."

"Derek understands." Celeste's smile was revealing. "I used a very intimate persuasion to convince him that he shouldn't come to the ranch again."

A familiar fear flitted across Madalane's mind. Derek and his gang of rustlers had been necessary to Celeste's plan. They had accomplished their purpose in severely damaging the stability of the Texas Star until Cal Star had caught up with all of them except Derek. However, months had passed since the activities of the gang had been brought to an end, and Derek had become all but useless to them. Yet he was still there, waiting.

Madalane's handsome face hardened. Derek was a degenerate, totally unworthy of her beautiful Celeste. Worse, he brought out a dark side of Celeste that Celeste enjoyed too well for Madalane not to fear it. She did not have to see the marks of rough handling on Celeste's beautiful body to know that while she was with Derek that afternoon, she had abandoned herself to a weakness that might eventually consume her.

Fearing for Celeste, cursing her throbbing leg, Madalane said, "If he understands the situation here, you will not need to see him again soon."

"Derek may yet be useful to me. I'll see him whenever I want."

"It is dangerous with the new woman in the kitchen. She will suspect. She will speak to your husband."

"Buck will never believe a word she might speak against me."

"If you continue your intimate association with that man, you will risk all we have worked for!"

"I risk nothing! Derek is my slave, although he be-

109

lieves the opposite to be true. He will do anything I ask rather than lose me."

"And when we leave this place to return to New Orleans?"

Celeste smiled. "Then I will establish myself in my rightful place in society, with a full stable of willing partners ready to satisfy my every whim."

"And Derek?"

"Crude Derek? *Unclean* Derek?" Celeste laughed. "I will not even remember his name."

A knock on the door turned Celeste with a start. She responded sharply, "What is it?"

Honor replied, "Your husband is calling you."

Celeste sneered as she whispered to Madalane, "And I will see to it that I am never summoned like a common servant again."

Taking a moment to affix an appropriate expression on her face, Celeste walked out toward her husband's room.

"I don't know if I like this."

Randy's softly voiced comment turned Jace toward him as they approached the kitchen for their evening meal. Tired, his muscles aching from stretching resistant fencing wire, Jace said nothing. One look at the pasture they were refencing, and Jace had understood the ranch hands' concern over the ranch's deterioration. No one had to tell him the ranch would have a hard way back with the limited help available to Buck.

Randy continued, "It's like waiting for the axe to

fall, with us coming to the house for our meals and Celeste holding her tongue for some reason. There's going to be hell to pay eventually."

The scent of roasting meat and baking sweet potatoes reached Jace's nostrils, and the men murmured appreciatively. A reluctant smile touched Randy's lips as he said, "But in the meantime, it sure is good to feel like a part of the family here again."

The men slipped into their seats at the table as Honor brought in the heaped platters. Jace waited patiently for the platters to reach him, his eyes intent on Honor's sober expression. Something had happened to upset her while he was gone.

Forcing that thought from his mind, Jace reached for the platter that had almost passed him by. What Honor did wasn't any of his business. She had stated that clearly to him on several occasions. It was about time he listened.

"Damn, we ain't had sweet potatoes in this house since Miz Emma died and her garden got grown over." Big John smiled as Honor turned his way. "Where'd you find these?"

Honor forced a smile. "I'm pretty good at scouting out things to eat. I've had a lot of practice."

"Just like that pecan pie you made last night," Mitch added. "It was mighty fine—just like Miz Emma used to make. It was her specialty."

Jace saw the way Honor went momentarily still at Mitch's comment before she turned away. He was still considering her reaction when a sudden flurry of movement from the far end of the hall turned all heads at the table. The sound of a heavy thud and Buck's loud groan brought everyone up.

Without conscious thought, Jace joined the rush toward the master bedroom and was only a few steps behind when Honor pushed open the door to find Buck lying on the floor with an expression of acute pain.

Jace heard Celeste's sputtering admonitions as the men joined to lift Buck back onto the bed and Honor said sharply, "Someone has to go for Doc Maggie."

"How dare you give orders in my house!" Her delicate features flushed with rage, Celeste railed at Honor. "I'll give the order to send for Doc Maggie if she's needed." Turning toward Buck without hesitation, she said in a softer tone, "I'm so sorry I couldn't help you when you slipped off the bed, but Doc Maggie isn't needed here, is she, Buck? You're all right now, aren't you?"

Honor rasped, "Get the doctor."

When Mitch moved toward the door, Celeste grated, "Stop where you are! I will not call Doc Maggie to this house if she isn't needed." Turning back again toward Buck as he struggled to catch his breath, Celeste whispered, "Tell me, darling . . . do you need to have Doc Maggie come out, or will you be all right?"

Buck gasped for breath.

"Darling . . . ?"

Laboring, Buck said, "No . . . I'm fine."

Celeste turned back toward Honor, her smile victorious as she said, "You heard him. You may all leave now. I don't need any help taking care of my husband."

The last to exit the room, Jace pulled the bedroom door closed behind him as the men walked back to the kitchen table. Seated beside them, Jace watched Honor as she placed the last of the platters on the table, then walked silently out the door.

Jace filled his plate. He cut the roasted beef into bite-sized pieces, smothered them with gravy, and with a piece of freshly baked bread in hand, began eating resolutely.

Honor took a stabilizing breath and wiped away a trailing tear. Why did it hurt so much to see Buck suffer so? She hardly knew him, and she probably wouldn't have wanted to know him any better if she'd had a chance.

The picture of Celeste's victorious smile flashed before Honor's mind, and Honor's distress became tinged with resentment. Buck had what he wanted. A beautiful young wife. A *doting* beautiful young wife. Even now when it appeared each breath might be his last, he bowed to her wishes.

Honor swallowed her tears. Betty Gannon had wasted her life loving a man who wasn't worth her love. It was as simple as that.

Yet the burning question remained. Why did she care?

"Honor . . ."

Honor wiped the tear from her cheek, then turned toward Jace, who stood behind her. His voice was flat, carrying little sign of emotion as he said, "Buck's a tough old man. He'll be all right."

Honor replied spontaneously, "He's in a bad way. Somebody should tell Cal."

She was unprepared when Jace replied harshly, "Is that what all this meant to you, an opportunity to see Cal again? He's married, Honor, or doesn't that matter?"

"Should it?"

Honor felt the full weight of Jace's gaze, and sudden realization dawned. The unexpected pain of Jace's assumption slashed deep as she said, "Cal is married, and I went chasing after him . . . Now I'm looking for an excuse to see him again—that's what you're thinking."

Honor stared at the shadowed planes of Jace's face, her distress profound. She had actually begun believing there was something special about him . . . about the way he seemed able to see through her, right to the heart. And she had made herself believe, somehow, that despite his obvious reluctance to do so, he actually cared. But he was no better than the rest of them, all the men she had known all her life who had chosen to condemn her and assume the worst.

She said in a soft, final tone that did not betray the ache inside her, "For a while, I thought you were different. Now I know you're not."

With nothing more to say, Honor left Jace standing behind her without a backward glance.

Chapter Six

"Yeah, Jace Rule worked here for a while." Larry Mott appraised the red-haired wrangler who had drawn up to his ranch-house porch as the sun was setting and a long day was coming to an end. Ranch hands moved around the yard behind them, finishing the final chores of the day. They had looked up briefly when the horseman rode in and asked for Rule, and had then gone back to their work when Mott walked out onto the porch.

Mott unconsciously rubbed his full stomach, his lined, bearded face composed in a half smile as he assessed the fellow more closely. Shadows obscured the man's features, but he looked like a hard worker, to judge by his muscular stature and the condition of his much-used saddle.

The burly rancher continued, "But Rule don't work here no more. I told him I didn't need him anymore after the first month. To tell you the truth, I didn't trust that fella. He worked hard enough and did a good job, but he was too quiet. Jailbirds are like that—quiet until they turn on you."

"How'd you know he was a jailbird?"

"He arrived in town on the stage. No horse, no money, and looking like he hadn't had a good time of it." Mott shrugged. "We're close enough to Huntsville for me to spot the look. I wouldn't have hired him if I didn't need an extra man real bad at the time. I paid him off and let him go as soon as I could."

"You were smart, but I wasn't."

"Meaning?"

"I got taken in by him. Rule owes me money, and I'm intending to get it."

"You're out of luck there, friend. When he left here, Rule didn't have much more than a few dollars in his pocket."

"After you paid him?"

"I paid him with room and board, and I gave him a horse he could call his own." Mott shrugged. "He didn't like it much, but I figure that's all he was worth, him being straight out of prison and all."

"Well, he has to set down somewhere, and I figure to get my money out of him then. Did he say where he was going?"

"No, sorry about that. He didn't say and I didn't ask."

"Thanks anyway." The rider tipped his hat and said, "I'll be on my way, then."

"Yeah, goodbye, uhhh . . . what did you say your name was?"

"Bellamy. My name's Bellamy."

"Good luck to you, Bellamy. I hope you find him."

"Oh, I'll find him all right." Bellamy smiled. "There's no doubt about it."

"I told you *only a pinch!* Now your husband hovers at the brink of death! You risk all we have planned!"

Celeste stared coldly at Madalane, who lay supported by pillows on her bed. She had come to check on Madalane's condition. Her husband had passed another difficult night after his "relapse" a few days earlier, and Madalane had obviously heard the sounds of his distress.

Celeste refused to be intimidated as she replied, "My husband is too ornery to die yet."

Obviously unimpressed by Celeste's response, Madalane demanded, "Give the powder back to me."

"No."

"Give it back!"

"No! He disgusted me with his mewling ways. I was angry and I gave him too much. It won't happen again."

"Put the bottle into my hand." Madalane's dark eyes drilled into Celeste's. "It is plain to see that you cannot be trusted when anger assumes control."

Relenting in the face of Madalane's determination, Celeste withdrew the bottle from her pocket and slapped it into her palm.

Madalane's fingers closed tightly around it as she continued more softly, "Since we have not yet accomplished our purpose, we have no choice but to make sure that your husband regains whatever health he can. Under other circumstances, I would already have administered some healing herbs with his food in order to accomplish this, and he would be recovering."

"But we're stuck with the situation as it stands. We have a stranger in the kitchen, a *nosy* stranger who does not hesitate to let her feelings be known; Doc Maggie hasn't brought the wheelchair yet; and you don't trust me with your powders."

Madalane did not need to reply.

Celeste gave a harsh laugh. "Don't worry. I'll see to it that my husband doesn't die until I'm ready. My care is meticulous and unceasing. It is earning me my husband's endless gratitude. Even the witch in the kitchen can't complain about it. I'll come up with a plan to slant the situation more in my favor if necessary. Derek is at my beck and call, just waiting for a chance to please me and put money in his pocket at the same time."

"Stay away from that man! We already have a plan. It is the same plan we have had since we came here. All that remains in order for it to be fully executed is for your husband to regain his health enough so you can convince him to change his will. Then we will choose the right time for the last dose, which I will administer carefully so there will be no cause for suspicion."

"I tire of waiting, Madalane!"

"As do I, but I will not have these last years spent in vain, and I *will* see my dear Jeanette fully avenged."

"Do you think it matters less to me that my mother is avenged than it matters to you? I am the one who suffered most because of Buck's callous treatment of her."

"You are wrong. Your mother suffered most."

"No, *I* suffered most, because my sacrifice is ongoing!"

"That may be true," Madalane responded softly, "but you will live to see your husband pay for his transgressions, and you will be well compensated for your efforts. Your mother did not have that opportunity."

"That was her choice."

"I will not have you speak of your mother in that way! She was shattered by Buck Star's betrayal. Her heart was broken. She had nothing left to live for."

"She had me."

"My dear Jeanette's spirit was too fragile to endure her heartbreak. Buck Star knew that when he seduced her with his handsome face and winning ways, and then tossed her aside. But you are stronger."

"I have learned to be strong."

"No, you were strong-willed and determined even as a child. You were resolved to get your way at any expense. You would never have allowed yourself to suffer as your mother suffered. My dear Jeanette was aware of that when she begged you to avenge her."

"I grow tired of your talk." Her ire rising, Celeste grated, "I want this finished once and for all."

Madalane questioned coldly, "Would you waste the years you have already devoted to this cause? Would you give your husband the satisfaction of passing on to his sons the ranch he valued above your mother's life—above her child? Would you allow his sons to flourish on the ranch he built into an empire at the price of your mother's blood?"

Celeste did not reply.

Madalane demanded, "Would you?"

Celeste ignored Madalane's question as she raised her chin defiantly and snapped, "Keep the powder in your possession, if that's what you want! It's yours."

"Celeste—"

"Do not speak to me again about this."

"Celeste—"

"Do you hear me?"

Celeste paused a moment to assess the silence that followed, then went into the hallway with her anger barely controlled. She struggled to put a concerned look on her face as she walked deliberately toward Buck's bedroom. She knew where true vengeance lay. She knew she would never rest until it was fully achieved. Yet she despised Madalane's reprimand, because she knew the adamant Negress was right. Her own momentary lapse of judgment had resulted in further delay in the completion of their goal.

More time . . . more pretending.

The wait had already gone on too long.

Jace flicked the reins sharply, increasing the buckboard's pace as it moved down Lowell's main street. A brilliant morning sun beat down on his shoulders, forecasting another balmy day as he glanced soberly at the seat beside him where Randy sat frowning. It occurred to him that there wasn't much to smile about at the Texas Star at present, despite the perfect weather.

Honor returned to mind as she had countless times since their angry exchange a few days earlier, and Jace's serious expression darkened. She had spoken to him very little since then. He missed the subtle intimacy they had shared. Although as guarded as he, she had seemed to turn to him instinctively, and the response within him had been spontaneous in return. He missed their candid conversations. He missed the look in her unusual eyes that sparked green and gold in reaction to her moods. He missed the trust he had seen reflected there. He missed . . . the honesty between them.

Jace amended that thought. There had been no *true* honesty between them.

Cal Star's image flashed to Jace's mind at that moment, and his frown tightened. Honor loved Cal Star. He could not seem to get that thought out of his head. Neither could he expel the ache inside him that the thought evoked. She had seemed so sincerely concerned about Buck Star. The way she had challenged Buck the first time she met him; the tears she had striven to hide when he became ill; her concern when he appeared to take a turn for the worse; and the way she looked at Celeste, like she was holding her tongue only because of the old man. He had never thought for a moment an ulterior motive might be hidden behind her concern.

"There's an open spot in front of the mercantile store, Jace. Pull up there. We'll be able to load the wire more easily then."

Jace nodded in compliance. He knew why Randy had taken him into town to help load the wire instead of one of the other men. Mitch and Big John were accustomed to working together and they knew what needed to be done without any explanations. Jace was "the new hand who wouldn't be with them very long," and was the logical choice to go on errands. He wondered if Big John or Mitch resented being left behind to work, and he wondered if they knew how much he wished he were they. He wondered if Honor felt the same way in a kitchen where Celeste resented her presence and was waiting for the moment when Madalane would be well enough for Honor to be fired.

Jace again corrected his trend of thought. Honor hadn't really come to the Texas Star because she needed a job. She had had Cal Star in mind all along.

Jace stepped down onto the boardwalk behind Randy and stretched his tall, lean frame. Years in prison had trimmed him down from the strapping youth who had first walked through those barred doors to the thinner, more tightly muscled man he had become. He had no doubt that Honor's cooking would change all that in time, but he doubted there would be enough time for either one of them at the Texas Star.

"Well, look who's walking toward us!"

Jace turned at Randy's suddenly jovial tone. His expression froze at the sight of Cal Star approaching with a dark-haired woman and a boy walking at his side. The warmth between the two men was obvious when they shook hands and Randy introduced him, saying, "This fella here is the new man your pa hired, Cal. His name's Jace Rule."

"Pleased to meet you." Cal extended his hand. "My name's Cal Star." Jace shook it without a smile, then looked at the woman as Cal said, "This is my wife, Pru, and our son, Jeremy."

Pru acknowledged the introduction as Jeremy extended his small hand toward Jace. The boy said unexpectedly, "My mother was a widow and Cal's not really my father, but he likes me to think of him that way." He added, "I do, too."

"Jeremy, that explanation wasn't necessary."

Jace noted Pru's embarrassed flush and Cal's amusement. There was love all over the smile he flashed at his wife as he said, "Jeremy always was a boy who spoke his mind." He then urged his wife, "Why don't you and Jeremy go ahead and place your order in the store, Pru? I need to talk to Randy for a few minutes."

"I'll stay with Cal, Mama."

"No, you won't." Gripping her son's hand firmly, Pru drew him along with her as Cal turned back to Randy and asked, "How's the old man doing?"

Randy's smile faded. "Not so good, Cal. I ain't never seen him this bad before. Doc's doing all she can, but even to hear her tell it, it ain't much."

"I came into town to ask Doc about him. I was hoping Pa was getting better."

"I wouldn't hope too hard."

Jace saw the distress Cal sought to hide. It was sincere . . . heartfelt, even though his father forced a distance between them.

Jace came instantly alert when Cal asked, "How's the new girl in the kitchen working out? Her name's Honor, isn't it? She seemed nice."

"You met her, did you?" Randy gave a surprised snort. "How'd that happen? Celeste keeps so close an eye on her that she can't move without Celeste telling her to do one thing or another."

"That little girl looked to me to be the type that has a mind of her own. I don't suppose Celeste gets too far with her."

"I figure only as far as Honor's willing to let her." Randy smiled. "She's a good cook, too. How'd you meet her, anyways?"

Cal sobered. "It was the damnedest thing. Celeste chased me off when I came to see Pa the other day, and Honor came riding up after me. She said she was sorry about the way Celeste acted and she'd do her best to look after Pa for me. It was real nice of her. I told her that, too." Cal paused. Jace saw confusion in his eyes when he said, "She's new around here, isn't she, Randy?"

"Right off the stage."

"That's what I heard, but she looked kind of familiar to me."

"Funny you should say that. The boys mentioned the same thing; but speaking for myself, there's no way I met her before." Randy smiled. "I would've remembered."

"She sure isn't somebody a man would easily forget." Cal shook his head. "Anyway, I told Pru about her, and . . . well, you know that woman of mine. She was real touched by what Honor said. She'd like to meet her."

"Short of coming to the Texas Star, there's no way Pru would be able to meet Honor right now. But the truth is, Honor probably won't last a day longer than it takes for Madalane to get back into the kitchen, so you can tell Pru she may get her chance sooner rather than later."

"Celeste doesn't want Honor there, huh?"

"Damned straight."

Turning to Jace, Cal said, "I'm sorry, Jace. I guess you can't make head or tail of all this, but I figure you'll hear the full story one way or another if you're in this town any length of time." He added, "I hope things work out for you on the Texas Star. My father sure can use your help."

Jace nodded and followed Cal and Randy into the store. He watched as Cal joined his wife. He saw the way Pru looked at Cal when he touched her shoulder. The brief loving glances they exchanged were so intimate that he looked away.

"The fencing wire's back here, Jace."

Jace joined Randy at the rear of the store as he rolled the bales forward.

Naked and sweating from their volatile sexual exchange, Celeste rolled off Derek's body and lay gasping beside him. She glanced at the dank cabin around them, then at Derek, who was as naked and sweaty as she.

Revulsion swelled inside her.

She had signaled for Derek to meet her at the cabin, but not for this. She had wanted to discuss a delicate matter, a plan she had not discussed with Madalane. She had wanted to get Derek's reaction to it and had left the ranch house with the thought that she'd be gone only long enough to talk to Derek. Once inside the cabin with Derek's hands on her, however, everything changed.

A warning note sounded in Celeste's mind. Derek was repulsive and unclean, but his aggressiveness somehow ignited a crazed sexual response in her that she could not resist. The great lengths she went to to satisfy that response were becoming startling, even to herself.

Celeste glanced again at Derek. Hair separated in greasy strands, coarse features, a repugnant odor . . . No, she refused to be caught in that trap. She must keep in mind that in New Orleans she would have as many men as she wanted to satisfy her needs.

Derek reached for her again and Celeste avoided his touch. She drew herself to a seated position, then stood and picked up her clothes.

"Where're you going?"

"I'm not going anywhere yet." Celeste turned back toward him, ignoring the heat stirring within her as she donned her undergarments under Derek's lascivious gaze. "I came here to discuss something with you."

"You wanted to talk, huh?" His knowing smile flashed. "But once you got here you changed your mind."

"Don't flatter yourself. I just wanted to forget my husband's shaky hands for a little while."

"Yeah."

Celeste growled through clenched teeth, "Get dressed! I want to talk to you seriously."

"Sure. Anything you say."

Fully dressed and jaw tight, Celeste looked up at Derek.

Also dressed, Derek said, "All right, out with it." He sauntered toward her. "What did you want to talk about?"

"Stay where you are."

"Why?"

"Just do it!"

Derek's hideous smile flashed again. "So talk."

Celeste began slowly. "Things aren't going exactly as planned at the Texas Star. My husband's 'relapse' took more out of him than I thought it would. Even Doc Maggie is starting to think he might not make it this time."

"So?"

"So, I haven't convinced him to change his will yet, and I may be running out of time."

"So?"

Celeste took a firm hold on her patience. "I know how my husband's will reads. If he dies, his sons will be included in the inheritance."

Derek shrugged, "Even so, after all the rustling we done and everything else, there can't be much left but bills."

Celeste glared. "I don't want *any* part of the Texas Star to be passed on to Buck's sons, no matter its condition! I want it all, so when I sell what's left, the Texas Star brand will vanish forever."

Derek stared at her. The venom in her response sobered him, and he said harshly, "What do you want me to do about it?"

"There's only one thing left that you can do. If things keep going the way they are . . . if it looks like Buck won't make it much longer, I want you to *kill* Cal Star."

"Kill him?" Derek took a backward step. "We tried that before, remember? It's easier said than done."

"Afraid, Derek?"

"I ain't afraid of nobody!"

"That isn't the way it sounds to me."

"Yeah?" Derek's unshaven jaw ticked with irritation. "What about the other son? Taylor's his name, ain't it? You'd still have to share the ranch with him."

"Nobody knows where Taylor is. I'm not worried about him."

Derek said abruptly, "What's in it for me? I was making money when we was running the rustling together, but I ain't seen any cash for a while now."

"If you kill Cal Star, I'll make it worth your while."

"That don't tell me nothing."

"Is half of what I get when I sell the Texas Star good enough?"

"Half of *not much*, you mean? I don't see how it'll be worth all the trouble either one of us would have to go through."

"I didn't waste my share of the rustling money like some did. Madalane saw to it that I have a sizable bank account in New Orleans, but you don't have to worry. When I sell the ranch, your share will be enough to make you happy. I guarantee it." Celeste's expression grew cold. "Well, will you do it or not?"

Derek stared at Celeste. Her jaw was set, and the look in her eyes chilled him to the bone. He said, "You're a cold-blooded witch, ain't you?"

"Answer me, yes or no."

When Derek did not immediately respond, Celeste assessed his expression more closely, then stipulated, "You won't have to go after Cal Star unless it looks like Buck won't make it. If Buck gets strong enough, I'll get him to change his will with no problem." Her brief smile was caustic. "My husband is so grateful to me for the care I've given him that he'll do anything I say if it looks like he's getting better."

"But he won't get better, will he?"

"Not a chance."

"It's a deal if"—Derek paused—"if I get half of what the ranch is worth either way."

"Even if you don't have to kill Cal Star?" Celeste shook her head. "No."

"Nothin' for nothin', Celeste. If you want me to do your dirty work, you gotta pay."

Celeste snarled, "You get paid every time I come to this cabin."

"But you do, too, darlin'!" Derek flashed his repulsive grin. "And don't tell me you don't."

Celeste's face flamed. She hesitated, then said, "It's a deal."

Taken by surprise when Derek reached out and

crushed her tightly to him, Celeste struggled against his wet kiss. He drove his tongue into her mouth as he groped her intimately, and Celeste felt a familiar response rising.

Stunned when Derek suddenly thrust her away from him, she heard him say, "Come back when you want more. I'll be waiting."

Celeste turned toward the door, head high. She did not look at Derek as she climbed into her buggy and snapped it into motion, because she knew.

Despite herself, she'd be back.

Honor approached Buck's room with a cup in hand. She hesitated at the door, uncertain. She had been simmering chicken broth most of the morning and it was now finished, but Celeste still had not returned.

Honor recalled Celeste's strict instructions.

I'll be back shortly. I'll bring the broth to Buck then. Stay out of my husband's room. Madalane will take care of things if Buck calls.

Honor silently scoffed—Madalane, who was still in pain and could hardly move from her bed. But Madalane was obviously sleeping and hadn't heard Buck calling or, despite her lack of a suitable conveyance, the determined Negress would have moved heaven and earth to respond.

Buck called out again. The sound of his voice, weak and weary, eliminated Honor's hesitation. She knocked, then entered at his invitation.

Honor caught her breath as she approached the bed. Surely this couldn't be the same man who had

130

greeted her with subdued arrogance when she showed up in his kitchen a few days previously, or even the same man she had spoken to shortly after he was again stricken. Surely such marked deterioration was impossible in so short a time. That man had been thin, but this man was skeletal. That man's voice had retained a semblance of authority, while this man's voice was reduced to a whisper when he asked, "Where's Celeste?"

But his eyes were the same. They pinned her as she responded, "Celeste took the buggy out. I think she went to town."

"Where's Madalane?"

"Asleep."

"Oh, that's how you got in here."

"If you want me to leave—"

"No point in that," he rasped. "What's that you've got in your hands?"

"Broth."

"I ain't been able to keep nothing down."

"Oh."

She felt Buck's keen eyes search her face. He said, "I'll give it a try."

Honor glanced around.

"There's a chair over there, girl." Buck instructed through gasping breaths, "Get it and sit down. But if you've got something against feeding me, you'd better leave now, 'cause there's no way I can drink that broth alone." He paused again at her tight expression. "And don't look at me that way. I'm still the boss on this spread."

Her jaw tight as she raised the spoon to his lips, Honor said, "My name isn't 'girl.' It's Honor."

Ignoring her, Buck swallowed tentatively. His eyes snapped back to her face when she hesitated with the next spoonful.

"What are you waiting for?"

"To see if the broth stays down."

"I'll let you know if it won't."

Honor stared at Buck's gray, lined face. He could hardly swallow, but his arrogance remained.

Buck asked abruptly, "Do I know you, girl?"

"You should." She lifted the spoon again to his lips. "You hired me."

"No . . . from before."

Honor mumbled under her breath and glanced away.

"What did you say?"

Honor looked up at him. "I said, why? Do I remind you of somebody?"

Buck stared harder. "I don't know." He swallowed the next spoonful, then sputtered and choked, his emaciated frame shuddering. Finally catching his breath, he looked at her and said, "Scared you, didn't I?"

"Yes."

"You want to quit?"

"No."

Buck opened his mouth when Honor raised the next spoonful to his lips. She held her breath as he swallowed more smoothly and then asked, "You're sure I don't know you?"

Honor stared at her father as his question reverberated in her mind. She opened her mouth to respond with the words she had wanted to say all her life, but they went unspoken. Now wasn't the time.

Instead, Honor responded evasively, "I never laid eyes on you before the day you hired me, if that helps you any."

Buck stared at her more keenly as she dipped the spoon back into the cup. He swallowed as a sound in the hallway turned them both toward the door. It opened to the sight of Celeste's raging countenance. "What's going on in here?" she demanded.

Honor responded, "Buck was calling and Madalane was asleep."

"Get out."

"Celeste, darlin' . . ." His voice weak, Buck explained, "I was thirsty. The girl brought me something to drink."

"I was only gone a little while." Celeste advanced toward the bed, her expression gravely apologetic. "I needed some air and I thought you'd sleep."

"I know. This has all been hard on you, but the girl was only trying to help."

The girl.

Honor glared at him as Buck continued, "She was real careful."

"I want her out of here. *I* want to take care of you."

Honor saw the distress in Buck's expression when he glanced her way. She noted his accelerated breathing, and the trembling that was again besetting his gaunt frame.

Aware that she had no choice, Honor stood up abruptly and announced, "There's more broth in the kitchen if you want it."

She heard the sound of Celeste's apologies and Buck's weak, placating whispers as she left the room.

The ranch house was silent as the men approached for their supper meal. Jace held back, allowing the others to enter first. He remembered pulling the wagon up to the porch earlier that day, with the wire bales and the roughly fashioned wheelchair that Doc had insisted they take for Madalane. He recalled how Randy had halted in the kitchen doorway to say to Honor's back, "Jace and me brought Madalane her wheelchair."

Jace knew he would never forget the look on Honor's face when she turned around to face them. Her skin was stark white and her eyes were bright with tears that Jace realized she refused to let herself shed.

He had taken a spontaneous step toward her when Randy said, "What's wrong? Is Buck all right?"

"He's fine. Celeste is with him," Honor had said flatly.

Jace had heard himself ask, "What happened? Did she say something to you?"

Honor had glanced at him coldly, then looked at Randy and said, "You can take the wheelchair to Madalane's room if you want. I know she'll be glad to have it."

Jace remembered he had remained rooted to the spot as an ache had twisted tight inside him. Honor had turned back to the stove without a word, and he had then helped Randy take the wheelchair down from the wagon. Honor had not looked at him again.

The screen door slammed closed behind Big John as Jace hesitated a moment longer. The other men were already seated at the table when he took his chair, and Honor put bowls of stew and freshly baked bread on the table. He eyed her closely. She still had a look about her that said something was wrong.

Big John asked between mouthfuls, "How's the boss today?"

"I don't know." Honor shrugged, "All right, I guess."

"You ain't seen him?" Mitch's voice dropped a note softer. "Won't she let you in his room at all?"

"Not if she can help it."

Randy asked, "What about that wheelchair? How's Madalane making out with it?"

The first sign of a smile twitched at Honor's lips. "I don't know. Celeste went in to help Madalane get up, but she left a little while later with a look on her face that said things hadn't gone so well." She added, "I haven't seen hide nor hair of Madalane."

"Oh, too bad." Randy's lips curved suspiciously upward. "I guess she won't be getting around the house too easy for a while."

Jace maintained his silence when the men finished their meal and started toward the door. He stood up when Randy walked up to Honor and whispered softly. The knot inside him tightened to the point of pain when Honor smiled back up at the graying cowpoke.

Jace told himself as he stepped out into the light of the setting sun that it was better this way. He didn't need or want to get involved in what appeared to be the complicated problems of a stubborn, independent woman who was determined to do things her own way, no matter how much it hurt. It wasn't hard to see, either, that for some reason that went unexplained, the situation at the Texas Star *did* hurt her.

Jace straightened up, his expression cold. As for himself, he'd had enough hurt and trouble to last a lifetime. It was time to walk away.

Honor cleaned up the last of the dishes and hung the drying cloth beside the stove. She then took a few weary steps toward the screen door and looked out into the twilight shadows. She turned toward the hallway at the sound of footsteps, but the click of Madalane's door closing indicated she'd see nothing.

The ever-present ache inside Honor deepened, and she shook her head, remotely amused at herself. She had come to Lowell intending to settle the past so she could face the future, but somewhere along the way her goal had changed. It had occurred to her more than once that perhaps Celeste was really saving her from herself by keeping her away from a man who didn't deserve her pity—but she couldn't make herself believe it.

Honor turned back toward the dry sink and the pail of dishwater waiting to be dumped. She lifted it and carried it to the door. The screen door slammed closed behind her as she started across the porch. She was tired, so tired, but it was not the exhaustion of physical labor. Rather, it was an exhaustion emanating from the endless circles in which her mind had traveled since she'd first met Buck Star.

She had hated him, but the man she had come to hate eluded her.

She despised his arrogance, but could not help admiring his fortitude.

She pitied him, when she knew he wasn't worth an ounce of her concern.

Only on one issue did her emotions remain unchallenged. She abhorred his subservience to Celeste, although she understood it well enough. The reason was simple.

Buck adored Celeste because she was the female version of the man he had once been.

Honor tossed the water out of the pail and watched as the earth consumed it. She then raised a weary hand to her forehead. About to return to the house, she took a backward step when she saw Jace approaching.

Angry at her own spontaneous retreat, Honor said, "You startled me."

"Did I?"

Jace walked closer.

He wasn't smiling as he came to stand close enough beside her that she could see how intently his gaze searched her face. She realized abruptly that she could not remember ever seeing him smile. She wondered how he would look with happiness in those dark eyes that even now seemed able to see straight into her soul.

Uncomfortable with that thought, she attempted to walk past him when he said, "I'd like to talk to you for a minute, Honor."

"Really?" Honor responded coldly. "I don't want to talk to you."

"Please."

The single word halted Honor in her tracks.

Jace continued, "I suppose I should start with, 'I'm sorry.'"

"You're sorry?"

"I met Cal Star today."

Her throat suddenly tight, Honor struggled to maintain her composure. "So you met Cal. What does that have to do with me?"

"Nothing . . . everything." Jace took a step closer. "Cal was in town with his wife, Pru, and his son, Jeremy."

"He has a son?" Honor's heart began a ragged beating.

"His wife's son by her first marriage, but as the boy said, Cal likes to think of him as *his* son."

A choking lump rose in Honor's throat as Jace continued resolutely, "I shouldn't have said what I did a few days ago. One look at Cal Star with his family, and I knew none of it could be true—but even if I hadn't seen them together, I should've known. I may not understand why you insisted on coming to the Texas Star, but I do know you didn't come here chasing after Cal." He repeated, "I'm sorry. I made a mistake. I didn't have any right to ask you such a personal question when you came back from talking to Cal, but once I did, I thought I read your response in your eyes."

"Really? What did you see?"

"That you love Cal Star."

Honor heard herself respond, "Maybe that's because I *do* love him."

Jace grew still. He stared at her with obvious uncertainty.

Unable to help herself, Honor said, "So you weren't wrong."

Honor made another attempt to brush past him but Jace caught her arm. His touch burned her skin, and she said roughly, "I'll say it again. I do love Cal. The truth is, I loved Cal from the first moment I saw him."

"Honor—"

"He's my brother."

Honor felt the shock that rippled through Jace. It mirrored her own shock at the words that had tumbled from her lips. Unable to rescind them, she tried again to pull away as Jace demanded, "You told me that much. Now tell me the rest."

"There is no rest."

"Buck's your father, isn't he?"

"There you go again, thinking you have the right to ask."

"Tell me!"

"Yes, he's my father—but he doesn't know it. Nor does he care."

139

"But you care."

"I care, all right! I cared so much that he never gave my mother or me a thought. It almost ate a hole clear through me. I came to town to tell him so, but . . ."

"But you didn't get what you expected."

Honor did not respond.

"Buck never even suspected you existed, did he?"

"It wouldn't have made any difference if he did. He had already made the decision to move on when my mother realized she was pregnant."

"Cal doesn't know you're his sister either, does he?"

"No, and he's not going to find out until I want to tell him."

"Honor—"

Honor said with a surface calm that did not reflect her inner turmoil, "I don't want either Buck or Cal to know . . . not with Celeste running the ranch, and with Buck so damned grateful to her that it makes me sick."

Jace responded softly, "If things were different, if it looked like Buck would regain his health completely, do you think his attitude toward Celeste would change?"

"No."

"Then why are you putting yourself through this?"

"Because . . . because I came here to set things straight between Buck and me, to tell him what I thought of him, and to expose him to the town for the man he was—a womanizer, an adulterer, a man who ruined lives without ever looking back. I needed to do that before I could move on."

"And the way he is now, you can't do it."

"No."

"Honor . . ." Jace slipped his arms around her. Despite herself, she closed her eyes, enjoying the comfort his arms afforded. She had missed talking to him. She had missed looking up into those dark eyes that spoke their concern even if he didn't seem able to say the words. She wished—

"Pack up your things tomorrow. I'll tell Randy I'm driving you back to town."

Honor jerked back from Jace's embrace. "What did you say?"

"You're only torturing yourself, Honor. Nothing is going to get better if you stay here. It'll only get worse."

"You don't know that."

"Open your eyes to the truth. Your father is sick. Celeste is making sure that he's totally dependent on her. If he gets better, he'll be even more beholden to her."

"That's not necessarily true."

"Celeste has a stranglehold on his affections. You know it, and I know it. She won't let anyone near him, and if you try to break through, she'll make you sorry."

"I'm not afraid of Celeste."

"Maybe you should be."

"What's that supposed to mean?"

"I don't trust her any more than anybody else does who ever met her. And there's Madalane—"

"Madalane isn't a threat. She can't even get out of bed."

141

"She has a wheelchair now. She'll be using it sooner or later to back Celeste up the way she always has."

"You can't be sure of that."

"I'm sure."

"So you want me to run away. You want me to leave before I do what I came here to do."

"I want you to stay clear of the trouble you're heading for."

"I won't run."

"Don't be a fool, Honor!"

"Better to be a fool than a coward!"

His hands grasped her shoulders as Jace said, "Listen to me! I know what I'm talking about. I know how things can be twisted into tragedy. All you're doing is heading for more heartache."

"Let me go."

"Honor—"

"I said, let me go!"

Wrenching herself free, Honor said, "You're not the man I thought you were. I thought there was some part of you that felt what I felt. I thought you understood, but I was wrong."

"You weren't wrong."

"Yes, I was."

"Celeste isn't to be trusted."

"All the more reason that I shouldn't abandon my father to her."

"Like he abandoned your mother, you mean?"

Jace's words struck a blow that stunned her. Taking a few seconds to recover, Honor said, "Yes, like he abandoned my mother. But there's a difference here that you can't seem to comprehend. *I'm not like him.* I don't *want* to be like him, which is all the more reason why I won't run away."

"Honor . . ."

Jace reached again for her, but Honor pulled away and said, "I can see I made a mistake telling you what I did. I guess I am a fool, after all."

Striding past him, she headed for the house. She gasped when Randy stepped out of the shadows and asked, "Is something wrong, Honor?"

"N . . . no."

Unwilling to say more, Honor returned to the house at a pace just short of a run.

Jace stood unmoving as Honor disappeared into the ranch house, the ache inside him expanding. She could never have been more wrong in what she had said. There *was* a part of him that felt what she felt, and he *did* understand. He understood too well how someone could hurt so badly inside about things that couldn't be changed. He knew about the invisible scars that kind of a hurt could leave . . . scars that throbbed and pounded, destroying peace of mind. He wanted to save her from suffering that kind of torment. He wanted to protect her, to keep her from remaining in a place where those scars could only burn deeper.

Jace took a breath, then shook his head. He hadn't intended to get involved when he took this job at the Texas Star, or when he first looked down into Honor's determined expression. But the look of her, the resolute set of her jaw, the subtle lift of her chin when the hurt cut deeper, and the damned aching need in

her eyes that gripped his vitals and wouldn't let go—
all were stronger than any resolution he seemed able
to make.

Then when he had held her briefly in his arms and
she had relaxed against him, he had wanted to make
all the wrongs right for her. In that moment he had
been so sure he could do it if she would give him a
chance.

But she had called him a coward and walked away.

Was he a coward? He supposed he was if being a
coward meant wanting to remove her from a place
where he knew instinctively she was heading for disas-
ter.

But he hadn't been able to explain because she
had walked away.

Jace stared at the ranch-house door through which
Honor had disappeared from sight.

Damn it, she had walked away!

The twilight shadows lengthened as Jace stood looking after Honor. He started toward the bunkhouse,
paused to answer a few questions from Randy, then
entered and closed the door behind him.

Randy followed slowly a few minutes later.

Twilight darkened into night, and the shadows behind the bunkhouse stirred. They assumed a male
shape that moved cautiously across the ranch yard to
a point where a horse was secured out of sight.

The shadowy figure mounted. A flash of moonlight
glinted on his curly red hair the moment before he
turned his horse back out onto the trail and melted
into the darkness.

Chapter Seven

"I feel better, I'm telling you. I want to get dressed. I haven't gone more than a few steps from this bed for more days than I want to count."

Doc looked down at Buck, her round face drawn into stern lines. Only a few days had passed since she had honestly believed Buck would soon be facing the hereafter, but she had arrived at the ranch that morning to find him clear-eyed and back to his old irritating, bullheaded self.

"Get my clothes."

"I'm not your servant, Buck Star. I'm your doctor, and I'm telling you not to try to do too much too soon."

"I'm not saying I'm going out to chase down mustangs, Doc. I'm telling you I'm going to get up so I can take my meals at the table with my wife like I should."

"Eat your meals with your wife?" Doc scoffed. "You couldn't even finish breakfast! If you try eating a full meal after what your stomach's been through, you'll find out how sick you still are."

"I'm not dumb enough to do that." Buck added, "Besides, I'm not that hungry."

"So why—"

"Because I want to, that's why!"

"You're a damned stubborn old man, Buck Star!"

"Maybe, but I'm getting up."

Annoyed when Celeste chose that moment to return to the room, Doc said flatly, "All right, have it your way, but don't send somebody running after me when you fall flat on your face."

"What's this all about?" Celeste approached the bed glaring. "Why are you upsetting my husband, Doctor? He's sick. You should know better."

"That's right, he's sick, but he's the one who should know better. He wants to get dressed and get up."

"Buck!"

Almost amused at the expression on Celeste's face, Doc said, "But you're right. I shouldn't upset him, so I'll leave it to you, Celeste, to convince your husband that he's a damned old fool who's going to end up in worse shape than before if he insists on overdoing it."

Celeste stared at her, momentarily at a loss for a reply, and Doc resisted the urge to laugh aloud. If she wasn't so mad at Buck, she'd give him a kiss smack on his lips for the pleasure of seeing Celeste wordless.

But the situation was only temporary.

"Buck, Doc's right." Celeste's voice oozed concern, "You're too weak to get up."

"No, I'm not."

"Give yourself another day or two," Celeste whispered. "I couldn't stand it if you hurt yourself."

"I need to get my blood moving around these bones of mine, Celeste, or I'll never get better." Buck's expression implored her understanding. "A few hours up this morning and I'll be ready to sit at the table for supper with you tonight."

"No, Buck, please."

"I want my clothes, Celeste."

"No, I can't do it."

"Then I'll call Honor to get them. She's not afraid of anything. She'll do what I say."

"I'm not afraid! I'm concerned about your welfare. Honor couldn't care less."

"If you're concerned about my welfare, you'll get my clothes."

"I can't!"

Enjoying the exchange too much to interfere, Doc was surprised to hear Buck call out, "Honor? Can you hear me?"

"I don't want that woman in here, Buck." Celeste flushed an angry red.

Doc turned at a knock on the door and the sound of Honor's voice inquiring, "Did someone call me?"

Celeste responded harshly, "We don't need you in here!"

Doc heard Buck reply, "Yes, I called you. Come on in."

The door opened, revealing Honor's uncertain expression. The tawny brown of her hair, those bright hazel eyes framed with thick brown lashes, the set of her mouth—Doc was struck with a sudden certainty she'd seen them before.

Buck said, "I want you to get me my clothes. I'm getting up." When Honor's frowning glance moved between Doc and Celeste, he continued, "My wife and the doc say I shouldn't get up yet, but I say I'm strong enough to give it a try, and I want to be dressed when I do it."

The momentary silence that followed Buck's request hung heavily in the room.

An indiscernible expression moved across Honor's face before she replied, "Your clothes are in the washroom. They're dry. I'll get them."

"No, you won't!" Celeste took an angry step toward the bed. "Buck, are you going to let this person disobey my orders? I'm only thinking of your welfare."

"And I'm thinking of yours, Celeste, darlin'. I'm not much of a man lying here in this bed, and I figure it's time for me to get up, one way or another."

"Tell that woman to leave this room, Buck."

His gaze lingered on Celeste's beautiful, tearful countenance for a moment, and then he looked at Honor and said, "Get my clothes."

Silent, Doc watched as Celeste turned on Buck, her rage barely controlled as she said, "I was only trying to follow Doc's orders. I just wanted to make sure you wouldn't have another relapse." A sob escaped Celeste's lips as she rasped, "But I see now how little that means to you. Well, I won't watch you hurt yourself. I won't!"

Celeste slammed out of the room, and Doc turned

toward Buck, to see his expression pained but adamant as he ordered, "Go ahead, Honor. Get my clothes."

Alone in the room with Buck once more, Doc said flatly, "You're going to pay for that, you know."

"You've got Celeste all wrong, Doc." Buck's face took on a desperate look as he said, "I love her and I know she loves me, but she's determined to coddle me. She won't let me make a move without her. I've been in this bed for more than a week, and if there's a spark of manhood left in me, I'm going to get dressed and be up on my feet for a few hours today."

"Celeste is furious."

Momentarily silent, Buck said, "I'll make her understand, and I'll make it up to her when I get everything running smoothly on the Texas Star again."

"I'm telling you it's too soon to push yourself."

"It's not too soon, I'm not going to push myself, and if I wait any longer, it'll be too late." Concern crept into Buck's tone as he whispered, "I'm losing control here on the Texas Star, Doc. I can't afford to do that if I want to bring the ranch back to what it was. Celeste has tried to take over, but she has no idea what needs to be done, and she listens too much to Madalane. I have to get back on my feet. I have to see what decisions need to be made, what steps need to be taken, what I can *afford* to do. There's nobody else who knows the extent of my debts except me, and nobody I can turn to."

"There's Cal. He'd come to help in a minute."

"No."

"He wants to."

"I don't want to talk about it! Bonnie's dead, and Cal is dead to me, too."

"Bullheaded, that's what you are!"

"There's nobody left but me and Celeste to think of now. Celeste will realize sooner or later that what I'm doing, I'm doing for her as well as myself."

At a knock on the door, Doc turned to see Honor with Buck's freshly washed clothes in hand. "Where do you want me to put these?" she asked him.

"On the bed, where else?"

Glaring at his tart reply, Honor placed the clothes on the bed and left.

Buck's weak snicker raised Doc's brows. She could almost believe she heard a touch of respect in his tone when he said, "That young woman's got backbone. I saw it in her the first day she set foot in my kitchen."

"You're making a mistake turning Celeste against her."

"I'm not doing that—not purposely. It's just that Celeste worries too much about me. She's done more than an old man like me has a right to expect."

"She knew what she was marrying when she married you."

"Yeah, a healthy fella in the prime of life—not a sick old man who isn't a real man anymore."

"Buck . . . you're sick. She knows that."

"I need to take my rightful place here, Doc. I need to be a man Celeste can respect."

"Respect—"

"I need to get up today. I'll make sure Celeste doesn't take it out on the girl."

Doc stared at the pitiful physical wreck of a man Buck had become. But the determined glint in his eye said it all.

Despite herself, Doc ordered, "Sit up. I'll help you get on your feet."

"I knew you'd see things my way."

"Don't deceive yourself into thinking I've changed my mind. I just figure it's either me or Honor who's going to get you up, and I guess it's best if Celeste is angry with me instead of Honor." She added candidly, "Celeste doesn't like me much anyway."

"No, she doesn't. She figures you haven't done enough to help me get better."

"She's *so* worried about you . . ."

"She says I'm her life."

Tempted to speak the words on the tip of her tongue, Doc ordered gruffly, "Sit up, you old fool. I'll help you get dressed."

"Your husband has chosen the kitchen girl over you."

Livid, Celeste stared at Madalane as the Negress sat propped up in bed with her splinted leg stretched out in front of her and her expression dark. Celeste had escaped to Madalane's room after leaving her husband in a huff, but she had arrived to discover that Madalane had overheard the scene in Buck's bedroom.

Responding to her servant's pronouncement in a voice that was a subdued screech, Celeste said, "How dare you say that? My husband idolizes me!"

"He has gone against your wishes and has turned to the kitchen girl. I say that only so you may realize what is happening."

"What is happening?" Celeste glared. "Has your mind been affected by your injury? My husband called the 'kitchen girl' when Doc Maggie and I both refused to accede to his wishes, simply because he knew she would do what he asked."

"Because there is a bond between them."

"Because he knows she will do her job without caring what happens to him!"

"You are wrong."

Celeste's delicate features twisted into an ugly sneer as she rasped, "You're trying to tell me my husband would prefer that thin, dowdy woman to *me*?"

"The girl is thin but she is not dowdy, and she has spirit that your husband recognizes and admires."

"He does not! How would you know anyway, lying here in this bed like a lump on a log while the world goes on outside your door?"

"I am not as isolated here as you choose to believe." Madalane's dark eyes reflected her conviction as she continued, "I have listened carefully to the conversations around the kitchen table when the ranch hands come in for supper. The fact that they eat there instead of in the bunkhouse is a victory for the kitchen girl that you have not yet reversed."

"I have more important things to think of right now."

"Perhaps, but the men admire her for it. They also speak of the way she has assumed full control of that room, a control you have not chosen to challenge."

"Control of the kitchen—you consider that a feat?"

"You have surrendered the kitchen to her. You also allow her to enter this room with increasing frequency, and have thus surrendered the privacy of this room to her also. You ought to concern yourself that you may soon lose yet another room to her—a very important room."

"What are you talking about?"

"She has now entered your husband's bedroom."

"Evil-tongued witch! My husband desires no woman but me."

"The girl is young."

"So am I!"

"And she is a new challenge."

"My husband isn't up to a 'challenge,' new or otherwise. He can't even handle his present 'challenge.'"

"His health is improving."

"Because I've allowed it."

"The men speak highly of her."

"I don't care what they think."

Madalane persisted. "It is time to guard against your husband's tendencies. He is an adulterer. Sick or well, he will always be an adulterer at heart."

Her chest heaving with fury, Celeste rasped, "Your mind has been affected by your inactivity, old woman! My husband is enamored of me, and *only* me. He desires me, and *only* me. And when the time comes, he will give me exactly what I want because he feels indebted to me and will not be able to resist my persuasion."

"I give you fair warning."

"And I choose to ignore it."

"To refuse to heed my warning is an error."

"The only error is on your part, old woman! And I advise you to heed *my* warning—that unless you're able to get out of that bed and into your wheelchair by yourself, you will remain where you lie today, because I'm not going to help you!"

"I suppose that then, like your husband, I will have to call the kitchen girl for help."

Infuriated, Celeste swept away from the stone-faced Negress and slammed the door behind her.

Randy stood up and stared at the fouled water hole the men had come upon after finishing a long day of fencing. He squinted against the unrelenting rays of the late afternoon sun, lifted his hat from his head, then wiped the perspiration from his forehead with the back of his arm before he said flatly, "Buck ain't going to like this."

"Hell, how'd this happen anyways?" Big John dismounted and kneeled to scoop some water into his hand. He grimaced at the stench. He turned toward Mitch with a frown. "Didn't you say you passed this way the day before yesterday and everything was all right?"

"As far as I could see."

Randy looked at the cattle grazing slowly toward the water hole. He frowned. "Seems like we got here just in time or we'd have a real sick herd on our hands."

"You're right, Buck ain't going to like this." Big John stood up slowly. "We ain't got no choice. Looks like we're going to have to move this herd to another pasture until we get this water hole fenced off and cleaned up. That'll set us back even further than we are now."

"Then we might as well get started. It's a good thing we finished the fencing in the north pasture or we'd really be in trouble." Randy instructed, "Big John and Mitch, you two can pull this herd together and start moving it there." He turned toward Jace, who sat his horse in silence. "I'll stay here and do the best I can, but you're going to have to go back to the house and load the wagon with some decent shovels and whatever wire we've got left. It's not going to be an easy job cleaning this place up."

Jace nodded and turned his horse back toward the ranch. He looked up at the position of the sun and unconsciously shook his head as he rode briskly along the trail. It had been a damned long work day, and it looked like it wasn't over yet.

He sure wished it was. As a matter of fact, he wished his whole stint at the Texas Star ranch was over and done with, as he was pretty sure it would be as soon as Buck was well enough to take over and send him packing.

Jace considered that thought. Just a few days ago he was envying Big John and Mitch for their stability as ranch hands on the Texas Star, but now . . . ?

The image of Honor's pale face and sober eyes flashed across his mind. No, he didn't want to stay there and see the pain in Honor's eyes grow deeper with every passing day. What he did want was to see her out of there. She needed to go someplace where a woman like her would be appreciated, not where seeing Buck every day impressed more keenly upon her mind that her father hadn't even cared enough to find out that she had been born; where the satisfaction she sought was no satisfaction at all while watching Buck waste away; where she had discovered she had a brother and an extended family who didn't even know she existed.

He had tried to explain that to her, but everything he said had come out wrong. Her coldness toward him in the time since was so apparent that Big John had commented dryly when they left the kitchen that morning, "You sure do have a way with women, Jace."

The remark smarted all over again, and Jace spurred his mount to a faster pace on the trail. The sooner he got back to the water hole with those shovels, the sooner they'd be done for the day—and it couldn't be soon enough for him. If he had a choice, he'd brush the dust of the Texas Star from his boots and leave the ranch far behind him, but the situation was such that he—

Jace's thought went unfinished when Whistler lurched suddenly forward. Unable to regain stability, the horse whinnied loudly as he tumbled so violently that Jace was thrown over his head.

A loud crack resounded inside Jace's skull as he struck the ground. The world jarred to a halt as he stirred and looked around him. He heard Whistler's pained whinnying and a moan that he realized belatedly was his own. He tried to get up and failed. He was staring helplessly up at the cloudless sky when darkness claimed him.

* * *

Honor wrinkled her nose with annoyance. Celeste was in a snit because Buck had called Honor to help him back to his bed at midmorning, and Madalane was rolling back and forth through the hallway in her wheelchair like a soldier on patrol. Honor did not deceive herself that Buck's call for her aid had been a mark of affection for her. He had been less than pleasant, and she knew he had asked her for help simply because he didn't want his young, beautiful wife to realize how weak he was.

The brief, satisfied glance she had exchanged with Doc Maggie before the older woman left had afforded her temporary satisfaction, but hearing Buck refer to her as "girl" when she helped him back to bed had since erased it. Her father couldn't even seem to remember her name, but she supposed she shouldn't have expected more. Despite the tense words exchanged between him and his wife that morning, there were only two people in Buck Star's world: himself and Celeste, the woman he adored.

Honor walked out onto the porch. She was unfamiliar with most of the seasonings on the kitchen shelf, which Madalane obviously was accustomed to using, but she had seen the remains of an herb garden behind the house that appeared to have been well tended at one time. Unfortunately, that day was long past and all that remained were a few sturdy plants. But she was accustomed to working in difficult circumstances.

When she heard a horse approaching, Honor raised her head from the fragrant stems she was gathering. The horse's uneven gait caused her to frown even before Whistler limped into view and started toward the water trough.

Honor's heart jumped a beat at the sight of Whistler's empty saddle.

The herbs forgotten, she approached Whistler cautiously. Her heartbeat rose to thunder in her ears when she saw his bruised and bleeding knees and the deep slashes across his fetlocks. The animal was obviously in pain from a bad fall, yet there was no sign of anyone coming after him.

Honor stared down the empty trail a moment longer, then started toward the barn. She was mounted and riding out through the doors when Celeste looked through the kitchen window and called out, "Where do you think you're going? If you value your job, you'll get down from that horse this minute!"

Her jaw tense, Honor called back, "Jace's mount came back without him. I'm going out to see what happened."

"Your job is here in the house. The men can take care of him."

Honor turned her mount out toward the trail as Celeste demanded more loudly, "Get back here! Do you hear me?"

Honor was riding cautiously through some dense undergrowth when she spotted him. The sight of Jace lying motionless on his back stole her breath. She swung down from the saddle and crouched beside him, spotting a bloody gash near his temple.

But he was breathing.

Her throat tight, Honor fought for control of her

rising panic as she said, "Jace, can you hear me?"

When there was no response, she said, "It's Honor, Jace. Open your eyes. I need to know you're all right."

She stared at him, awaiting his response. He was so still. He had tried to warn her from the first that she was making a mistake coming to the Texas Star. When she chose to ignore him, he had made it clear he wanted no part of the problems she would encounter—but his actions had contradicted his words. She had felt his concern even while they had argued every step of the way. She had continued to ignore his warnings; then, without conscious intent, she had revealed to him her most intimate secret.

Why?

Because, for a reason neither of them seemed to understand, she knew he cared.

Honor stared down into Jace's bloodied face, her heart pounding. She needed to know he would be all right.

Her voice shaking, Honor begged, "Jace, speak to me . . . please."

Please . . .

The word was a whispered plea that stirred the veil of darkness engulfing Jace. He attempted to respond, but the words came out in a muffled groan.

Honor entreated, "Open your eyes, Jace. Talk to me."

Jace's heavy eyelids admitted narrow slits of light as he attempted to comply. He saw Honor leaning over him, her small features tight with concern. He wanted to reach up and stroke the strain from her expression, to brush the tears from her eyes, to still her trembling lips with his. The need was strong, but he was strangely unable to move.

"Jace?"

He wanted to respond. He wanted to say so much more . . . but his eyes slowly closed.

"How in hell do you suppose it happened?"

"Who knows? It ain't like none of us never had a spill from a horse before."

"I ain't ever had a spill like his. Hell, Jace is lucky he ain't dead!"

The muted conversation filtered slowly through the shadows surrounding Jace. His mind reacted despite the persistent throbbing in his head, and Jace fought to respond. Able to open his eyes at last, he saw the plain bunkhouse walls, the ranch hands standing a few feet away, and Doc Maggie leaning over him, frowning as she dabbed at his forehead.

But he didn't see Honor.

Jace scanned the room and finally saw her standing in the shadows, apart from the ranch hands. She took a tentative step forward when their gazes met, but halted when Doc Maggie said, "So you're waking up at last, Jace." Her round face creased into a smile. "You had a helluva fall."

"Yeah . . . I suppose."

"You don't remember?"

Jace took a breath. "Not much." He raised a hand to his head and touched the bandage Doc had applied.

"You couldn't just take a simple spill from your

horse, you had to hit your head on a rock when you landed. I was worried for a few minutes when I first got here and you were unconscious. I had to put in some stitches to close up that cut, but you're lucky you have such a hard head. You'll have a headache for a few days, but I figure everything will go back to normal afterwards."

Jace frowned. "How's Whistler?"

Randy responded, "He's all right. He's a little shook up. His knees took a hard hit when he fell and he's cut up a bit, but it looks like that old fella will be all right with a little rest."

Jace winced when he attempted to nod.

Doc added, "Whistler went back to the barn after your spill. That's how Honor knew something had happened. She rode out after you. It's a good thing she did, 'cause I was going out on a call and I wouldn't have been home if somebody had come to get me a little later."

Jace looked at Honor, but she did not react.

Doc said, "I've done all I can right now. I'll leave you some powders for the pain and come back to look at you, but you'll probably just have to stay off your feet for a day or two."

"I'll be all right tomorrow."

"Oh, no, you won't!" Doc's round face grew stern. "You bumped your head real hard, Jace Rule. You probably have what we in the profession call a concussion. Not to get technical with you, but it could kill you if you don't take the proper care."

Jace's expression said it all.

"Don't look at me like that! I know what I'm talking about. At the very least, you're going to be dizzy for a while, and if you try getting up on a horse and you fall off again . . . well, it'll probably be a waste of time for anybody to come to get me."

When Jace still did not respond, Doc turned toward Randy and instructed, "You make sure he stays right where he is, you hear?"

Randy responded flatly, "I ain't his keeper, Doc."

"Don't worry, Doc." All eyes turned toward Honor when she spoke up unexpectedly. "I'll take care of it."

Doc flashed a triumphant smile at Jace. "And if I know that young woman at all, she means what she says."

Jace did not reply.

"Not in a mood for arguing, huh?" Doc gathered up her bag, then turned to Randy. "You can tell your boss, in case he's interested, that he's going to be short a ranch hand for a few days. He won't like it, but there isn't much Buck does like these days."

Ignoring the round of head-nodding and mumbling that her comment elicited, Doc turned back to Jace. "Rest. You won't be able to do much else for a while anyway. Like I said, I'll check on you when I come out to see Buck and Madalane." Doc gave a caustic snort. "Buck, Madalane, and now you. Hell, the Texas Star is starting to look like a hospital ward!"

His head pounded harder and Jace closed his eyes. He opened them again when Doc pressed a glass to his lips.

"Drink this. It'll take care of the pain."

Jace grimaced at the bitter taste as he swallowed.

"You'd better be lying in that bunk when I come back tomorrow," Doc said as she stood up to leave.

Jace's eyes drooped closed. He heard the sound of retreating footsteps. Consciousness was drifting away when he felt a gentle touch and looked up to see Honor adjusting the coverlet across his chest. He reached up to take her small hand in his. Her expression was solemn, and he was content when she made no effort to pull away.

Standing unseen a little distance from the bunkhouse, Bellamy scowled as the sober-faced parade of visitors left. He cursed softly. Things hadn't gone exactly the way he had planned, and he didn't like it.

Bellamy consoled himself that it wasn't his fault. Walter Coburn's "conditions" had complicated a job that should have been straightforward and easy to accomplish. It hadn't been good enough for the old man to have his son's killer shot. He had to make sure Rule suffered first.

Bellamy had received Coburn's inquiry at a post office box address that was known to very few. He had been flattered that his reputation had reached the ears of the wealthy in a place as distant as New York City, and he had cautiously accepted Coburn's offer to come east to consult with him. Despite his easy acquiescence when Coburn stated what he wanted done, Bellamy hadn't liked the conditions attached. He disliked skulking and planning. He much preferred a simple shot in the dark without a long-term commitment, and was actually thinking of turning down the job when Coburn mentioned that blank check. Setting his own price had been too much to turn down—but now he was beginning to regret his decision.

The fiasco today was supposed to have been a simple accident. He had watched the Texas Star long enough to know the ranch hands would finish fencing the north pasture that day. He also knew they'd ride by the water hole on the way back to the ranch house and wouldn't be able to miss its fouled condition after he finished with it. Anticipating the foreman's decision was easy. Rule as the new man was the one most likely to be sent back to the ranch for the materials needed to fence off the water hole. Bellamy had prepared by rigging up a wire, which he jerked taut just as Rule rode past. What he hadn't figured on was that Rule would be riding at a pace that would send his old nag tumbling hard. Nor had he figured on Rule striking his head on a rock when he hit the ground. He supposed he was lucky Rule wasn't killed instantly. Coburn would've been furious to have had him finished off so fast, and Bellamy probably would have lost the tidy sum waiting for him at the completion of the job.

But he disliked delay, and from what he could gather from snips of conversation he'd heard as the men exited the bunkhouse, it would be a few days before Rule would be back on his feet. He would have to wait before he was able to put his plans back into action.

Bellamy mentally reviewed the strategy he had devised to make a man like Rule suffer enough to satisfy Coburn. It was inspired. Rule had already lost everything he owned. All he had left was his life and his pride. He would lose the first one soon enough, but attacking the second one was a more delicate matter. Bellamy had finally chosen to stage a series of "accidents" that would make Rule suffer physically while also appearing incompetent in his work. Attacked on both fronts, Rule would lose the confidence of his employer and the men he worked with. He might even begin to doubt himself. He'd be fired, of course, and be unable to find another job. When Rule was hungry and at his lowest, Bellamy would kill him; but he would make sure Rule knew his death would appear a suicide—that it would appear he had taken the cowardly way out and ended his own life.

Yes . . . inspired.

But slow.

Bellamy shrugged. He'd have to make the best of it. Lowell had a decent saloon and a house that would accommodate his baser desires while he waited.

Encouraged by those alternatives, Bellamy made his way cautiously back to his mount. A few days more or less. . . . he could afford to wait.

Buck looked out his bedroom window toward the setting sun, then determinedly slipped his legs over the side of the bed and prepared to stand up. Bitterly amused, he admitted to himself that Doc had been right that morning when she said he wasn't really up to spending the morning sitting in the parlor as he wished. But she had yielded to his pleas and helped him out of bed and into the parlor. Settling him into a chair, she had left to attend to her other duties, hoping for the best.

Celeste had been shocked to find him sitting in the parlor when she returned to the house after a walk to "settle her anxieties." Her anxieties again unsettled, she had refused to have anything to do with his "stubborn behavior" and just let him sit there for hours.

When he found he couldn't push himself out of the chair, he had refused to call Celeste, unwilling to reveal to her the full extent of his weakness. Instead, he had called Honor. To her credit, the girl had ignored Celeste's irritated mumblings and had helped him out of the chair and back to his room.

Now Buck braced himself as he prepared to stand. But Doc had been correct about another thing, too. He was bullheaded, and for that reason he was determined to make it to the dining-room table to have supper with Celeste as he had said he would.

Buck's stomach rumbled, to his pleasant surprise. The aromas wafting into his room from the kitchen had been teasing him for hours, and he realized that he was hungry for the first time in days.

On his feet at last, Buck stood stock-still until he got his balance. It was only a short distance to the dining room. He'd make it or die trying.

". . . when the boss finds out, he ain't going to be happy."

Buck steadied himself against the hallway wall at the sound of Mitch's voice in the kitchen. The click of silverware indicated the boys were already eating.

"He don't know yet, huh?"

Randy responded, "He was sleeping when I came in. I figured it could wait to tell him what happened. He's so sick that there's nothing he can do about it anyways."

Anger washed through Buck in a hot flash. So sick that he couldn't function, huh?

Making it to the kitchen doorway in a few unsteady steps, Buck growled, "I'm too sick to do what?"

Taking satisfaction in the fact that all heads snapped up with surprise at the sound of his voice, Buck waited for a reply.

"Boss . . . hey, are you all right?"

Buck glared at Big John. "You see me standing here, don't you? What were you boys holding back from me?"

"We wasn't holding nothing back from you, boss. You were sleeping."

Ignoring Mitch's response, Buck approached the table and addressed Randy flatly. "What's going on here?"

Buck heard the scrape of the chair Honor moved up to the table behind him. He sat and demanded, "Well?"

"The water hole just over the line of the north pasture is fouled," Randy said.

"Fouled. Did you get the herd out of there in time?"

"Sure did."

Buck shook his head. "We've never had trouble with that water hole before."

"I know."

"What caused it?"

"I don't know yet. We've got it fenced off for now."

Buck cursed under his breath.

"I figured on going to town to get what we needed and then trying to clear it up tomorrow," Randy said.

"Tomorrow? Why didn't you go to town to get what you need today?"

The men glanced at each other, and Buck heard Honor move restlessly behind him. He waited.

"Jace, the new fella, had an accident," Randy said. "He got thrown from his horse and we had to get the wagon to bring him back here. Mitch went for Doc Maggie in a hurry, 'cause none of us were sure he was going to make it."

"That doesn't make sense. That fella knows how to handle a horse."

"Yeah, well, he's all right now, but Doc says he'll have to stay in bed for a few days."

"A few days!" Buck felt his blood rise. "Hell, I'm not going to feed a wrangler who can't work. Get him on his feet tomorrow."

"We can't, boss. Doc says he hit his head pretty hard. If he moves, it might not be too good."

"I don't care. If he doesn't work, he doesn't eat. That's it."

"Boss—"

"You heard me! If he won't work, run him off this spread. We don't want him here."

"You *are* an ornery old coot, aren't you?"

Silence followed Honor's unexpected interjection. Buck saw the angry sparks that flashed in her eyes when she stepped around to face him and continued hotly, "If you needed another wrangler on this place when you hired Jace Rule, you surely need one even more now that you're sick again. Another thing that's sure is that Jace will be ready to get back on his horse long before you are."

Buck snapped, "You got some gall, girl! This isn't your ranch. It's mine, and I make the decisions here."

Honor snapped back, "I told you before, my name's not 'girl,' but you're right. You make the decisions here—but that doesn't mean you always make the right ones. This time you're wrong."

"Says who?"

"Just tell me this." Honor ignored his question as she asked, "Did you need help when you hired Jace?"

"That's beside the point. He can't work if he's flat on his back."

"Like you've been, you mean?"

"I can lie on my back all I want. I own this place."

"But at the rate you're going, this ranch won't be yours much longer."

"That's not your business, neither!"

Honor turned to Randy and said, "How has Jace been working out?"

Randy glanced at Buck, then said, "He does as good a job as any one of us."

Honor pressed, "Has he been pulling his weight?"

"More than that, I'd say."

She looked back at Buck. "You heard him. Where're you going to get another good wrangler for the money you're paying Jace if you let him go?"

"What . . . did Rule tell you what I'm paying him?"

"He didn't have to."

Buck's lips twitched. The girl had gall, all right. He

looked back at Randy. "How'd Rule get thrown anyway? Was it that old nag of his?"

Randy shrugged. "I can't say."

"If that nag is feeble-footed, you should've put Rule on one of the other horses."

"That horse seemed all right to me."

"Where is it now?"

"In the barn . . . pretty cut up."

Buck looked at Honor. He studied her face. There was something about her that drew him.

Buck made an abrupt decision. Again facing Randy, he said, "Rule's supposed to be able to ride again in a couple of days?"

Honor responded, "More or less."

Buck frowned back at her. "I'm not running a rest home here. He'd better be able to work again in a couple of days or he's out."

Buck felt the astonishment that swept the table at his sudden about-face, but he ignored it. The girl had gall, but she made sense. Where would he get another good hand for what he was paying Rule—especially now when he needed help more than ever?

Buck knew without turning who had walked into view when the hands glanced up suddenly at the hall doorway. Nor did it miss his notice that Honor didn't back up an inch.

Buck gathered his strength and stood up. Satisfied with his effort, he looked at the hands and grated, "I don't expect to have to tell you all again that I want to know what's happening on the Texas Star *when* it's happening. No excuses. Is that understood?"

Mumbled acquiescence rounded the table. "I'm hungry," he said to Honor. "Celeste and I are going to eat in the dining room. And don't let that food get cold before you bring it."

The girl's nose twitched. He had put her in her place. It wouldn't do to let the little twit think she had worn him down.

Buck turned toward the hallway in time to see Celeste leave in a huff. Celeste didn't like Honor. He had no doubt that she liked her even less after hearing the conversation that had just transpired.

The thought occurred to him that Celeste was acting as if she were jealous of Honor, but he dismissed it. Celeste could never be jealous over an old wreck like him.

Buck walked resolutely toward the dining room with an apologetic smile ready for his beautiful wife.

Chapter Eight

He had a helluva headache.

Jace opened his eyes and mumbled under his breath as he squinted at the morning sun beaming through the window. The bunkhouse was empty. No one had to tell him that the rest of the hands had been up at dawn and had already been working for hours while he was lying abed.

Annoyed by that thought, Jace threw back the coverlet and attempted to stand, but piercing pain and a whirl of dizziness knocked him back against the pillow. He closed his eyes, barely breathing as his stomach momentarily rebelled. He waited for the nausea to cease, then forced his eyes open at the sound of a light step.

"You tried to get up, didn't you?" Seeming to appear out of nowhere, Honor looked down at him, her expression unreadable. "You know you weren't supposed to."

His breathing easier, Jace replied, "I do?"

Honor moved closer. "Are you being stubborn, or don't you remember what Doc said?"

He felt the weight of her gaze. His head hurt and his stomach was churning, but the sight of her so nearby stirred feelings he dared not identify as he replied, "A little of both, I guess."

Honor sat on the chair beside the bed. The tawny brown of her hair glinted in a ray of the morning sun, but her clear skin seemed unnaturally pale as she said, "You were thrown from your horse. Do you remember that?"

He responded honestly, "Some of it."

"You were on the way back to the ranch when Whistler must have lost his footing." Anticipating his next question, Honor said, "Whistler's in the barn. He's all right. Doc says you'll be all right, too, if you stay where you are for a couple of days."

"A couple of days!" Jace exclaimed. "I'll be up on my feet as soon as I catch my breath."

"You could try, but Doc advises against it."

"She does?"

"You don't remember?"

The pounding in Jace's head was increasing. He tried to think.

"Does your head hurt?"

Jace did not reply, and Honor reached for a packet on the table. Seconds later, she raised a glass to his lips. When he hesitated, she said, "Doc left this for you. It'll help."

Jace swallowed. The bitter taste was familiar, and he grimaced. "I remember that all right."

"It'll probably make you sleep. I'll bring you something to eat in a few hours."

Without realizing his intent, Jace grasped Honor's hand as she was about to stand. Fragmented images flashed into his mind. He remembered striking the ground, the pain, the darkness . . . and he remembered something else.

. . . Please.

His pained gaze locked with hers as he whispered, "I'm glad you're not mad at me anymore."

Jace was still holding her hand when his eyes closed, and Honor's throat choked tight. She stood up when his grip loosened, hardly resisting the urge to stroke back the unruly dark hair that spilled onto his forehead. He looked terrible. Doc's bandage covered most of his forehead, and traces of dried blood were visible where his wound had bled during the night. His face was so pale that his thick, stubby eyelashes stood out like dark fans against his stubbled cheeks. He was breathing unevenly, and it worried her. She watched as his lips moved with indiscernible words in his uneasy slumber.

Lips that seldom smiled.

But Jace's lips were full and well shaped. His teeth were straight and white. She supposed a spontaneous grin from him would be a sight to behold. She knew so little about him. She wondered if there had ever been a time when he had smiled easily and often, and she wondered how it would feel to have him smile just for her.

Refusing to follow that thought, Honor stood up abruptly. She had come to the Texas Star to settle a torment that left her no peace. Nothing else mattered, and everything that had happened since she came was secondary to that purpose.

She needed to remember that, no matter how difficult it was beginning to be.

Bellamy rode slowly down Lowell's main thoroughfare, barely restraining a sneer. False-fronted buildings; a single, unpaved street; board sidewalks that had suffered much wear; poorly dressed pedestrians who had no sense of style. He had seen dozens of similar unimpressive Western towns in his travels.

Bellamy glanced at the stores in passing. He doubted there was a single person in town who had ever walked the streets of a city as civilized as New York, or as exciting as New Orleans. He suspected they had no inkling of what they were missing.

He knew.

Bellamy smiled. There had been a time when he was as backward as they were, but that time was long past. His situation had changed because he had made it change, and the second blank check he would receive when he walked back through Coburn's door would guarantee that he would never be like these people again.

Bellamy's smile faded. Everything had changed for him the day he had learned how easy it was to kill. In most cases, it was a matter of a single gunshot without a backward look. That had been the most valuable lesson he had learned. The second most valuable lesson had been to make sure the price was right.

Bellamy straightened his broad shoulders and tipped his hat to a young matron who looked at him with an appreciative smile. He wasn't handsome, but he knew women liked him. He enjoyed them, too, even if he had little respect for them. Women were undependable and not to be trusted past the emotion of the moment. He had learned *that* the hard way, when a spurned lover had reported him to the law. But that had been many years earlier. He was a different man now, in appearance and personality. He was successful and sought-after in his chosen profession, and with the exception of that single instance years earlier, the law had never been a problem. He was careful enough that it would never be a problem again.

Bellamy's smile returned when he spotted the sprawling Last Chance Saloon and Dancehall at the end of the street. He'd make himself comfortable there for a few days. He had no doubt there would be women enough to amuse him and time enough to indulge himself in the pleasures they provided. Rule wasn't going anywhere, and he had already accepted the necessity of delay.

Yes, he had plenty of time.

Doc Maggie approached her buggy with a frown. She wasn't much in the mood for the long ride ahead of her, and she was glad she had made arrangements at the livery stable to have her buggy brought to her door at midday. She would be spared a few steps and a few minutes of valuable time.

"On your way out again, Doc?" Doc turned at the sound of Cal Star's familiar voice. It occurred to her not for the first time that he was damned handsome with that heavy sun-streaked hair, those honey-gold eyes, and shoulders that looked as if they could carry the weight of the world. Few men could match Cal in height and breadth of shoulder. A possible exception was Jace Rule, despite the fact that the Texas Star's injured wrangler was thinner than should be normal for his frame.

Doc remembered the moment she had delivered Cal into the world. She recalled the joy on Emma's face, and she wished the dear woman could be there now to share her pride in him.

She also wished Buck wasn't such a damned fool that he couldn't appreciate the man his son had become. But Buck had always been a fool for women. She just hadn't believed how far his folly would take him.

Smiling her first true smile of the day, Doc replied, "You know how it is, Cal. A woman's work is never done, especially when she's the only doctor hereabouts."

"Oh . . . I was hoping I'd get a few minutes to talk to you about Pa. You weren't in your office the last time Pru and I were in town."

"I'm on my way to the Texas Star now." Doc shook her head. "There isn't too much to say about your pa, Cal. He's sick again, but being the man he is, he's determined to get better. And it looks like he's improving." She shrugged. "That's all I can tell you, except that the Texas Star has had its share of difficulties lately. They're sure keeping me busy there."

"What do you mean?"

"Your pa's off his feet when work needs to be done at the ranch; Madalane is mobile now with that wheelchair, but I'm thinking she might be doing herself more harm than good the way she bumps her leg around getting into it; and the new wrangler your pa hired got thrown from his horse. He'll be flat on his back for a few days and more hindrance than help."

"That new fella, Jace Rule?"

"That's him . . . flat on his back. It's a good thing Honor's there. She's the one who found him when his horse came back to the ranch with an empty saddle. She's putting Celeste through her paces, too—and I don't think Celeste likes it."

Silent, Cal stared at her, and Doc prompted, "Does that bother you, Cal?"

"No, it's just that Honor said she'd take care of Pa for me. It's funny, but I believed she'd try. I just didn't think she could do anything that would make a difference."

"I'm not sure she is making a difference on the ranch. Things haven't changed much. Celeste is still wrapping your pa around her finger." Doc couldn't help smiling when she added, "But it isn't as easy as it used to be."

"Why's that?"

"I don't know. Honor's got spunk, and your pa seems to be amused by it."

Cal frowned.

Understanding his expression, Doc said, "No, it's not that way. Your pa still worships the ground Celeste walks on. It's different with Honor. She tells him what she thinks, whether he likes it or not. I figure your pa actually listens to what she has to say because she doesn't have any reason not to tell him the truth—and he knows she makes sense."

Cal remained silent.

"I know," Doc said. "He won't listen to a damned word you say, and it hurts—but the truth is, your pa always had a weakness for women, one way or another."

"Tell me something, Doc. Does Honor look familiar to you?"

"I was thinking that the other day, but I'll be damned if I know who she reminds me of."

Cal nodded. "So Pa's more shorthanded than he was before."

"And rumor has it that he's got a real ways to go before he can meet his next mortgage payment."

Cal's expression grew clouded. "None of this would've happened if Bonnie—"

"Bonnie's dead. It was an accident. It wasn't your fault. Don't let Buck make you think it was."

"I believed it was my fault for a long time. I still think about it."

"Listen to me, Cal." Suddenly angry, Doc said, "Your pa's putting the guilt he feels about Bonnie's death onto you. It's the only way he can deal with it."

Cal did not reply.

"You've got a good life now. A damned good wife,

and a boy who's pleased as pink to call himself your son. Don't let your pa spoil it for you."

"It's that letter, Doc, the one saying it was time to come home. I still don't know who sent it, or why."

"It's a mystery to me. Your pa sure didn't send it, and Celeste didn't even pretend to welcome you. I figure you might never know."

"I feel like Honor is another mystery. I need to talk to her, Doc."

"Are you sure you want to do that? It might cause complications for her at the Texas Star if Buck finds out."

"I need to." The honey-gold of Cal's eyes held hers as his voice grew softer. "Could you ask her to meet me? Anywhere, anytime will be fine with me."

"Cal . . ." Doc sighed. "All right. It's probably better than letting you ride up to the ranch house so your pa can drive you off with his six-shooter."

Doc was unprepared for Cal's brief appreciative hug. The soft words of thanks he whispered in her ear tightened her throat. She whispered, "Your ma would've been proud to have a son like you, Cal."

Doc did not miss the moisture in Cal's gaze as he swung her up easily into the wagon, and with a wordless smile walked away.

A sound at the bunkhouse door turned Jace toward Honor as she entered with a tray in her hands. Never more aware of his infirmity, he remained where he had lain the morning long, unable to lift his head from the pillow. He didn't like being helpless. He had learned the dangers of debility during the five long years he was confined. And strangely, intuition told him he was in danger now.

His gaze followed Honor as she approached and placed the tray on a nearby table. She was no physical threat to him. He knew that instinctively—just as he knew that the kind of danger she represented was growing more real for him with every day that passed.

"I brought you something to eat."

Jace's stomach did a rebellious somersault at the thought, and he responded tensely, "I don't think so."

"Broth. Doc recommended it. I'm getting a real knack for making broth around here."

"I'm not hungry."

"Doc said—"

"I said, I'm not hungry."

"But you sure are short tempered, aren't you?"

"Maybe I am." Jace continued solemnly, "When I should be thanking you."

"For what?"

"For riding out to find me."

"The hands would've found you sooner or later."

"But you found me sooner."

Honor avoided his gaze as she picked up the plate and spoon. She raised the spoon to his lips. Irritated at her persistence, Jace took a sip. It warmed him down to his toes.

"Taste good?"

Jace did not respond.

Honor said more soberly, "Doc said you need fluids. I let it go as long as I could because you were sleeping so soundly, but a few more sips would make her happy, if you could manage it."

Please.

The memory flashed again across his mind, and Jace pinned Honor with his gaze. "Why does it matter to you if I do what Doc says or not?"

Honor was uncharacteristically silent.

Jace pressed, "Is it for the same reason that you rode out to find me when Whistler came back alone?"

When Honor again refused to reply, Jace said with harshness, "It isn't smart to care what happens to me, Honor—for any reason."

Suddenly defensive, Honor responded, "Why not? You cared about me."

"I gave you some good advice, that's all."

"And despite all your protests, you tried to help me from the first moment we met."

"I'm a stranger to you. You don't know anything about me."

"You tried to help me. I'm just returning the favor."

"We're two different people, with two different reasons for ending up on the Texas Star. You came here looking to settle the past so you could go forward. This place is just another stop on a long trail for me."

"I don't believe it's as simple as that."

Jace took a breath, then said, "I'm an ex-convict, Honor, straight out of Huntsville. I spent five years there because I killed a man."

"Killed . . ." Honor's voice trailed away.

"I shot him, and I've never regretted it."

"What did he do?"

"Does it matter?"

"Yes."

"He's dead, whatever my reason was."

"Jace—"

"How long do you think I'll last here, or on any decent ranch, when my record becomes general knowledge?"

Honor took a breath. "The past is past. It's over and done."

"If that's true, what are you doing here?"

"That's different."

"Is it?"

Silent a moment, Honor said, "You hit your head. You're confused. Now isn't the time to talk."

"There'll never be a better time." Grasping her hand, Jace rasped, "You're right, I knew what you were walking into the first day you came here, and I didn't want to see you get in the middle of a situation where you couldn't win. Without knowing why, I cared. I didn't have the right to be jealous of your feelings for Cal when he showed up, but I was. Then when you told me the truth, I cared even more."

Jace took a breath. "We fought, and I was miserable every moment you avoided me. Now you're sitting beside my bed and I'm wishing with all my heart that I was feeling well enough to do something about it. Honor . . . dammit . . . I'm warning you. Get away from me while you still have the chance!"

His heartbeat keeping pace with the renewed pounding in his head, Jace watched Honor's throat work. He saw her eyes search his face before she said, "Suppose I don't want to go away."

"Then you'll be sorry, because I don't have the strength to make you."

"Jace—"

The strangled sound of need that escaped his throat was almost simultaneous with the click of approaching footsteps that turned his attention to the door. Not daring to look at Honor, he watched as Doc Maggie walked in and said, "I'm glad to see Honor's taking care of you. Did you eat something? You need fluids, you know."

"That's what I told him." Jace turned at Honor's response. Her voice was strong, devoid of emotion as she continued, "But he won't listen."

"Then I'm going to sit here until he finishes every spoonful of that broth you're holding." Doc directed a stern glance in Jace's direction. "Did you hear what I said?"

He heard her.

And he was thankful she had stopped him from making a mistake that Honor and he would both have regretted.

"Wait a minute, Honor."

Honor looked at Doc Maggie as the older woman halted her on the way back from the bunkhouse. True to her word, Doc had watched as she had fed Jace every spoonful of the broth she had brought him. Honor had avoided Jace's gaze and had struggled to still the trembling of her hand as she fed him. She had never been more grateful to see the bottom of a bowl, and when she did, she had risen quickly from the chair, hopeful of leaving before she betrayed herself.

Because she ached inside. Jace was an ex-convict. He had admitted killing someone—a crime for which he had served five years in prison. She could not imagine the horror of those years or the weight of knowing he had taken a man's life.

Jace had warned her not to care, and she had wanted to escape, to run away.

But Doc had had other ideas that had kept her standing at the older woman's side until she was done treating Jace's wound.

"Honor . . . ?"

Brought abruptly back to the present, Honor turned toward Doc Maggie as the older woman took her arm to stay her, saying, "I need to talk to you for a few minutes before we go into the house. I met Cal in town this morning. He wants to talk to you. He's concerned about his father. He figures you could tell him more about what's happening here than anybody else can right now."

Honor went still. She saw the concern in Doc's expression as the older woman said, "Cal's a nice fella. His father's an ornery old bastard who doesn't deserve a son like him, but that doesn't stop Cal from caring."

. . . caring.

"Cal just wants a chance to talk to you."

"I have nothing to tell him."

"I think it would relieve his mind even to hear you say that."

"I'm too busy here to meet him. I can't get away."

"You could if you wanted to."

"I don't want to, then."

"Honor . . . Cal's a fine man. His father disowned him for something he didn't do. He needs to set things right."

Doc's words rebounded inside Honor. Cal had suffered because of Buck. Just like her.

"You can set the time and place."

"I have nothing to say to him right now."

"Tell him that, then. It breaks my heart to know how Emma would feel if she could see the way Buck is treating Cal. It would break any mother's heart."

As her own mother's heart had been broken.

Honor took a breath. "All right. I'll meet him."

"When?"

"Things will start going back to normal when Jace is on his feet again. I'll meet Cal at your office in town then."

"You're a dear girl, Honor." Doc's eyes were suspiciously bright as she said, "Well, I guess it's time to check on Buck." She added with a wry twist of her lips, "Then Madalane." She sighed. "Sometimes that Hippocratic oath really smarts, you know?"

"There they were, Doc and the kitchen girl, whispering like conspirators on the way back from the bunkhouse."

Celeste stood beside Madalane's bed, her expression rabid. She had waited only until Doc's buggy disappeared from sight around the bend in the trail before going directly to Madalane's room. She continued heatedly, "They're planning something, and I don't like it. I didn't leave Buck alone with Doc Maggie for a minute."

"I warned you, Celeste." Perspiration dotted Madalane's forehead as she struggled to pull herself into her chair. She had dressed herself and finished her toilette. She had sat up to endure Doc's visit—all without getting help of any kind. She was exhausted, though Celeste took no notice of her discomfort.

In truth, Madalane had known she could expect nothing else. Celeste had always been self-centered and self-absorbed, even as a child. Celeste trusted her with her life, but Madalane did not deceive herself that Celeste would ever care about anyone but herself.

Irritated, Madalane snapped, "I am doing all I can for you right now. I told you earlier that the kitchen girl was gaining strength in this house—that it was time for you to do something about it."

"Like what?" Celeste's delicate features grew haughty. "Would you have me fire her? With you lying abed like you are, I would then have no recourse but to assume her work. Would you have me sweat and scramble like a common housemaid to provide for my husband and the wranglers alike?"

"As I have done, you mean?"

"Yes, as you have done! Because that is *your* place, not mine!"

"For a woman who resented the kitchen girl when she first came to the Texas Star, that is a change of attitude on your part. I am suspicious of your reasoning. Is it because your husband would not tolerate firing the girl for any reason?"

"No. My husband would do whatever I wanted him to do, including firing the kitchen girl if I wanted it that way."

"You fool yourself! Your husband is growing to rely on the kitchen girl. He admires the way the ranch hands have responded to her."

"That is not true."

"And now she is joining forces with the doctor, who despises you."

Celeste did not reply, and Madalane rasped, "You must do something to drive a wedge between those two before it is too late."

"It will never be too late. All that an alliance between the kitchen girl and the doctor could do would be to cause me some discomfort—a situation I do not intend to tolerate."

"Then you must put more pressure on your husband to change his will so you are free to finish up with him quickly."

Celeste's expression grew tight. "My husband is not a fool. He will see through any plan that is not carefully executed."

"Find a way."

"I intend to."

"Soon . . . or it may be too late."

"I remind you, Madalane—you are the servant here, not I! I do not take your orders and I will not follow any course I do not approve. Is that understood?"

Madalane did not reply.

"Is that understood!"

"I understand . . . completely."

Her head high, Celeste stepped out into the hallway and pulled the door firmly closed behind her. She paused outside the door. She listened to the sounds of Madalane's struggle as the Negress attempted to swing herself into her wheelchair.

Satisfaction twitched at Celeste's lips. Reminding Madalane of her place was becoming increasingly difficult. She was determined not to allow it to become a problem.

It was worse than he had expected.

Bellamy leaned against the back of the rickety wooden chair, a glass in hand and a bottle on the table in front of him as he scrutinized the interior of the Last Chance Saloon and Dancehall with a critical eye. The establishment was aptly named. Despite the early-afternoon hour, a cloud of smoke already hung over the place. Several cowpokes stood swaying uncertainly at the bar, a few silent customers sat morosely at tables around the room, while two brightly dressed saloon girls laughed uproariously at comments made by the scruffy customers who filled their glasses. The piano stool stood empty, and the absence of music added to the bleakness of the scene as two other saloon girls lingered at the end of the bar watching the door for potential customers. Bellamy had already turned both women away. He wasn't that desperate for female company. His only hope was that the evening hours would bring in a few more palatable women for him to pass the time with.

Bellamy swallowed his drink in a gulp and poured

another. The atmosphere was depressing to a man with his zest for life. He was beginning to think he would earn the money Coburn was paying him just by enduring the primitive conditions Lowell had to offer.

Agitation crawled up Bellamy's spine as he tossed down another drink and refilled his glass. He needed to get this job over and done. And he needed to get back to New York for that blank check that was waiting for him.

Bellamy's attention was caught by a slovenly, bearded fellow who stood briefly in the doorway before entering. There was a look about the man that seemed familiar. His expression was hungry, almost bestial, and transparently corrupt. A few greetings along the bar indicated he was a frequent patron of the establishment. Snide, whispered remarks from some of the tables beside Bellamy indicated his assessment of the fellow was correct.

Bellamy almost smiled. He had never met the man before, but he probably knew him better than that fellow knew himself—because he had been that man when he was younger. The difference was that he had outgrown that part of his life. He had learned how to make the best use of his talents, whereas this fellow, evidently, never would.

Perversely amused, Bellamy succumbed to impulse, picking up his bottle and heading for the bar. He reached it just as the fellow said, "Yeah, I got plenty of things going for me—things I ain't sharing with none of you old boys."

An unsteady cowpoke responded with a smile, "Well, you always got money in your pocket, that's for sure. I wish I knew how you do it, Derek."

"I'm smart, that's how. And I got me a situation that suits me too fine to change it."

"Yeah, what's that?"

"Wouldn't you like to know?" Derek's unshaven face creased into a leering smile, and Bellamy felt his interest heighten. It had been years since he had indulged the side of himself that this fellow seemed to be enjoying so well. It occurred to him that stepping back in time a bit might be the only enjoyment he'd be able to find in this desolate town.

"Let me buy you a drink." Bellamy smiled as the fellow turned toward him. He continued, "Your name's Derek, right? Mine's Bellamy." He looked down at the gun Derek wore on his hip and said, "It looks like that gun on your hip has seen good use. I expect you know how to use it."

Derek's leer widened. "Better than most, I'd say."

"Not better than me."

Derek searched Bellamy's expression, then said, "That stands to be proved, don't it?"

"Maybe." Beginning to enjoy himself, Bellamy continued, "But not now. I figure we both came here to do some drinking."

Bellamy filled Derek's glass to the brim. Derek studied him a moment longer, then picked up the glass and emptied it in a gulp. He belched loudly.

Smiling, Bellamy refilled both their glasses. It looked like a boring afternoon was coming to an end.

Chapter Nine

He was feeling better with every step he took.

Jace glanced around the ranch yard as he stepped out into the light of early morning. The other hands had left an hour earlier. It had been three days since his injury, during which time he had grown stronger every day. To their credit, the hands had been as considerate as they could be. They had made as little noise as possible when returning to the bunkhouse each evening. They had taken to holding their conversations outside the door so as not to disturb his sleep, but he had heard them talking.

Big John had bemoaned the difficulty they'd had cleaning up the fouled water hole, especially since they hadn't been able to ascertain what had caused the problem. Randy had voiced his concern that they were falling seriously behind with all the other chores Buck had set for them. Mitch had commented that Buck seemed to be getting better but was growing more ornery every day.

Evidently, Madalane was still pushing herself around the house and irritating everybody she came in contact with. The men groaned at the thought of what Honor had to put up with while they were gone, but they were thankful Madalane was so exhausted by the time they came home that she barely put in an appearance before retiring to her room.

It seemed that Buck continued to cater to Celeste's every whim, nauseating the men and leaving Honor cold. The hands couldn't understand how Honor managed to speak her mind so openly with so few repercussions from Buck. They knew that Honor's candid comments infuriated Celeste. They could not understand why Celeste put up with her. They figured Honor would be made to pay sooner or later.

That thought had stopped Jace cold. He wondered what Buck's reaction would be when Honor finally told him who she was.

He wondered if Honor would ever tell him.

Admittedly, during the past few days he'd done little else but sleep; but he had not been free of thoughts of Honor whether awake or sleeping.

He had come to both dread and anxiously await the moment when she would walk though the bunkhouse door to bring him his meals. The realization that she had obviously heeded his warning to distance herself from him both pleased and upset him. Relief alternated with a nagging ache inside him when she avoided his gaze. He reminded himself that Honor's problems did not concern him, yet he longed to share again the sweet intimacy of her confidence.

Confusion had reigned over his thoughts so completely that he had begun wishing he had never set foot on the Texas Star. He had then decided to leave the ranch as soon as he was able, for both their sakes.

Steady and resolute, Jace walked through the barn doors. Whistler's whinny of recognition brought a smile to his lips that faded when he viewed the extent of the gelding's injuries. He winced at the sight of the animal's bruised knees. The poor old fella must have fallen hard, to do that much damage to himself. There was something strange about that. The part of the trail where the accident had occurred was heavily foliated, but it was level and smooth, and he had never considered it particularly treacherous.

Jace crouched down to examine Whistler's legs more closely. His knees were healing, but deep horizontal slashes across his fetlocks would need more time.

Jace squinted at the slashes more intently. They were sharp and clean, as if made by a blade.

Jace shook his head at the absurdity of that notion. He supposed the only way he would satisfy himself as to how Whistler had gotten such a strange injury would be to examine the site of his fall.

He needed to know.

Jace stroked Whistler's muzzle. Unfortunately, it would be a while before the old fellow was ready to travel.

"I brought your breakfast to the bunkhouse, but you weren't there." Jace turned toward Honor as she approached. Her concern was obvious as she said, "Doc Maggie won't like seeing you up and about so soon."

Jace silently cursed as Honor drew closer. What was there about this woman that stirred familiar longings? She wasn't a beauty in the way Celeste was, with startling coloring and perfect features. But the sparkling strands of red and gold in the tawny brown of her hair seemed to capture the warmth of the sun, mesmerizing him; those heavily fringed eyes that burst into sparks of riotous color with her emotions numbed his mind to everything but her; and her lips, so soft and gently curved, drew him. She was successful in hiding her emotions from other people, yet he seemed able to sense them without effort.

He wanted to protect her, to keep her safe from the hurts and anxieties of the world, but what made him think he was up to the job? He had failed in a similar situation before. That failure had changed his life forever. Honor deserved better than to accept the protection of a man like him.

With those thoughts in mind, he responded sharply, "I don't need anybody's approval to be out here."

"If you got dizzy and fell—"

"I'm not dizzy and I'm not going to fall. Neither am I going to stay in bed to satisfy an old woman, even if she is a doctor."

"Doc Maggie would be happy to hear you say that, I'm sure."

"Doc Maggie would be happy to see me on my feet. That's one less person she'd have to worry about on this ranch."

"She's up to the job, no matter how many people she has to tend to here."

"I didn't say she wasn't."

"What did you say, then?"

Jace paused at the sharpness of Honor's response, then replied, "I can see your father's disposition is rubbing off on you."

Honor went suddenly white. She stared at him, then turned silently toward the doorway. She was making rapid strides away from him when Jace caught her arm. Sincerely regretting his remark, he said gruffly, "I'm sorry. I don't know what made me say that."

Honor did not reply.

"Honor, I didn't mean to hurt you."

Attempting to shake off Jace's grip, Honor responded, "I was a fool to confide in you. I don't know why I did, but I can see now that I only added to the long line of mistakes I'd already made."

"You didn't make a mistake." The ache inside Jace expanded. "I'm sorry I said what I did. I'm sorry about a lot of things."

"I accept your apology, so let me go."

"Honor . . ."

She looked up at him. Her lips were trembling. She was at the point of tears, and the realization that he had brought her to that state disturbed him. How could he explain that he had come out into the barn ready to run away from a problem for the first time in his life—because he was losing a fight he couldn't afford to lose? How could he make her understand that, however determined he had been to maintain an emotional distance from her, he was rapidly weakening now that she was so close? How could he make her comprehend that, despite his sober reasoning, all he really wanted now was to—

Jace dropped his hands back to his sides. "Maybe I should go back to the bunkhouse for my breakfast."

"Yes, maybe you should." Trembling, Honor added heatedly, "And afterwards, maybe you should leave the Texas Star and never come back."

Honor's words slashed deeply. Hardly aware of his response, Jace said, "Is that what you really want, Honor?"

"I only know one thing for sure." Fighting back her tears, she said adamantly, "I'm not going to leave the Texas Star until I settle everything I came here for— no matter what it costs me."

Honor's reply resonated deep inside him. Jace returned solemnly, "You're right, and what I advised you to do was wrong. I realize that now. Your path to the Texas Star was long and hard. You need to settle the past. You have to do what you have to do." His own heartbeat pounded in his ears as he added in a harsh whisper, "And, dammit . . . so do I."

Jace swept her into his arms.

The beauty . . . the warmth . . . the taste of her.

Elation swept Jace's senses as Honor's brief resistance faded and she melded to his strength . . . as the wonder of the moment he had sought so desperately to avoid consumed him.

Wanting . . . needing, Jace pressed his kiss deeper. It felt so good, so right to hold Honor at last. He had been lost and wandering for so long. His arms had been empty, but he'd had no desire to fill them.

Somehow he had known the first moment he met Honor that it could be like this.

Jace crushed Honor closer. Her arms slid around his neck, and his passion flared. Tearing his lips from hers, he tasted her fluttering eyelids, her smooth cheek, the delicate contours of her ear. He trailed his lips to the curve of her jaw, whispering loving words before he covered her mouth once more. Yes, he wanted her. He needed her. She had somehow become an innate part of him that he longed to finally claim for his own.

His kisses surged deeper. His caresses grew more intimate. She was returning kiss for kiss, caress for caress—when reality returned in a heated flash that jerked him back from her as if he had been stung.

Holding Honor an arm's length from him, his chest heaving with the power of emotions barely restrained, Jace rasped, "This is a mistake."

Motionless, Honor did not reply as Jace continued haltingly, "This isn't what I intended. I came out to the barn this morning for one reason, to see if Whistler was well enough to travel—so I could leave the Texas Star. I would've done it, too. I would've turned my back on the ranch and you without a backward look if his injuries were healed. That's the kind of man I am, Honor, and you deserve better."

Jace lowered his hands to his sides as he continued hoarsely, "I don't know what else to say except to repeat that I'm no good for you, and to warn you to stay away from me—because I know now that I don't have the strength to stay away from you."

With nothing else to say, Jace strode from the barn, leaving a deadening silence in his wake.

Honor stared at Jace's retreating figure. Unable to move, she watched him disappear from view.

Her lips were still warm from his kiss, her body still trembling as she berated herself silently. What was wrong with her? She had fallen into the arms of a man she hardly knew, a person who had confessed to spending five years in prison for killing someone with no regrets, a man who admitted he would have left her and the Texas Star far behind him if he were able.

Honor took a shaky breath. Jace had warned her of the danger of caring, yet she had ignored him. He had cautioned her about getting too close—but it had been he who had had the sense to pull away.

Harsh reality forced Honor's eyes briefly closed. She had grown up living with the repercussions of her mother's brief submission to passion—an act that could never be rescinded. She had matured knowing that her mother and she had been defined by that moment. She had sworn she would never make the same mistake that had caused a lifetime of pain—but in the warmth of Jace's arms, with his dark eyes speaking the words she longed to hear, resolution had slipped away.

How could anything that felt so right be wrong?

Shaking her head in confusion, Honor listened to the sound of Jace's departing footsteps.

Seconds later, she heard Doc Maggie admonish,

"What are you doing walking around, Jace? You're not a well man yet."

Moving to the shadow of the barn doorway, Honor saw Jace's sober expression as he replied, "I'm fine. You can cancel me off your list of patients."

"Oh? When did you get your medical degree, young man?"

"I don't need a medical degree to know how I feel. I should think you'd be happy to see me on my feet. If I don't miss my guess, Buck's been after you to get me back on my horse as soon as possible."

Doc responded tightly, "That's not far from right, but Buck Star doesn't tell me what to do. You should know that by now. You should also know that I won't take sass from a young fella like you, Jace Rule."

"No sass intended, Doc."

Apparently satisfied by his response, Doc said stiffly, "How do you feel?"

"Fine."

"No headaches, dizziness, weakness, blurred vision . . . no instability of any kind?"

"No, ma'am."

"Stand still a moment." Doc stepped forward to assess him more closely. She nodded. "Your eyes are clear. That's good. How's your stomach feel? No queasiness?" She warned, "Tell me the truth or you'll end up flat on your back again."

"Like I said, I'm fine. I wish I could say the same for Whistler."

"He'll be a while healing. Buck already told Randy

to let you use one of the other horses when you're ready to go back to work."

"I guess that says it all."

"Maybe, but I'd test myself out for a day or so before I went back to a full day's work. It might be sensible to busy yourself around the ranch yard first. Ride around a bit. Make sure you can handle being back in the saddle." When Jace remained silent, she added, "There's plenty of work to be done in the barn, you know, and Whistler could use a little more attention, too."

Jace nodded. "Maybe you're right."

"I *know* I'm right, but I'm glad to hear you say it. If you're wise, you'll eat something that will test your stomach, too. And you'll take it easy the first day back."

"Any more orders, Doc?"

"Not right now, but remember this." Her expression stern, Doc continued, "I'm the doctor here and I know what I'm talking about, so you'd do well to do what I tell you to do."

"Anything you say, Doc."

Honor stepped back out of sight as Doc started toward the house. She followed Jace with her gaze until he disappeared inside the bunkhouse.

And she wondered again . . . how could anything that had felt so right be wrong?

This was a day of days.

Doc stopped in her tracks as the door to Buck's room opened and he walked boldly out into the hallway. She shook her head and snapped, "What, you, too?"

"What are you talking about, old woman?" Nothing more than a bag of skin and bones, Buck was obviously beginning to feel his oats as he questioned, "You're late, aren't you? I expected you half an hour ago."

Her brief amusement fading when Celeste walked out into the hallway behind Buck, Doc replied, "You should be glad I came at all, especially since my patients here see fit to ignore my orders."

Buck stopped a few feet from her. He questioned, "Meaning?"

"Meaning you should be taking care not to overdo, and Jace should have more sense than to think he's well enough to go back to work already."

"Already? I've been paying that fella for doing nothing but lying in his cot for three days! It's about time he started earning his keep again."

Honor entered the kitchen. Doc glanced briefly in her direction before instructing, "Get back in your room, old man, so I can examine you the way I should."

"I'm all right." Ignoring his own wavering stance, Buck continued, "I'm feeling better every minute—just like happened before. I'll be back on my horse in a couple of days."

"And I'll be ready to fly then, too."

"You're not funny, Doc."

"Neither are you." A hand on her ample hip, Doc ordered, "Get back in your room like I said so I can do my job. You can do whatever you want after I leave, but while I'm here, you follow my orders."

"How dare you speak to my husband like that in his own house?" Stepping out from behind Buck, Celeste continued, "You're here because we *allow* you to be here."

"I'm here because you panicked when Buck had a relapse and you sent for me."

Interrupting the angry exchange, Buck said, "There's no reason for either of you to get huffy." Addressing his livid wife, he said, "Like Doc says, she's only doing her job."

"She shows you no respect!"

"Celeste, darlin'," Buck almost purred. "That's just Doc's way."

Her stomach close to rebelling at Buck's placating tone, Doc remained adamant. She'd give him another minute, then she'd head right out the door.

As if reading her mind, Buck turned back toward his room, saying, "You win this time, Doc, but I'm telling you, I'm fine."

Grateful to be on her way after finishing up with Buck and making an obligatory visit to Madalane's room afterwards, Doc started across the kitchen toward the door. She stopped beside Honor. Responding to Honor's unspoken question, she said, "Well, it looks like Buck's done it again. That old man is actually improving. Damned if he doesn't have more lives than a cat!"

Honor responded unexpectedly, "You know what they say, 'Only the good die young.'" Honor added just as unexpectedly, "I have to go into town to pick up some supplies around noon tomorrow. If Cal still wants to talk to me, I can see him then."

Doc responded without hesitation, "He'll be there."

Jace kept his mount to a steady pace along the leafy trail. As much as he hated to admit it, Doc's comments that morning had been correct. He was already tiring, and the day was barely half over.

Determined to occupy his mind, he had followed Doc's suggestions by going to the bunkhouse to eat the breakfast Honor had left for him, and had spent the morning mucking out the barn. He had then returned to the bunkhouse to find his afternoon meal on a tray, with Honor nowhere in sight.

He had told himself it was better that way.

He had struggled to convince himself it was true as he ate with dogged determination and returned to the barn to examine Whistler's injuries again. When the slashes on Whistler's fetlocks continued to mystify him, he had saddled the buckskin in the corral and mounted up.

Jace slowed his pace as a familiar section of the trail came into view. Dismounting, he led his horse behind him to study the area more closely. He halted when flattened and broken shrubbery indicated the place where Whistler and he had gone down. On close inspection, he saw dried bloodstains still visible where Whistler's blood had mixed with his own. The ground was level. There was no sign of anything that could have made Whistler lurch forward with such force as to cause the injuries they had both sustained.

Jace sighed and shook his head. He supposed he had to face the fact that Whistler was getting on in years and wasn't as surefooted as he had once been—but the notion wasn't easy to accept. Whistler hadn't shown any signs of age in his performance prior to the accident. On the contrary, he had worked exceedingly well despite the occasional gray hairs on his muzzle, outperforming younger horses at certain tasks.

Obeying an impulse, Jace tied his mount to a tree and entered the heavy brush beside the trail. He examined the ground, frowning at the bootprints visible there. His frown deepened at the sight of a circular cut about a foot off the ground around the bark of a tree a few feet away.

Jace walked stiffly to the opposite side of the trail. His blood ran cold when he saw similar bootprints and the same type of cut on the bark of a tree there.

Wire would cut a horse's forelock as sharply as a knife if it tripped him up while he was traveling at a brisk pace.

Wire would cause a circular scar on the bark of a tree if it was pulled taut against a sudden thrust forward.

There could be only one reason for a wire to be strung that low across a trail.

Jace stood up and looked around him. He searched the foliage carefully but could find no sign of a wire, or clues as to the person who had strung it.

The size and depth of the bootprints suggested that the fellow was a man of medium height. Jace could not imagine the who or the why of it, but he was determined to find out.

Honor's image appeared unexpectedly in his mind, and Jace went still. She had ridden out after him as soon as Whistler returned to the ranch, perhaps missing the culprit by minutes. If she had seen the fellow, or if he had seen her—

Jace felt the blood drain from his face at the possible consequences.

No, he wouldn't let that happen again!

Jace mounted up and turned his horse back toward the ranch house. He had told Honor to keep her distance from him, but only now did he realize the full danger to which he had exposed her. Sober resolution turned Jace cold. No, he didn't know the who or the why of the "accident" that had been manufactured for him, but two things he did know for sure:

He would find out.

And he would protect Honor with his life.

Dressed in riding clothes, Honor walked briskly down Lowell's boardwalk as the new day moved rapidly into afternoon. Her destination was the storefront that bore Doc Maggie's name. She glanced up at the sun that had dropped past its zenith, annoyed that circumstances at the ranch had prevented her from coming to town earlier as she had planned.

Circumstances.

Buck had awakened early, and he was on a tear. Obviously feeling better than he had in days, he had swiftly made everyone on the ranch suffer because of it. No one had to tell Honor that Celeste had enjoyed every minute as he'd walked boldly into the kitchen where the hands were eating breakfast, and demanded a report from Randy on what had been accomplished while he was ill.

Honor had kept her silence as Randy had attempted to relate the difficulties they had encountered with the fouled water hole and the shortage of help that handicapped them even further. She had not looked at Jace as Buck had turned his full attention on him, outlining how he expected Jace to make up for the days of work he had lost. It had been all she could do not to tell Buck straight out that he was an ungrateful, demanding old man without a speck of humanity, but she had held the words back. It had not been the right time.

She had taken great pleasure, however, in choosing that moment to inform Buck that she intended to go into town. As expected, he had ranted about her earning her keep in the kitchen, but she had stood her ground until he agreed. She had then added as if in an afterthought that she was going to pick up some supplies for the ranch. When he had surprised her by saying he would send one of the men with her to drive the wagon, she had declined, telling him that taking a packhorse would be easier. When Randy had protested her traveling alone, she had added that her gun was all the company she would need.

She had felt Jace's gaze burning into her, but she had ignored it. She had convinced herself during the sleepless night past that, however right it had felt to be in his arms, it had indeed been wrong. She was determined not to allow herself to forget it.

Honor was uncertain if Celeste's persistent demands had deliberately delayed her intended early start for town, but the result was the same. She had arrived in Lowell only a few minutes previously, had dropped off her list at the mercantile, and had headed for Doc's office aware that she was late.

Honor's steady stride faltered. In truth, she didn't really want to meet with Cal. She had consented only because of her realization that Cal's situation wasn't terribly different from her own, that Buck had caused Cal a misery he couldn't entirely overcome despite the happiness he had achieved in other areas of his life. She knew how it felt to suffer because of that old man's selfishness. She felt the need to help Cal as best she could.

Honor paused briefly at Doc's office door, then pushed it open and walked inside. The office was empty.

Uncertain whether the emotion that surged through her at that moment was relief or pain, she looked at the curtain covering the entrance to Doc's living quarters in the rear and called out, "Doc, are you in there?"

She smiled when Doc's rounded figure pushed into view. Her smile froze when Cal stepped into sight behind Doc.

"We thought you weren't coming." Doc advanced toward her with a welcoming smile. "I was just about to make Cal a cup of tea."

"Oh, don't let me stop you." Honor took a backward step. "I can come back a little later."

Tall, handsome, his gaze intense, Cal advanced toward her, saying, "No, we were waiting for you. Come on in."

Hardly aware that Doc had slipped out onto the street to allow them privacy, Honor waited for Cal to speak.

Her heart was pounding as Cal began, "First of all, I want to thank you for coming. I figure you probably have enough to do on the ranch without taking time out to meet me." Cal's half smile faded. "But I needed to talk to you, Honor. Doc tells me you've been standing up to my father and trying to set things as right as you can on the ranch. I know the situation there isn't easy, especially with Celeste's influence on my father. She doesn't bring out the best in him."

Honor was unable to respond as Cal continued with obvious difficulty, "I don't want you to take this the wrong way, Honor. I know what you said, how wrong my father's behavior seems to you. What I don't understand is why you care."

Care.

Honor shuddered as the word somersaulted in her mind. Yes, it was all about caring . . . the caring Buck had never felt for anyone but himself, and the caring she had missed because he had deprived her of any chance of family.

She managed in reply, "I know how hopeless it feels when you want so badly to set things right and you can't."

"You probably know the story behind my trouble with my father." Cal's face darkened. "My father blames me for my sister's death. I don't know . . . I suppose in a way I do blame myself. I was supposed to be looking out for her when the accident happened. Pa loved Bonnie. She was his only daughter. I don't think he'll ever get over her loss."

Honor averted her gaze. A sister, Bonnie, whom she might've known; a brother, Taylor, who was out of touch with the family, whom she'd never get to know; and Cal, standing only a few feet away without any realization that the same blood ran in their veins.

"Honor . . ."

Honor looked back up at him.

"Do I know you from somewhere?" Cal's eyes searched hers. "I asked you that before and you said no, but is there some way we might've come into contact somewhere?"

"I told you, we've never met."

"You seem so familiar."

Honor could not help asking, "What's familiar about me?"

"I don't know . . ." Cal studied her more closely. "Your coloring strikes a bell somewhere in the back of my mind. Those eyes . . ." He laughed. "They're not easy to forget."

"They're my mother's eyes. I have her coloring."

"Did she have that same way of looking at a person . . . of pinning them with her gaze? There aren't too many people with that intensity."

"No, there aren't. My mother always said I took after my father that way."

"Where is your mother?"

"Dead."

"And your father?"

"He was never a part of my life."

"Oh. That was his mistake."

Honor's eyes brimmed.

Cal frowned. "I didn't mean to stir up old hurts."

"You didn't."

"Honor . . ." Cal moved an uncertain step closer. "I don't know how to explain the way I feel . . . like you know exactly what I'm trying to say, even though I haven't been able to say it worth a damn."

"Are you trying to say you feel like we share something you don't quite understand?"

"Yes, I guess that's it."

A tear slipped down her cheek as Honor whispered, "Don't you recognize me, Cal?"

"Recognize you?"

"I'm your sister."

Cal's sharp intake of breath was simultaneous with his backward step as he said, "Bonnie's dead. I saw her lying at the bottom of that well."

"Yes, Bonnie's dead, and I wish I had known her. I wish I had known all of you instead of growing up alone, with only a mother who loved me despite living in shame because she had borne me."

"What are you saying?"

"My name is Honor Gannon because my mother took back her maiden name when she decided to start her life over. Her married name was Montgomery . . . Betty Montgomery."

"Montgomery." Cal hardly breathed. "My mother's best friend was named Betty Montgomery. Betty moved away from Lowell without even saying good-bye after her husband died."

Another tear slipped down her cheek and Honor brushed it away.

"Honor . . . it can't be."

Hardly able to speak past the lump in her throat, Honor whispered, "Then it isn't. It isn't anything that you don't want it to be, Cal."

Honor made an attempt to turn away, only to feel Cal's hands grip her shoulders, holding her fast.

"It's true, isn't it?" He searched her face more closely. "I remember Betty. You have her same hair and eyes, but other than that . . ." Cal's eyes misted. "Damn, Honor . . . I know why I thought I had met you before." He took a rasping breath. "You look like Bonnie."

A sob escaped Honor's throat as Cal wrapped his arms around her and hugged her tight. She struggled to restrain tears as he whispered, "I'm sorry, Honor. I'm so sorry for all the time we lost—all those wasted years."

She was sorry, too.

"I wish I could make them up to you."

She wished she could speak so she could tell him that he had.

Cal separated himself from her abruptly. "Pa doesn't know, does he?"

Honor shook her head. "I came back to tell him. I wanted to expose him as an adulterer in front of the whole town. I wanted to make him suffer." She took a breath. "Then I saw him, weak . . . just hanging on to life, and I couldn't make myself do it."

"But you stayed."

"Nothing's changed." Honor took a backward step. "I *am* going to tell him who I am, Cal. I *am* going to expose him for what he is, but I need to wait until he's strong enough to look me in the eye when I tell him what he did to my mother and me. I need to wait so he can tell me he doesn't care, and I can tell him I don't care about him, either; so I can tell him he deserves Celeste, because she's just like him—conniving, a person who pretends to love but only loves herself. I need to wait until I can tell him Celeste will use him up and throw him away when she gets what she wants, whatever that is, just like he used my mother. And I need to wait until I can tell Buck that I hope he lives a long life to suffer his regrets when they come back to haunt him, one by one."

"Honor—"

"I'm sorry." She smiled shakily. "I didn't come here today intending to tell you who I am, or to burden you with all this. I came only because Doc Maggie said you were upset. I didn't want that."

"I don't want you to be upset, either."

"Cal . . ." Honor took a breath. "I didn't even know you existed before I came here, but I'm so proud to have a brother like you."

"I'll tell Pa who you are. I'll make him—"

"No!"

"He has to know!"

"I'll tell him when I'm ready—not before."

"He's sick, Honor. He may never get well enough for you to do what you want to do."

Suddenly uneasy, Honor said, "I don't want you to tell him. Give me your word you won't tell him, Cal—that you won't tell anybody who I am."

"But—"

"Please. I've waited so long. I want to do it my way."

"Honor . . . how can I keep a secret like this?"

"The same way I did."

"You haven't told anybody?"

"Only one person, and he won't tell."

"You can trust him with your secret?"

Honor nodded. "I'd trust him with my life."

Momentarily silent, Cal said, "There's one person I trust like that. My wife, Pru." He continued solemnly, "I'll keep your secret, but I want you to know how much it means to me to have you for a sister. Thanks for that, Honor."

The irony of the moment tightened Honor's throat. Cal had thanked *her*, without realizing he was the greatest gift she had ever received.

With Cal's words still ringing in her ears, Honor walked out of Doc's office richer at that moment than she had ever expected to be.

Bellamy strolled leisurely along Lowell's boardwalk, doing his best to ignore Derek's presence beside him. Derek served his purpose by distracting him from his boredom during the evening hours, but in the bright light of day, the fellow disgusted him.

Unfortunately, Bellamy had awakened that morning in his hotel room with a heavy head, with dim memories of active nights past while he and Derek had indulged their vices to excess, and with the realization that Derek was probably lying abed in the next room with the playmate he had chosen for the night. His association with Derek had been timely. It had brought him back to a period of his life when he had been as great a degenerate as Derek now was. It had also awakened him to the fact that he needed to get back to business and the new life he had made for himself before bad habits became too deeply entrenched.

Yet his time had not been wasted. Initially bored with Derek's drunken ramblings, he had come to full attention when the Texas Star was mentioned. The Star family history had come out in enticing bits and pieces that Bellamy was certain he could use to his advantage when he was ready to finish up with Jace Rule. It amused him that Derek did not realize he had betrayed himself, that his intimate knowledge of the inner workings of the Texas Star could only come from someone close to its owner.

Someone who was also close to Derek.

There was only one person that could be—and it amazed Bellamy.

He had seen Celeste Star while he had watched the Texas Star covertly. She was a young, beautiful woman, apparently devoted to the sick old man who owned the ranch. He had had his suspicions about that from the first, and only a few days of Derek's company had confirmed them. Not that he cared that Celeste Star's tastes were secretly debauched enough to allow Derek to entertain her. He had briefly considered the thought of offering her a step up in the world after his present job was concluded. The idea was still in the back of his mind.

His steps slowed to a halt when he saw Honor Gannon leave Doc's office on the opposite side of the street. He had seen that woman before, and he knew who she was. She was the little twit who had ridden out to find Jace Rule when his horse came back to the ranch alone. She had ridden up the trail just as he had finished removing the wire and had attached it to his saddle. He had gotten away in the nick of time. A few minutes sooner and she would have seen him.

Bellamy scrutinized Honor's trim figure as she continued down the street. Slim, but womanly. He liked that. She walked like a woman with spirit. He liked that, too.

"What are you looking at? Oh!" Derek laughed. "You're wasting your time thinking about that fancy little piece."

"Is that so?" Bellamy smiled. "I figure you're speaking from experience."

"You don't have to figure nothin', because I never gave that woman a second look. I got me something better than that whenever I want it."

"This 'something better'—she doesn't mind that you spent the past three nights with other women?"

"What she don't know won't hurt her."

"You're sure?"

"I take care of her real good. She knows where to come when she needs what I got to offer."

"Oh, you don't have a say as to when or where? She comes to you when she's in need?"

Derek's sweaty face turned hard. "That ain't none of your business."

"Neither is it any of your business what woman I want to look at."

Silent for long moments, Derek said, "You're right. I was just trying to warn you. That Honor Gannon's got too much to say for a woman."

"How would you know?"

Derek smiled. "I got my ways."

"I got my ways, too, and I say she's pretty interesting. From the look of her, nothing much scares her."

"You hit the nail on the head that time. She wasn't in town but a few hours when she hooked onto the Texas Star's new rider, Jace Rule, and traveled out to the ranch with him to get herself a job that most people in town wouldn't touch with a ten-foot pole."

"Really?"

"I hear Rule and her hit it off real fine, too."

Interesting.

Turning toward Doc's office as a big, light-haired cowpoke walked out onto the street, Derek said slowly, "Well, what do you know."

"You know him?"

"Everybody in town knows him. He's the town hero, Cal Star." Derek's expression darkened. "I told you about him. He became a big hero to everybody but his own pa when he sneaked up on the rustlers who were working the ranches around here and got every one of them killed."

"Is that right?"

"Yeah. His pa don't want nothing to do with him,

but it looks to me like he's found a way in on the Texas Star after all." Derek said abruptly, "I got to get going. I got things to do."

"Where are you going?" Bellamy pressed, "I thought you were going to stay in town a few days longer."

"Yeah, well, I changed my plans. I'll see you around."

Leaving without another word, Derek turned in the direction of the livery stable, and Bellamy almost laughed aloud. Derek was so transparent Bellamy wondered that the whole town didn't know whose lady Derek was vigorously "pleasing" on the sly.

Bellamy considered the information about Honor Gannon and Jace Rule more closely. It just might come in handy.

It was time to get back to work.

Bellamy turned back toward the hotel so abruptly that he bumped hard into the heavily jowled man walking behind him. He was about to growl his annoyance when he saw the badge on the old man's chest. Instead, he smiled and said, "Sorry. I guess I should look where I'm going."

Bellamy retained his smile with pure strength of will as the old man scrutinized him, then grunted in return and continued on his way. His smile faded as he made his way more carefully down the boardwalk. Sheriff Carter. Bellamy made it his business to find out who and where the local peace officers were in any town he entered, just to be safe. He also made it a point not to bring himself to their attention, even if the sheriff turned out to be nothing more than a figurehead like that old man.

Bellamy dismissed the sheriff from his mind as he increased his pace. Yes, he had things to do.

Chapter Ten

"What in hell happened? It doesn't look like this fella is going to make it."

Randy stood beside the stall where Jace's buckskin gelding lay, its breathing labored. Jace had no answer to give him. He had returned from a long day of work, his second day back, with his mount staggering so badly that he had been forced to dismount and lead the animal the rest of the way home. He had barely put the horse back in its stall when it collapsed. He was at a loss to explain the animal's sudden malady.

The buckskin's condition had rapidly deteriorated, although Jace had done his best to treat it with the medicines available. Nothing had seemed to help; and now, with twilight shadows lengthening, it indeed appeared the gelding would not live through the night.

Randy glanced back at Big John and Mitch as they approached the stall. He shook his head, then addressed Jace again. "This horse was fine a couple of days ago. He shows no signs of a disease even now— just stomach problems. Did he get into something he shouldn't have? If he did, we need to know."

"He was with the rest of the horses all day, by the stream."

"Well, the rest of them are fine," Randy mumbled. "Buck is going to be madder than a hornet when he hears about this. We can't afford to lose any stock on this ranch."

At a loss, Jace maintained his silence. Everything Randy said was true, and if it weren't for the fresh bootprints and the marks on the tree Jace had discovered a few days previously, he might have considered this nothing but bad luck.

Jace took a quick step forward as the buckskin shuddered abruptly and breathed its last.

The silence in the barn grew almost palpable.

Sincere, Jace said, "I'm sorry. I don't know what to say except that I don't know how this happened to him."

"It ain't your fault, Jace." Speaking up for the first time, Big John consoled, "That big fella must've had something working in him when you started riding him, but Randy's right. Buck's going to have a fit over this one." He shrugged. "I'm glad I don't have to tell him."

Jace said, "I'll tell him. He'll want to talk to me anyway to find out what happened."

"No, I'll handle it." Randy's mouth was a hard line. "Buck would expect me to. Get rid of the carcass as fast as you can, just in case." He added in an afterthought, "Whistler isn't ready to ride yet, Jace, so you'd better rustle up one of the other horses from the pasture to ride tomorrow."

Jace watched in silence as Randy headed for the house.

Mitch spoke up quietly, "Come on, we'll help you clean up this stall."

Jace had seen the looks the men had exchanged despite their offers of help. An accident that temporarily disabled his own horse, and now a mystery that had killed his temporary mount. What was next?

It was a question he could not answer.

Impatient, Bellamy trained his monocular on the barn doorway. It was getting dark. He had seen Randy leave the barn and walk resolutely toward the house. If things went as planned, he would soon see—

A slow smile slid across Bellamy's lips as Rule and Mitch, both mounted, dragged the buckskin's carcass out of the barn. His satisfaction expanded as Big John walked out after them carrying shovels, his expression grim.

This second unexplained incident had been accomplished with the use of a simple poison that the greedy buckskin had eagerly consumed. The future incidents Bellamy intended for Rule wouldn't be as easily accomplished, but he was in no rush now. The complex situation at the Texas Star intrigued him. Rule had no way to escape what was in store for him with his mount temporarily disabled. Bellamy had all the time in the world to accomplish his purpose.

He lowered his monocular and turned toward his horse. Actually, he had a plan in mind that would allow him to achieve his goal and gain a very special, intimate bonus besides.

Poor Rule. He was going to end up wishing he was never born.

Buck was aggravated, and he didn't care who knew it.

Honor worked silently in the kitchen, cleaning up the last of the supper dishes as Buck met with Randy in the parlor. She could not miss hearing Buck as he ranted, "More trouble? I thought I recognized a good cowhand when I saw one, but it looks like I was wrong about that Rule fella."

"His horse falling was an accident, boss." Randy's tone was level . . . controlled. "As for the buckskin, that animal had to have been sick already when he took him out."

"There was nothing wrong with that buckskin! He was one of the healthiest horses on this ranch!"

"He was . . . but he ain't anymore."

There was a moment's silence before Buck asked unexpectedly, "What do you think of all this, Randy? Is this Rule fella just plain bad luck? Because I'm telling you, I don't need no more bad luck than I already got."

"I don't know what to say about that. Things haven't been going right for Jace, but he's a hard worker and we need him out there with us, especially now that—"

"Now that I'm lying around this house like an old sack of bones waiting for the grim reaper?" Not waiting for Randy's response, Buck continued harshly, "All right, we'll keep Rule on because we need him, but if he gets to be more trouble than he's worth, I'll put an end to it."

"It ain't right to start thinking like that, boss, about yourself or about Jace. You got sick. That could've happened to any one of us, just like any one of us could've had an accident like Jace. As for that buckskin, that wasn't Jace's fault."

"We need him now anyway. I'll get rid of him as soon as I can."

"Boss—"

"I didn't expect to keep him on, even if he worked out."

"Rule is a good worker."

"That's my last word!"

"You ain't being fair to him."

"Nobody ever said I was fair."

The sound of Randy's departing footsteps marked the end of the conversation, but Honor's sigh was cut short by Celeste's clipped voice behind her as she asked, "Did you hear all you wanted to hear?"

Honor turned toward Celeste. How Buck could fail to see beyond Celeste's calculated exterior was a mystery to her.

"Nothing to say? Your 'friend' Rule will soon be out on his ear."

Honor ignored Celeste's innuendo as she said, "You heard Randy. Jace is a hard worker. Buck needs him."

"Just like Buck needs you here—temporarily." Celeste smiled. "Don't get too comfortable. Buck lets you get away with speaking up, but that doesn't mean anything. You're temporary help—remember that. You won't be needed here once Madalane is able to take over again."

Halting her vicious diatribe at the sound of Buck's unsteady step approaching, Celeste turned in time to say, "Buck, are you all right, dear? You look upset."

"I'm upset, all right. I'm damned if I do and damned if I don't around here."

"What's wrong, darling?" ·

"Nothing. I'm going to bed. Are you coming?"

Honor turned away, her stomach churning as Celeste responded softly, "If you want me to."

Honor stiffened as Buck addressed her unexpectedly. "Make sure breakfast is on time tomorrow, girl."

Girl.

Honor's gaze was cold. "It always is."

"And make sure it's hearty. Me and the boys are going to have a long day tomorrow."

Me and the boys.

Honor stared at the shaky old man who had just uttered those words. She said incredulously, "You're expecting to ride out with the men tomorrow?"

Celeste glared at Honor before stepping between them to say, "It wouldn't be wise for you to attempt to do too much too soon, Buck. You're not well enough yet. You need more time. There's plenty of paperwork that needs to be done right here. We could do it together."

"Paperwork?" Buck turned sharply toward his wife, startling her with his intensity as he said, "Are you trying to say scribbling my name on some pieces of paper is more important than getting this ranch on its feet, when it sure as hell doesn't look like it's going to happen without me?"

"Buck!"

Honor stepped out from behind Celeste and said, "Maybe you *should* ride out tomorrow. That way you'll spend the rest of the week flat on your back in bed where you belong."

Buck turned his wrath in Honor's direction with a sharp, "What I do or don't do is none of your business!"

"You're not in any condition to ride out yet, and you know it."

Obviously furious that Honor had assumed control of the conversation, Celeste said, "You heard my husband! This is none of your affair, *girl*. We neither want nor need your opinion. You're hired help here, and nothing more."

Honor went silent. Their attention was riveted on her. There would never be a better time.

Honor faced Buck, furiously determined to speak her piece, but her fury dissipated at the visible effort Buck was expending to keep himself upright.

No . . . she couldn't attack a sick old man, no matter how she felt about him.

Instead, Honor responded, "I may be just hired help here, but I do my job and I do it well." She concluded coldly, "Breakfast will be on the table at the regular time tomorrow morning."

Honor turned back to her work, the sound of Celeste's cooing and pampering nauseating her as she guided Buck back to their room.

Honor's stomach twisted into knots. She couldn't take much more of this.

Celeste snapped the reins against the horse's back, picking up the buggy's pace as she traveled the familiar trail. It had been a damned long morning after a damned long night.

A familiar distaste crawled up Celeste's spine at the memory of Buck's bony hands on her skin when they had been abed the previous night. Not that she had needed to worry he would be able to consummate his pathetic attempts at lovemaking. Even *he* hadn't believed himself capable of that.

Celeste grimaced as the rendezvous cabin came into view.

Rendezvous.

At one time she had actually avidly anticipated reaching it. Derek had been an integral part of her plan then, and he and his gang of rustlers had been doing their part well. However, his effectiveness since the death of his men had become nil, and the fact that their relationship was presently purely physical was beginning to chafe at her.

She had seen the neckerchief tied in a distant tree two days earlier—Derek's signal to meet. She had not felt pressed to accommodate him under the existing circumstances, but she knew it might be dangerous to put him off any longer. Buck had fallen asleep and would be asleep for hours. Despite his protests that he would be able to ride out with the men that morning, he had been too weak to even try, but she needed to make sure Derek understood that she couldn't be gone long.

Derek was becoming too sure of her anyway. She didn't like the part of herself he seemed to bring to life so easily. It was gaining too great a control of her senses. Derek had no part in the overall plan to which she and Madalane had devoted so much of their lives. She had already resolved that no matter how Derek affected her physically, she would dispense with him if he became an impediment.

Celeste drew her buggy up behind the cabin and stepped down. She was wearing a yellow dress which clung to her in a way that proclaimed innocence while leaving men salivating. Derek was no exception, and she did enjoy her power over him. She would keep him salivating . . . until the end.

Celeste approached the cabin doorway. She stepped back with a gasp as it was jerked open to reveal Derek's livid countenance. "I don't like being kept waiting!"

Recovering, Celeste replied, "Don't you? That's too bad, because I couldn't get away."

"You never had trouble getting away before."

"Well, things are different now. There's so much going on at the ranch . . . so much trouble." Celeste couldn't help smiling. "Buck is a wreck with worry, poor fellow. The new ranch hand was injured—"

"You're talking about Jace Rule. He's the fellow who brought that Honor Gannon to the ranch."

"Yes, that's right."

Derek sneered, and Celeste went still. She asked, "Do you have something to tell me about that?"

Celeste felt the slow shift of power as Derek's appalling smile flashed. Impatient with his enjoyment of her uncertainty, she snapped, "Out with it, then!"

Derek took a step closer. The sour scent of him was perversely titillating as he asked, "What will I get for it?"

"I'm not in the mood for your games, Derek!" Despising her reaction, Celeste felt a carnal craving gaining life as she demanded, "Tell me!"

"It's something important." Derek took another step. He cupped her breast and squeezed it roughly. "It's something you need to hear."

"Derek . . ."

Derek slipped the bodice of her dress off her shoulder. She could hear his intake of breath . . . or was it her own as she demanded, "Tell me!"

"Not now. Later."

His thick fingers were fumbling at the buttons on her bodice. He wasn't opening them fast enough, and she brushed away his hands and loosened the buttons, allowing her breasts to slip free. She felt his hands on her nipples as she whispered, "Tell me."

"Not now." His mouth closed over a roseate crest, and Celeste gasped aloud, her senses rioting. She was groaning, writhing. Regaining brief control, she commanded sharply, "Stop! You'll tear my dress. Let me take it off."

At Derek's nauseating smile, she ordered, "Strip down, too, damn you, and I'll give you a time you won't forget. Then I'll listen while you tell me everything I want to hear."

Standing as naked as he moments later, Celeste repeated, "*Everything* I want to hear."

Not bothering to reply, Derek thrust her down on the unclean cot beside them and fell on top of her.

Honor walked slowly across the ranch yard. Celeste had taken the buggy out, the hands were at work, and Buck was sleeping. Yet despite the silence surrounding her, she was unable to think clearly.

What was she really doing on the Texas Star? If she had hoped to gain some respect for the man who had sired her, that effort had fallen flat. Buck Star was what she had always believed him to be: self-centered, demanding, ungrateful, unscrupulous. The list went on. He had no loyalty except to the Texas Star ranch and the young wife who manipulated him at will.

Even the joy of the moment when Cal had accepted her as his sister had somehow faded to an ache inside her. What had she accomplished by revealing their relationship to him? She had seen his face when she left him. He was worried about her, about the way Buck treated her, about how long she would be able to hold her tongue if Buck verbally abused her. And he was worried about her future—where she would go from there—when she knew he wasn't even sure what the future held for himself.

It was general knowledge that circumstances on the Rocky W ranch Cal shared with his new wife were almost as uncertain as those on the Texas Star. Cal couldn't afford to have his concentration split in yet another way with so much at stake in his own life. Unfortunately, Honor had realized belatedly that in telling him, she had merely added to his already mounting concerns.

Honor approached the bunkhouse. She needed to retrieve the baking tin the men had taken back with them the previous night. She remembered that Jace had remained silent when the hands had elected to draw cards for the last piece of apple pie.

Jace.

Honor swallowed against the ever-present lump in her throat each time he came to mind. True to his word, he had kept his distance from her, but she had felt his gaze burning into her whenever he was near.

He had confessed that he was an ex-convict and a killer. Yet that confession seemed at odds with the concern he had evinced for her from the first moment they met; with the emotion she had seen in Jace's eyes when he held her in his arms; with the tenderness of his kiss when he crushed her close—or with the beauty she had felt stirring to life within her as his kiss had deepened.

But he had pushed her away.

And he had walked away.

The reason was obvious, and she needed to force herself to face it. She had all but melted in his arms, and he had panicked. He cared about her—but not enough. It had been easier for him to walk away.

It occurred to Honor that she should be grateful to Jace for his honesty.

That sober truth resonated painfully inside her as she pushed open the bunkhouse door.

* * *

Jace glanced up as the bunkhouse door swung open and Honor stood silhouetted there. His heart began a heavy thumping at the sight of her. She was wearing that faded blue dress with an overly large apron wrapped tightly around her that inadvertently outlined her slender form too clearly for comfort.

And she was looking at him.

Damn, he wished she wouldn't look at him that way! She didn't seem to realize how her gaze affected him: how it made him long to stroke back those silky wisps of hair around her face, how it made him want to erase the wariness in those incredible eyes with his kiss, how it brought back the taste of her parted lips.

The memory of the wire scars around the trees bordering the trail unexpectedly conjured up the image of Peg's lifeless body. The image was a reminder too clear to ignore.

Jace straightened up. His hand was tight on the rifle he had been loading when Honor asked, "What are you doing here, Jace? I thought you were out working with the men."

"Randy sent me back for something he needed."

Her gaze dropped to his rifle. "He needed a rifle?"

Jace's expression hardened. "No, Randy needed some nails. _I_ needed the rifle."

The question in Honor's eyes went unspoken, and the knot in Jace's gut tightened. The wire marks on the trees where Whistler had tumbled couldn't be explained. The sensation of being watched had made no sense to him either.

Jace continued, "I saw signs of some varmints on the trail. I figured I might need my rifle."

"Oh."

He had the feeling she didn't believe a word of it. But there was something else bothering her, and Jace's heart pounded uncertainly as he asked, "Is something wrong?"

"No . . . nothing."

"Did something happen to scare you?"

"No." She raised her chin. "Besides, I don't scare easily."

"What's the matter, then?"

Honor avoided his gaze, and Jace studied her more intently. "Did Buck say something to you?"

"No." Those incredible eyes glanced up to meet his with a flash of anger. "What do you care anyway?"

Oh, he cared, all right.

He took a step closer, his concern deepening. "You'd tell me if something was bothering you—if something didn't seem right around here—wouldn't you, Honor?"

Her gaze challenged him. "Why should I?"

"Because I'm . . . a friend."

"Are you?"

Honor's response stung, and Jace took another step forward. "I need to know if something is making you feel uneasy. It's important."

"Why?"

She was holding something back, and a cold fear rose inside him. He had ignored the warnings the last time. He couldn't let that happen again.

In a few strides he had grasped her shoulders to hold her fast as he said, "Tell me."

"Tell you what?" Honor attempted to shake herself free of his grip, her eyes suddenly brimming with tears. "What do you want me to tell you? That I made another mistake yesterday that's haunting me?"

Another mistake?

Jace demanded, "Tell me what happened, Honor."

Honor replied defiantly, "I met Cal in Doc Maggie's office in town. He . . . he was so confused. He looked at me—" A sob escaped her throat and she rasped, "I told him who I was. I shouldn't have, but I did."

"What did he say?" Jace asked.

"He believed me, and he was happy—can you imagine? He said there was a part of him that had somehow known because . . . because I reminded him of his dead sister, Bonnie."

The heaviness in Jace's chest tightened.

"But I've only added to Cal's problems by telling him. He's worried about me now. He's afraid of what Buck will say when I tell him who I am—and in his heart, I know he's thinking about how Buck deceived his ma. Cal's suffering, because of me." Honor was suddenly trembling, "I didn't come here to do that, to make things better for myself by making things worse for him."

"Honor, darlin' . . ." Hardly aware that he had slipped his arms around her, Jace drew her close. He felt her shuddering and he clutched her closer. He heard her sob, and his own throat tightened. He whispered, "Cal had to find out sooner or later."

"No, he didn't. He would never have found out if I didn't come here. What have I accomplished anyway? All I've done is confirm that my father is a hateful old man who wasn't worthy of my mother's love, and that my mother wasted her life pining for a man who probably doesn't even remember her name. All I've done is cause more problems for the only family I've got."

"That's not true." Jace continued softly, "Love is special. You gave that to your brother, and he cherishes it because love makes a man feel he's worthy of much more than he ever dreamed. Love also makes a man feel he wants to take care of the person who loves him, that he'll do whatever he has to do to protect her."

Honor looked up at him. She whispered, "Is that really true, Jace?"

Honor's lips were so close. Yes, it was true. With Honor in his arms, that truth was so clear that he could hardly breathe.

Scarcely aware of his intent, Jace lowered his mouth toward Honor's to taste its sweetness—but a taste was not enough. Overwhelmed by the emotion that surged through him at the touch, he covered her lips fully with his own. Intoxicated by the beauty that swelled between them, he crushed Honor closer, sliding his hands into the silky warmth of her hair to hold her fast as his heart pounded and his hunger deepened.

Honor was made for his arms, he knew that instinctively as her softness melded to his strength, as her arms slid around his neck. He gave a soft groan of yearning. Her body fit snugly to his, and his yearning became a longing so deep that he scooped her up into his arms and carried her to the cot nearby.

He indulged himself in the taste of her mouth, the column of her throat, the hollows at its base that throbbed with her fluttering pulse. Her breasts were rounded and warm as he explored them with his lips. The bared flesh was exhilarating as he luxuriated in their heat.

Clothing that separated them slipped away. Flesh to flesh with her at last, Jace paused to look down into Honor's face. Her skin was flushed, her eyes glowing. His heartbeat rose to thunder in his ears as he whispered, "I didn't want this . . . not for you. I wanted to keep you safe, untouched by the dark cloud that seems to follow me . . . but I need this for *me*, Honor. I've wanted it from the first moment I saw you because I somehow knew how good it could be."

He slid himself inside her, and the world stood still.

Jace filled her. Honor gasped as the wonder of the moment soared. He had said he was no good for her. He had warned her to stay away from him because he couldn't stay away from her, but all the words fell away as Jace held himself still within her.

Jace lowered his mouth to hers to kiss her more deeply. He mumbled loving words as he began a heated rhythm inside her. She joined him, wanting him because she knew it was right; needing him, not out of fear, but out of a longing so intense that it stole her breath.

She felt him throbbing within her, and she knew the moment was coming. She felt her body respond with waves of ecstasy at each gasping breath, at each breathless thrust. His soft cry of culmination took her with him to soaring heights where she remained suspended for endless, exquisite moments.

The throbbing ceased, but the loving lingered as Honor lay in Jace's arms. He was still joined to her, his lips against her cheek, his warm breath against her hair when she whispered, "Jace, you were mistaken."

She saw anguish flash in his eyes as Jace raised his head to search her gaze. "You said you were wrong for me, but you're not. I know now that no one could ever be more right."

He kissed her then, a soul-searching kiss to which she surrendered with all the love in her heart.

Bellamy followed at a discreet distance as Rule rode away from the bunkhouse. He had been watching Rule the morning long, waiting for his opportunity. The buckskin Rule had ridden the previous day had been eager to cooperate when Bellamy had slipped up secretly to feed him. He had no doubt that the chestnut Rule was presently riding would do the same.

Bellamy was certain, however, that the reaction at the ranch wouldn't be the same when Rule's second mount fell. The men would look at Rule curiously, maybe suspiciously. They'd begin avoiding him, thinking Rule might be a part of something sinister. The old geezer, Buck Star, would raise the roof when told he had lost another horse.

He wondered how Rule would handle it. Even if Buck Star fired him, there was nowhere he could go with an injured mount and limited funds.

What a dilemma he'd be in!

Satisfied that the situation was moving in the direction he intended, Bellamy smiled, then lifted his hat from his head and ran a hand through red hair darkened with perspiration. Though his plan was working smoothly, he still hadn't been entirely sure how to finish Rule off in a way that would fully satisfy Coburn's need for vengeance. Rule himself, however, had provided the perfect solution when he had pushed that bunkhouse door closed behind him and Honor.

Bellamy had realized from the beginning that providing proof of the painful circumstances preceding Rule's death—a condition Coburn had demanded— would be the most difficult part of his task. News items in a local paper relating in detail the story of Rule's death would be exactly what was needed, but he had known Rule wouldn't get more than a few brief lines unless he could provide circumstances bizarre enough to warrant more.

The answer was now clear. Coburn's son had raped and killed Rule's wife, and, in a rage, Rule had killed Coburn's son. How bizarre would it be for Rule to find his new love, the Gannon girl, raped and killed in the same way as his wife?

Bellamy was sure Rule would come after him, just as Rule had gone after Coburn's son. That, of course, would be a fatal mistake, because he would be waiting for Rule in a place where Rule's intentions would be clear to all, where Bellamy knew he, himself, could be accused of nothing more than defending himself against a killer.

The irony of it all! When the story came out, it would be too delicious for a local newspaper to ignore.

Of course, the success of his plan depended on Rule's reaction to Honor Gannon's fate. The affair between them had to be more than a simple roll in the hay. Rule had to care strongly about the woman.

Bellamy considered that point a moment longer. Rule obviously didn't give his affections lightly. If Bellamy didn't miss his guess, Rule was a one-woman kind of fool who would have remained married and true to his wife for the rest of his life if not for Coburn's son, yet he couldn't rely on that assumption. He'd have to give Rule's feelings for the Gannon woman a little more room to grow, and in the meantime he'd satisfy Coburn's sadistic nature by producing a series of damaging incidents wherever Rule went, incidents which would surely be reported when Rule's story came out.

As for Honor Gannon, it wouldn't be difficult to lure her off when the time was right. The thought of the private time he would spend with her before he carried his plan to its conclusion warmed him in an area far distant from his heart.

Yes, he had always liked the look of her.

Bellamy mounted up and started for the pasture where the hands were waiting for Rule to return. He'd find a spot there and await his opportunity.

Bellamy's smile broadened. He was damned pleased with himself. He had become a real expert at his trade.

"What kept you?" Big John looked up as Jace approached. He glanced at the sun's position as it climbed toward its apex and said, "Randy's been looking for you for an hour, and he ain't happy."

"I went back to the bunkhouse for my rifle and I got delayed."

"If you had trouble with your rifle, you could've fixed it some other time. We was waiting for you."

"I didn't expect to take so long."

"I'm surprised Buck didn't come out on the porch to chase you off."

"Celeste was gone with her buggy, and Buck and Madalane were both asleep."

"It figures that Honor would be the only person left working on that ranch."

Jace did not reply.

"Well, you're here now." Randy walked up behind them, frowning. "There'd be hell to pay if Buck knew how much time we've lost this morning, so we'll have to make up for it."

"Just as long as we're not back late for supper." Big John shrugged. "That Honor is a damned good cook."

Randy did not smile. "Let's get back to work. I want to finish up here before the day is over." He turned back to Jace. "We put our horses down by that stand of trees. You might as well tie yours up there, too. We're going to be here for a while."

Jace nodded. It had been hard to leave Honor. It would be harder still to see her again when he returned to the ranch and act as if nothing had happened between them. But he had held Honor in his arms and made love to her, and if he was sure of nothing else, he knew it would not be the last time.

Celeste drove her buggy at a furious pace back toward the Texas Star ranch. Her delicate jaw tightened when she turned a curve and the house finally came into view. Derek had been insatiable, but she had not been of the same mind as he. With the thought of Derek's "important news" on her mind, she had quickly had her fill of him, but convincing him of that had been another story. She had finally been forced to make promises she was not sure she intended to keep before he would tell her what he had seen in town.

Honor Gannon and Cal Star meeting alone behind the closed door of Doc Maggie's office . . .

She had always known there was more to Honor Gannon than met the eye, and she was furious at the implications of the meeting. Was the bold witch a spy that Cal had placed on the ranch? She intended to get to the bottom of it, but she was not fool enough to tell Buck. No, she needed no complications when she was so close to achieving her end.

Celeste drew back on the reins, slackening the buggy's speed as she neared the ranch house. It would not do to appear upset. If he was awake, Buck would immediately notice, and she couldn't risk his suspicions. She had already placed Buck's will in the stack of paperwork that she and Buck intended to clear up before the week was out. She needed him calm and totally engrossed in her when that document rose to the top of the pile. She would then appeal to him, touching on every weak spot in his nature, areas she had come to know so well—and this time she would not be put off.

But the mystery remained. Who was Honor Gannon, and what interest did she have in Cal Star? Admittedly, Cal was handsome. Perhaps Cal was more like his father than she had realized. Perhaps Honor was an old flame hoping to stir the embers of their romance anew by allowing him to use her to report on conditions at the Texas Star. Or perhaps, more simply, the appeal of a new young woman in town had surpassed the appeal of the wife who waited for Cal at home. Celeste could not imagine that Doc Maggie would have any part in a situation like that, but Doc doted on Cal. The old woman would do anything that she could be convinced was in his best interest.

Celeste drew her buggy to a halt at the corral, stepped down, and started toward the house. She entered the kitchen and stopped short at the sight of Honor's back turned toward her.

The deceitful witch.

She asked coldly, "Has my husband awakened yet?"

Honor turned toward her, and Celeste paused. Honor looked different somehow.

"He's still sleeping. At least, he's still in his room. So is Madalane."

"So you've had a leisurely day amusing yourself at the stove."

Honor did not reply, and Celeste stepped forward to say more softly, "Remember what I said. Don't get too comfortable here, because you won't be here long."

Surprising her, Honor replied, "I never expected to stay."

Celeste countered, "Why did you come, then?"

"I thought that was obvious. I needed a job."

"That's all?"

"Should there be more?"

She acted so innocent. If Buck only knew that the kitchen girl whose spirit he obviously admired was involved with his son, he would be furious. She would be thrown out of the house in a minute.

But no, it wouldn't be wise to tell Buck, no matter how much she'd enjoy it. The girl was cunning, but she certainly hadn't learned anything important to convey to Cal. There was, however, always the possibility that Celeste could learn something about Honor Gannon if she tried.

Celeste started toward the hallway, then turned back to command, "Make sure supper is on time. Buck will be hungry, and I don't tolerate tardiness." When Honor did not reply, she snapped, "Did you hear me?"

Celeste saw the contempt Honor made no attempt to conceal as she responded, "I'd have to be deaf not to."

Celeste made a cold decision.

Honor Gannon would suffer for her arrogance before all was said and done.

* * *

Sheriff Carter's jowled face sagged as he took another stack of Wanted posters out of his bottom drawer and placed them on his desk. He hesitated a moment before removing his spectacles from his middle drawer, then glanced toward the doorway self-consciously as he adjusted them firmly on his nose.

Damn, it was tough getting old! He had been Lowell's sheriff for more years than he cared to count. The fact that he had been ineffective in catching the rustlers who had played havoc on the surrounding ranches a few months earlier, and that Cal Star had succeeded where he had failed, was a sore point with him. Cal was a nice fella. Carter liked Cal and he was glad that Cal had managed to put a stop to the rustling when he couldn't, but even though his eyesight was not what it used to be and his girth was broadening, he knew he was still a good sheriff.

One reason he was good was that he never forgot a face.

Sheriff Carter studied the posters more closely. The incident on the street a few days earlier still nagged at him. There was something about that fella who had bumped into him so abruptly on the boardwalk that allowed him no rest. He had originally attributed his feelings to annoyance at having almost been knocked off his feet by the man's haste. The fact that the fella had looked like he was about to give him guff until he saw his badge hadn't missed his notice, either. Yet he would have dismissed the entire episode except for that niggling feeling that he'd seen the man's face before.

Sheriff Carter frowned at the dust the ancient Wanted posters had raised. They were years old. He couldn't remember the last time he had looked at that particular stack, but he had gone through all the others without any results, and he could not let the matter rest.

His patient expression froze when he turned the next sheet. Studying it more closely, he read:

REWARD: $1,000 FOR THE CAPTURE DEAD OR ALIVE OF BARNEY HORN.
WANTED: FOR THE MURDER OF JOSHUA MILLER IN WACO, TEXAS.
DESCRIPTION: EARLY TWENTIES, MEDIUM HEIGHT, MEDIUM WEIGHT, CURLY RED HAIR AND DARK EYES. NO VISIBLE SCARS.

Sheriff Carter studied the picture on the poster more closely. That curly, shoulder-length hair was the same as the curly, carrot-red hair on the man who had bumped into him. That was probably what had rung a bell in his mind. The black-and-white picture on the poster had been professionally taken, obviously a vanity picture, to judge by the fellow's smile and the way he was staring so openly into the camera, and supplied to the law by an acquaintance. It looked like the kind of picture a man would get taken to please a woman. He was sure that Horn had his regrets about having had that picture taken. Yet there was no doubt about it. The fellow who had bumped into him on the street was older and probably craftier, but he definitely was Barney Horn.

Sheriff Carter took off his spectacles, folded the poster and shoved it into his shirt pocket, then returned the rest of the stack and his spectacles to the drawer. His heart was thumping as he stood up slowly, snatched his hat from the hook by the door, and headed for the Last Chance Saloon.

He told himself that there was no point in getting excited. It was likely that Barney Horn—if the fellow was still using that name—felt safe from the law after all the years since that poster had been issued. If Horn was still in town, he'd show up at the Last Chance sooner or later.

He'd get Horn then. That was the kind of lawman he was.

The setting sun shone fading pink rays through the barn doorway as the four wranglers inside stood motionless beside the front stall. The barn was so silent that Jace could hear himself breathe. He looked down at the body of his second temporary mount, the chestnut gelding that had been so full of life when he had saddled him up that morning to ride out with the men. The gelding wasn't full of life anymore.

Jace looked up as Randy questioned, "What happened this time, Jace? Buck is going to hit the ceiling when he hears about this, and I need an explanation."

"I don't have one." As incredulous as the other wranglers beside him, he said, "He was fine when I mounted up this morning. I didn't notice anything wrong with him until we started back to the ranch tonight, when he started stumbling."

"Like Whistler and the buckskin."

"No, Whistler didn't stumble. Whistler was steady on the trail. I mean, there was no warning. His legs went out from underneath him suddenly. It wasn't like that with the buckskin yesterday, or with the chestnut today. Both of them were staggering so bad that they were hardly able to walk by the time we reached the ranch."

"None of the other horses are sick, and the chestnut was out in the pasture most of the time, so he never got close enough to the buckskin for the ailment to have been passed between them."

"I can't explain it."

Randy frowned. "Buck's not going to stand for this, Jace."

"I don't blame him. I wish I could tell him more, but I can't."

Mitch asked, "Did you use the same saddle on both horses? Maybe there was something on the saddle blanket that might've—"

"I purposely used the spare saddle in the tack room."

Randy stared at him. "So, what do you want me to tell Buck?"

"You don't have to tell him anything. I'll talk to him."

"That won't do no good. Buck ain't the forgiving kind."

"At least I'll get a chance to have my say . . . and to apologize."

"You know what Buck will say to that—apologies don't do him no good." Randy stared at Jace a few moments longer, then said, "If you still want to talk to him anyway, give me a few minutes first. No use springing this on him without warning."

Jace looked back at the lifeless gelding. The brief time he had spent with Honor that morning had almost made him believe his life could still work out well. With Honor in his arms, he'd believed things were taking a turn for the better. He now knew he'd been wrong.

Randy waited for his reply, and Jace said, "I'll start cleaning up this stall while you're talking to Buck. Call me when he's ready to see me."

As Randy cleared the doorway, Mitch said soberly, "To put it plain, Jace, all these problems with your mounts don't look right to any of us. None of us knows you that well, but as far as *I'm* concerned, there ain't a reason in the world you'd have cause to start killing off the boss's stock. So I'm thinking this has to be a fluke."

Big John added, "We all know it ain't because you don't know your job. You're as good a cowman as any one of us, and I figure no fella in his right mind would purposely put himself in your position here." Big John forced a smile. "So come on, let's get rid of this carcass. We'll get it done in no time flat if we work together."

"No, I'll do it myself."

"Jace—"

"I want to."

Big John shrugged his beefy shoulders. "All right.

Whatever you say." He looked at Mitch. "We may as well go in to supper. Honor probably has it waiting."

Jace turned to look back at the gelding's lifeless body as they walked out the door. Yes, no fella in his right mind would put himself in the position he was in at the Texas Star.

The thought lingered.

"Who put you up to this? Tell me! I want to know!"

Buck's eyes were blazing as he awaited Jace's reply. He was raving, and Jace couldn't blame him; he had expected as much when he'd walked into the parlor to face him.

Jace eyed Buck soberly in return. Celeste stood silently behind him, her expression imperious. If Jace didn't know better, he'd think she was enjoying the situation, but that didn't make any sense either.

Without realizing it, Jace searched Buck's countenance for a resemblance to Honor. He saw none. No, that was wrong. There was no resemblance in the color of their eyes, but there was in the intensity of their gazes.

Jace responded under Buck's scalding stare, "Nobody put me up to anything. I can't explain what happened to those horses any more than you can."

"That's it, huh? That's all you got to say?"

"There's nothing else *to* say, except I'm sorry. Losing one horse that way was bad enough, but two . . ." Jace shook his head. "I won't forget it easily."

"You won't forget it and I can't afford it, even if I wanted to forget it." Buck grabbed the chair beside him to steady himself, but his harsh expression negated his apparently fragile physical condition as he said, "I told Randy if anything like this happened again, you were done for on this ranch, but I wasn't expecting you'd kill another horse the way you killed that buckskin."

"I didn't kill him. I didn't kill either one of them."

"What happened to them, then? It wasn't no disease."

"Stomach distress."

"That's bull!"

"It's the only answer I can give you." Jace paused, then continued softly, "I came in here to tell you personally that I'm sorry this happened, not to make excuses. I had nothing to do with the deaths of those horses. I happened to be riding them for the day, that's all."

"Coincidence, huh?"

"I don't know what it was."

"So what are you saying?"

"I'm saying exactly that. I don't know what killed those horses, but I know it wasn't me."

"Somebody else?"

"I told you, I don't know."

Buck's pale eyes narrowed. "Are you suggesting that somebody is trying to kill the stock on my ranch?"

"I told you—"

"I know what you *said*. Now I want to know what you meant."

Jace stared at Buck for silent moments. This was his opportunity to speak up, to let it be known that he had discovered the footprints and the wire marks that indicated his "accident" wasn't an accident at all. It followed that the deaths of his two mounts weren't coincidental, but there was no way for him to prove any of it—and nobody had to tell him that Buck had a less than understanding ear.

Jace replied cautiously, "I don't know if anybody is trying to kill the stock on your ranch. I only know that I'm not."

Buck's pale blue eyes pinned him. "It isn't you. It's just the bad luck you brought with you."

"Maybe."

"Not to say I hadn't been having my share of bad luck before you came."

Jace remained silent, waiting for the axe to fall.

Buck said unexpectedly, "We're short of help on this ranch. Randy says you're a hard worker, so I guess we need you here whether I like it or not. But I'll tell you now"—Buck took a shaky step—"if another horse falls under you, you're done!"

Stunned, Jace did not reply as Celeste grasped Buck's arm and said, "What are you saying, Buck? This man has brought nothing but trouble to the ranch. We're better off without him."

"Are we?" Buck turned toward Celeste sharply. "Doesn't it seem strange to you that everything's been happening to this fella? Like it's too coincidental? Hell, if he had fallen a little harder that first time, he wouldn't have made it up! That's straight from Doc's mouth, and I can't see somebody doing that to himself for any reason."

"So what are you saying?"

"I'm saying somebody's trying to cause trouble on

this ranch and make it look like him . . . and I want to know why."

"Why? Why?" Celeste shook Buck's arm angrily, her bright eyes brimming. "Do you have to ask that question? Your son wants to get back in your good graces, doesn't he? He's come to this ranch countless times pretending to want to help you get the Texas Star back on its feet, hasn't he? You've refused to talk to him every time."

"Cal gave up on that a while back. He doesn't care anymore."

"Really? For your information, Cal was at our door when you had a relapse, saying he wanted to talk to you. I sent him away."

"You didn't tell me that."

"Should I have allowed him to anger you when you were barely clinging to life?"

Buck frowned. "What's Cal got to do with this anyway?"

Celeste brushed away a tear. "You're getting desperate to fix all the problems that are happening, aren't you, darling? If you get desperate enough, he thinks you'll turn to him."

"Never!"

"He doesn't know that."

Buck glanced at Jace, then said to Celeste, "Are you trying to say you think Rule is working for Cal?"

Interrupting the exchange, Jace said coldly, "I'm not working for anybody but the Texas Star."

Celeste responded as if Jace had not spoken, "He's the new man here, isn't he? This new trouble came with him."

"I'd be more likely to say the trouble came *to* him."

"Are you blind, Buck? Your son—"

"Cal wouldn't do that . . . he wouldn't try to hurt the Texas Star in any way."

"You're not being realistic, Buck."

"Cal would never do anything to harm the Texas Star, I tell you."

"Why not?"

"Because his mother loved this ranch, that's why not! Because he loved her. His mother's buried on this land, and it's all he's got left of her."

"Your daughter, whom he killed, is buried next to her."

Buck did not reply.

"Well?"

"Cal wouldn't try to harm the Texas Star. There's more to what's going on here than is apparent, and I'll be damned if I'm not going to get to the bottom of it." Buck took a deep breath, then turned to Jace and said, "You heard everything I said, and I meant every word of it. I'm going to find out what's happening here. In the meantime, I want you working with the boys." He warned, "But keep an eye on your horse, because if you lose another mount, you're done."

Jace nodded. He heard Celeste whispering a soft appeal as he walked out the door. He did not glance back at the kitchen where he could feel Honor watching him.

Bellamy cursed low in his throat, damning the twilight shadows as he adjusted his monocular to no avail. He went still when he saw Rule emerge from the house, then saw the other cowpokes leave the kitchen to converse with him for a few moments before slapping him on the back.

He couldn't see their faces clearly, but something had gone wrong for his plan. The men showed no sign of either suspicion or aversion in the way they treated him. They actually seemed to be welcoming him back into the fold.

He didn't like it.

Honor watched as the men congratulated Jace. They had heard everything that had been said between Jace and Buck, just as she had. Every word had been audible, with Buck ranting the way he was.

Jace had deliberately avoided looking her way when he walked toward the barn. She supposed that was wise. If any of them knew why he had been delayed that morning . . .

Honor unconsciously sighed. She didn't like deceit of any kind, and there was already more than enough at the Texas Star. She wished she could talk to Jace, but she knew that would be a mistake at present.

Honor breathed a sigh of relief when the hands followed Jace into the barn and emerged with shovels in hand. They were going to help Jace whether he wanted help or not, and her heart warmed. They were good men. Buck didn't appreciate what he had in them.

With that thought in mind, Honor went back to her work. It would be dark before she was done in the kitchen. She shrugged. She supposed that was good.

She'd be exhausted before she went to bed and exhaustion would be her only chance of sleep after this eventful day. Her mind was whirling in endless circles.

Honor stored the last of the pans and looked up at the clock on the kitchen wall. Two hours had elapsed, but the kitchen was clean and she had made all the necessary preparations for breakfast. She was glad that Celeste had chosen to bring Madalane her meal. She had heard them conversing and was grateful that Madalane had not even bothered to come out of her room. The Negress's hostile gaze would've been more than she could handle that evening.

The house was quiet. Buck had retired to his room and Celeste had joined him shortly afterwards. The steady murmur of Celeste's voice had continued on endlessly, with Buck apparently saying little. Silence had fallen between them abruptly, and Honor had no doubt that Celeste was ensuring in the most intimate of ways that she had made her point.

The thought sickened her. Her father was a fool. She told herself that the angry, bitter old man she saw now must have been different when he was younger. She could not believe her mother could have fallen in love with a man so filled with hate as to disown his own son.

Her confusion exhausting her, Honor picked up the trash and walked out into the darkened yard. The men had long since dragged the gelding's carcass from the barn and disposed of it, and the bunkhouse was as dark as the house. It appeared she was the only person still working. That thought was amusingly ironic. She had come to Lowell to tell her father what she thought of him. She had intended to humiliate him by exposing his sins of the past; yet here she was, working in his house as much a slave to her emotions as her mother had been.

The only difference was that it wasn't love for Buck that kept her silent. It was compassion for a frail, sick old man who didn't really deserve compassion.

"Honor . . ."

Honor started. She stared into the darkness as Jace stepped into view. Her heart pounded as a shaft of moonlight lifted the shadows from Jace's face. She saw his hesitation as he said, "I have to talk to you."

"I heard everything, Jace." His expression was tight, emotionless, as if the intimate moments they had spent had never been. Anxiety nudged her senses as she said, "Even Buck realized that everything Celeste said about you and Cal working together against him is untrue. I don't really know what made Buck change his mind about firing you, but I'm glad. Maybe he does have some sense after all."

"I want you to leave the Texas Star, Honor."

"What?" Startled, she said, "Why?"

"It's too dangerous for you here."

"What are you talking about?"

"Your father was right about one thing he said tonight. Something's going on here that he can't figure out. Nothing that's been happening to me here has been an accident. I don't understand it, but it's true."

"I admit that this thing with the horses sounds strange—"

"It's more than strange. It's deliberate. Somebody is after me."

"No."

Jace moved closer. She could feel his body heat only inches from her as he whispered, "That first accident . . . I knew from Whistler's injuries that something was wrong. I went back to the trail to look around. A trip wire had been strung between the trees at the edge of the trail. That's why Whistler fell."

"That can't be. It must've been the remains of old fencing."

"The bootprints were fresh, and there was no sign of the wire, rusted or otherwise, except for fresh circular cuts into the bark of two trees where it had been pulled suddenly taut."

"But why would anybody do that?"

"I don't know."

"And you think the deaths of the horses—"

"One horse with stomach problems severe enough to kill it could be understood. Two horses, both my mounts, two days in succession, can't be coincidence."

"Maybe it's like Buck said . . . somebody wants to cause trouble for the Texas Star. Buck surely has made enough enemies in his life."

"It's not *him* somebody's after, Honor. Nobody would attack me to get to Buck. He couldn't care less."

Unable to deny his statement, Honor looked up into Jace's tense expression. She raised a hand to stroke the lines of strain from his cheek. He caught it and pressed it back to her side.

Uncertain, Honor questioned, "Even if you're right, why should I leave the Texas Star?"

"Because I can't. Whistler's injuries will need another week at least to heal."

"Jace—"

"I want you to pack your things and tell Buck you're leaving tomorrow morning. Celeste and Madalane will have to manage without you."

"I don't want to leave."

Honor unconsciously raised her hand again toward him, but Jace restrained it as he whispered, "You have to. I don't want you getting in the middle of whatever happens here."

"That doesn't make sense."

"It makes more sense than you realize." Jace clenched her hand almost painfully tight. She heard the anxiety in his tone as he whispered, "I told you I spent five years in prison for killing a man."

"Yes, but—"

"I came home to my ranch to find my wife raped and murdered. I went after the man who did it and I killed him."

"Jace—"

"It was my fault, Honor. Peg was town bred. I told her she should learn how to use a gun to defend herself on the ranch, but she was young and she thought I was worrying needlessly. She resisted, and I didn't insist. If she had known how to use a gun, it wouldn't have happened. I failed her."

"How could you have known what was going to happen?"

"There were signs. I just didn't see them until it was too late. The way Coburn looked at her. The way he always sidled up to her when he saw her. I laughed about it when she was uneasy."

"You couldn't have known, Jace."

"Well, I know now. It's not going to happen again. I want you out of harm's way."

"Why would anyone want to hurt me?"

"To get at me."

"But nobody knows . . . I mean—"

Jace's voice dropped a note softer. "I know what you mean, but I can't depend on that." He took a breath, then said in a rush, "Dammit, Honor, I can't even look at you for fear of somebody reading the way I feel about you on my face."

The look in Jace's eyes set Honor to trembling as she whispered, "How *do* you feel about me, Jace?"

"Do I need to tell you?"

Honor moved a step closer. The hard steel of Jace's body was warm against hers as she said, "Yes, you do."

Jace looked down at her for silent moments, then whispered, "I never thought I could love again when I came out of prison, Honor. I never *wanted* to love again. I fought loving you with all my strength, but the battle was lost the moment you strode so determinedly into my life—because in that first moment, I knew I cared." He whispered, "Surrendering to my feelings for you was a risk I wasn't prepared to take, but that choice was taken from me the first time I touched you. Yet I know now, that was a mistake."

"What are you saying?"

"I put you at risk when I took you into my arms."

"That's not true."

"It is. I can't let you stay alone here while I'm out working, don't you understand?"

"I'm not alone here."

"You might as well be."

"Besides, I know how to use a gun."

"Honor, please . . ."

Please.

But she could not yield to the plea in Jace's voice. Instead, she whispered, "I won't leave you, Jace. I can't. Don't you know that?"

Silence. Then with a soft groan, Jace crushed her close with his kiss. Held tight in his embrace, Honor reveled in her joy as his mouth moved warmly against hers, separating her lips to deepen the wonder. She loved him. That truth was clear in Honor's mind when Jace pulled back from her unexpectedly to whisper, "I want you securely away from here, but you feel so damned good in my arms that I can hardly bear to let you go."

She whispered in return, "I'm glad, because I won't leave."

"Honor—"

"You don't have to worry about me, Jace. I need to stay here, and I can take care of myself."

"I want you to be safe."

"And I want to be near you."

Jace's mouth closed over hers then, and the magic began again. She was mesmerized by its power when the sounds of footsteps nearby and clipped male voices startled them apart.

"It's Randy and Mitch," Jace said hoarsely. "They're

261

going back to check on the barn. They must think they heard something. You'd better get back to the house."

Honor nodded. She was about to leave when Jace drew her back into his arms. Her heart was pounding when he tore his mouth from hers at last and they parted to slip away through the darkness.

Chapter Eleven

Things weren't going exactly as Bellamy had planned, and his frustration was mounting. He stared through his monocular at the Texas Star ranch hands working in the sunny pasture. His stomach growled a reminder that the noon hour was fast approaching. He had camped on Texas Star land and had been on hand when the men went into the house for breakfast at dawn. The aromas wafting out from the kitchen had taunted him while the hands ate their hot breakfast and he had dined on stringy dried beef and warm water from his canteen.

Admittedly confused by the hands' attitude toward Rule, he had followed them covertly when they returned to the pasture where they had been working the day before. The simple fact that Rule was still employed on the Texas Star, and riding yet another Texas Star mount, amazed him. Buck Star was known to be a bastard who was quick to anger, a man who would not stand for losing two of his best horses to a new wrangler. The old man had to be suspicious that something was going on, but it appeared he wasn't looking in Rule's direction as expected. Evidently, the long history of misfortune connected to the Texas Star ranch was causing complications that he'd had no way of anticipating.

Bellamy considered that thought a moment longer. He still wasn't sure what to expect, and he couldn't afford any surprises about what Star and the men were thinking.

Bellamy made a decision. If he needed to adjust his plans, he would; but not before he cleared his mind about what was really going on at the Texas Star, and not before he could hear for himself the ranch hands' reactions to the events he had masterminded.

The men would soon stop for a noon break. They'd unpack their food, eat, and talk, and he would be there to listen. Aware as he was of the spot where they normally took refuge from the sun, he had positioned himself close by.

Bellamy lowered his spyglass and returned it to its case. He was suddenly impatient for the job to be done.

As if on cue, the hands dropped their tools to the ground and started toward the stand of trees where he was concealed. Bellamy moved deeper into the foliage with a smile. They'd never know he was there.

"That bay gelding looks as healthy as he did when you took him out this morning, Jace." Indicating with his chin the spot where Jace's mount grazed in full view beside the other men's mounts, Mitch said, "There's no way that horse is going to fall down underneath you tonight."

"He'd better not." Randy took another drink from his canteen, then added, "Buck's not expecting us to let that happen again."

"I'm not saying anything against Jace, but we didn't 'let it happen' the first two times, and I ain't letting the boss blame us," Big John said adamantly. "The only problem is, I still can't figure out how it did happen."

Randy addressed Jace soberly, "I don't know what the boss is thinking, either. I'd say you're a lucky man, considering that you're still alive and have a job at the Texas Star. I figure the boss has decided there's more to all of this than meets the eye."

Jace looked up, aware that the men were awaiting his input. They had trusted and accepted him. He owed them some explanation. The problem was, he didn't have any.

Jace responded, "I don't know any more than you do about what the boss is thinking. I only know *I'm* thinking that all the things that have been happening aren't a coincidence. I've had my share of bad luck in the past, but two horses dropping out from under me is pushing it."

"You're saying somebody's got it in for you." Randy was frowning. "Do you know who it is?"

"No."

Big John looked at him, openly doubtful. "If somebody had it in for *me* bad enough to do all the things that've been happening to you, I'd have an idea who it was."

"Maybe *you* would, but I don't."

"Come on, Jace!" Displaying sudden impatience, Mitch ran a hand through his graying hair. "I figure you have a right to your secrets, but those secrets are boiling over onto us, and we need to know what we're in for."

Jace eyed each man in turn, then said, "None of you fellas ever asked me where I come from or why I showed up at your door like I did—broke and hungry and looking for a place to set myself down."

"We figured you was the restless type." Randy flashed a smile. "I might've been the restless type, too, if I hadn't met up with Emma Star and this bunch. Emma was a good woman. She gave every one of us a direction to work toward on this ranch, a sense of being part of something worth striving for—except for Buck, who always seemed to have his own way of thinking. Emma died too soon. She didn't live to get all the good things out of life that she deserved; but speaking for myself, and I think for these fellas, too, she left us with a feeling that if we stuck it out, her dream would come true for her whole family, and we'd be a part of it all."

Jace listened in silence, then responded, "I'm not the restless type, Randy. I never was. I always had a clear idea of what I wanted out of life. It just didn't work out the way I hoped." Jace paused briefly, then said, "That's why I spent the last five years in prison."

"Prison!" Big John's eyes flew open wide. "I never would've figured you for that."

His reaction restrained, Randy asked, "What did you do to get yourself put there?"

266

"I killed a man."

"Damn!" Mitch almost dropped his canteen. "That fella must've done something pretty bad to make you angry enough to do that."

"He killed my wife." Jace stood up, restless as a familiar agitation returned. His face darkened as he said, "Don't ask me for details, because I won't give them. It's enough to say that the picture of how I found her won't ever leave my mind."

"I'm sorry, Jace."

"Yeah, I'm sorry."

"But that fella's dead . . . right?" Randy pressed, "It can't be him who's after you."

"Right."

"Then who?"

"I made some enemies in prison, and some enemies before I went to prison, but if I knew who could've done all this, I would've taken care of it." Jace added, "There's something else you got a right to know. That accident I had with Whistler, it wasn't an accident. Somebody strung wire across the trail and pulled it taut so Whistler would take a spill. I found fresh bootprints and marks on the—"

Jace halted abruptly and turned toward a sound in the brush behind them.

"What's the matter?"

Jace raised a hand to halt any further talk. He heard another sound, then dashed into the brush at the same time a male figure stood up and fled into the brush. Hardly aware that the hands were right behind him, Jace chased after the man. He ran faster, pushing aside the leafy obstacles in his path before becoming suddenly uncertain of his direction. He had lost sight of the fellow he was chasing.

Jace slowed his steps to a halt and looked around him, then turned abruptly at the sound of hoofbeats as a rider raced away from the scene. The fellow's shoulder-length, curly red hair was a burst of color that was easily visible underneath his hat as he rode out of sight.

Jace ran back for his horse. He took up the chase moments later, with the clatter of horses' hooves to his rear indicating that the hands were right behind him.

Jace slowed his mount to a halt when the thick foliage and hard-packed ground left him uncertain which direction the intruder had taken.

The moment stretched into minutes as the men drew up beside him and Jace realized the chase was over.

Randy asked breathlessly, "Who in hell was that, and why was he spying on us?"

"I don't know."

"You don't know?"

"You heard me."

"Well, he ran for a reason." Randy's expression was grim. "And since this is Buck's land, and whatever's going on is affecting him, too, I figure it's time you let him in on as much as you do know about all this."

His angular features grimly composed, Jace was forced to agree.

Bellamy cursed as he glanced behind him, then kicked his mount to a faster pace. He had lost the riders pursuing him, but that fact granted him little satisfaction. Despite his caution, he had not been able to control his reaction to the coiled rattler he had glimpsed nearby while concealed in the brush. He had jumped out of range of the rattler's strike, but in doing so, had alerted Rule to his presence.

A damned bad turn of luck!

Bellamy drew back gradually on his laboring mount's reins as he assessed a situation that seemed to change minute by minute. His own planning could not be blamed. It was the unknown factors at the Texas Star that continued to plague him. He needed to know more about what was going on there. He needed to know how deeply Derek Beecher fit into the scheme of things, and how Derek's actions might inadvertently have affected him. In short, he needed to be filled in fully about the Texas Star's past before he could expect to carry his plans through to a successful conclusion. There was only one man who could do that without causing suspicion.

Bellamy glanced again behind him, then drew his horse back to a moderate pace. Rule was smart. Not only had he insinuated himself into the perfect place for a man like him to hide, but he had also given up pursuit the minute he realized pursuit was useless.

No wasted effort.

Well, he would waste no effort either. Derek would give him the intimate insight into the workings of the Texas Star that he needed.

He had no doubt where to find him.

Bellamy turned his horse back toward Lowell and the Last Chance Saloon.

* * *

"Who was this red-haired fella you're talking about, and why was he spying on you boys?"

Facing Randy and Rule across the silent parlor, Buck stood rigidly still, awaiting a response. Celeste stood at his rear, ominously silent as Buck's intense, pale-eyed gaze moved between the two men. The silence grew strained, and Buck urged impatiently, "Well?"

Breaking the silence, Randy replied, "I reckon Jace is the person who can best answer your questions, boss."

Jace felt the heat of Buck's stare as he responded, "I don't know who the red-haired fella was, and I don't know why he was spying on us, but what I do know is that he was up to no good."

"That's easy enough to figure," Buck replied irritably. "He wouldn't have run otherwise."

Randy interrupted, "That ain't all, boss. Jace has more to tell you, and I'm thinking none of it makes sense to anybody but that fella who ran away."

Facing Jace, Buck said with obviously waning forbearance, "Spit it out, Rule! I'm getting tired of waiting."

Jace replied flatly, "My accident with Whistler wasn't an accident. I found fresh bootprints beside the trail and fresh cuts on two trees, indicating a wire had been strung across the trail to trip Whistler up so I'd be thrown."

"Why would anybody do that?"

"I don't know."

Buck's pale eyes narrowed. "You don't know, but it

follows that the deaths of those Texas Star mounts that fell underneath you weren't just coincidences, either."

"No, I suppose they weren't."

"You figure that red-haired fella was responsible for it all?"

"It would seem that way, but I never saw that man before."

"You're sure?"

"I'd remember a man with hair that color."

"You're saying that fella followed you to this ranch and started a war here for no reason at all?"

"Tell him the rest, Jace," Randy interjected. "About where you were for the past five years."

"Where you were?" Buck squinted. "Where would that be?"

"Prison, for shooting the man who killed my wife."

Buck heard Celeste's restless movement behind him, and he turned toward her with a tender solicitude in sharp contrast with his brusque manner. "Maybe you should go back to our room, darlin'. This might turn out to be too much for you."

"I'm fine." Celeste's exquisite features moved into lines of loving compassion as she continued, "Just as long as I'm near you."

Buck accepted Celeste's response without comment, appearing oblivious to the men's reaction to her fawning reply. He looked back at Jace and said harshly, "Tell me the rest, Rule. I need to hear all of it . . . now."

Jace told his tale from the beginning.

The room was silent when he finished speaking. He

271

was still uncertain what Buck was thinking when the old man said, "I figure this isn't all about you anymore, Rule. Whoever this fella is, he involved the Texas Star in his scheme, and there's no way he's going to get away with it." His expression strained, Buck continued, "Under other circumstances, I'd hunt out that fella right now and make sure he paid for those two horses he killed and the trouble he started here—one way or another—but that isn't going to be. So I figure I don't have any choice but to tell you both to go into town and report all this to the sheriff so you can hear what he's got to say."

"The sheriff?" Randy was incredulous. "Sheriff Carter's a nice enough fella, but he's an old man! He couldn't even get close to catching those rustlers who were running wild over this territory. It took Cal to put an end to that gang. You'd be better off getting Cal and his wranglers in on this than you would be—"

"I don't want to hear about it!" Buck flushed with wrath. "I don't want anything to do with Cal. He's not my son. He never will be my son again."

"Boss—"

Randy took a backward step when Buck ordered hotly, "Do what I told you to do! You and Rule get into town and tell that sheriff all you know. Carter may be old, but he's smarter than you think. He'll put you all on the right track."

"Yeah, sure, boss."

Conviction absent from his tone, Randy took another backward step before he turned to Jace and said, "You heard the boss. Let's head for town."

Hesitating, Jace stared at the old man who stood swaying unsteadily a few feet away. As frail as a twig, he was still a formidable force who would not be denied. Aware that Honor could hear all that had progressed from the kitchen, his heart sank.

When Jace remained motionless, Buck snapped, "Well, what are you waiting for?"

Yes, indeed, what was he waiting for?

The familiar din of the Last Chance Saloon and Dancehall was subdued as Bellamy swallowed the drink the bartender had placed in front of him, then asked casually, "Have you seen Derek Beecher in here today?"

The bartender's full mustache twitched with a half grin. "He ain't been in . . . yet."

Bellamy concealed his frustration as he motioned toward his glass and downed the contents as soon as it was refilled. He didn't like delay. A familiar apprehension was crawling up his spine. He could not afford to ignore its warning. That certainty set him on edge as he asked, "I guess that means you're expecting him in here later."

"Yeah." Apparently curious, the bartender asked, "Why the interest in Derek? You got something he should know?"

Irritated at the bartender's prying, Bellamy sneered, "That wouldn't be any of your business now, would it?"

Aware that his normally controlled temper was nearing the flashpoint, Bellamy slapped a coin down on the bar and turned toward the door. He stepped out onto the boardwalk, a bitter smile flashing across his lips when he glanced back at the sign over the saloon entrance. The Last Chance Saloon. Whether Derek knew it or not, that name suited his present situation. Remembering Derek's suspiciously hasty departure the last time they were together, Bellamy was still uncertain if his inadvertent association with Derek was one of the causes of the problems he had encountered. Derek was a loser. If he should refuse to provide the information Bellamy needed, it would prove a fatal mistake.

Bellamy looked up at the position of the sun in the cloudless sky. He was hungry and tired, and it seemed he would have hours to wait before Derek would show up at the Last Chance. He'd go to the restaurant for a decent meal, then go upstairs to his hotel room and sleep for a while before returning to the saloon. If Derek showed up as expected, he'd put a few drinks in front of him and flatter him into revealing all he knew about the Texas Star. It shouldn't prove difficult.

Bellamy's expression sobered. He'd then adjust his plans accordingly, and he'd get this damned job done with no more unexpected occurrences. He only wished he could be there to see Rule's face when he arrived just a few minutes too late to save his new love.

Afterwards the rest would fall into place easily.

Rule didn't stand a chance.

Sheriff Carter looked at Randy, then at Jace Rule as the two men stood a few feet away in his small office.

He considered the story Rule had related. Rule was a virtual stranger to him, yet Carter's old heart had begun a slow pounding at his mention of the red-haired man.

Still uncertain, Sheriff Carter looked at Rule more closely. "Five years in prison, you say."

"That's right."

"For killing the man who killed your wife."

"And I'd do it again," Jace replied stiffly. "No matter what it cost me."

Sheriff Carter studied the fellow's tight countenance for long moments before replying, "Normally, I'd say you was a fool for taking the law into your own hands, but there are times when a man behaves by instinct. I was married for thirty years before my woman died; and right or wrong, lawman or not, I'm thinking I might've done the same if I was in your place."

Jace did not reply as the sheriff continued slowly, "That aside, this fella who was watching you . . . he had red hair, you say?"

Randy replied in his stead, "It couldn't have been more red. I didn't get much of a look at him, but there was no mistaking that color."

Sheriff Carter opened his center drawer and pulled out a yellowed poster, then said tentatively, "How about this fella? Do you recognize him?"

Jace turned the Wanted poster toward himself so he might view it more clearly. The name on top was Barney Horn. He shook his head, uncertain. "I can't rightly say I've seen this fella before, but that long, curly hair sure looks the same, and if it's as red as the description says, I'd say he could be the fella we saw today."

"This here fella was in town a couple of days ago."

Jace's heart leaped. "How do you know?"

"He almost ran me down on the sidewalk." Sheriff Carter frowned. "He wasn't about to apologize, either, until he saw my badge and turned all smiles. That bothered me. I figured anybody who reacted like that to a piece of tin on somebody's chest had to be hiding something, so I dug out these old Wanted posters and there he was, smiling that same smile. The only problem was that when I went over to the Last Chance to find him, the bartender said he had already left town, and nobody knew where he'd gone."

Agitation flushed Jace's face a bright red as he said, "Did you try organizing a posse so you could go after him?

"I reckoned there was no need for that. That poster was years old and nothing new had come in here about him, so I figured he'd be coming back. No reason not to."

Impatient with the sheriff's seemingly indifferent attitude, Jace questioned, "What made you think he'd be back?"

"Because he paid for his hotel room in advance and left some of his things there, that's why. I didn't want anybody to know I was watching out for the fella, so I purposely didn't ask the desk clerk to tell me when he returned. The name he's using now is Bellamy. It seems he spent a lot of time at the Last Chance with one of the regular customers there, a fella named Derek Beecher. Nobody seemed to know or even care where Derek was, so I've just been biding my time. I had no idea that Bellamy might be up to something at the Texas Star."

Jace questioned, "Did you check on him today?"

"I've been keeping my eye out for him. He didn't come back last night, so I figured I'd check again later. I didn't want to look too interested."

With a growing respect for the aging sheriff, Jace responded, "If Bellamy is the fella who was on the Texas Star this morning, I need to talk to him."

Jace turned to the sober wrangler beside him. "I'll take it from here, Randy. There's no need for you to get involved in something that has nothing to do with you."

Randy's slight frame tensed as he said, "I'm already involved, and I'm not leaving until this is all settled." He added, "It seems to me that if this Bellamy fella is the same one who was on the Texas Star this morning, he's probably hot and thirsty. As far as I'm concerned, if he's in town, the best place to start looking for him would be at the Last Chance."

Sheriff Carter stood up in silent agreement. His jowled face creased into hard lines as they walked out the door.

Hardly conscious of the light buzz of conversation around him in the small restaurant, Bellamy shoved another piece of steak into his mouth and chewed distractedly. It seemed ironic that the slovenly, drunken companion whom he had silently scorned throughout their brief association in Lowell should end up being so important to him at this crucial point in his plans. Even more annoying was his realization that Derek was thoroughly undependable, that something as simple as a woman's agreeable nod or a bottle that was still half full might determine whether Derek showed up when expected or not.

Hardly acknowledging the waitress as she appeared beside him to refill his cup, Bellamy looked out the window. He had hours to wait until evening, yet he knew he dared not take another step until he—

Bellamy's thoughts stopped cold as three men strode into view on the boardwalk across the street. He watched, hardly moving as Jace Rule, a cowpoke from the Texas Star, and Sheriff Carter continued their steady pace toward the end of the street. The sight jolted him. Somehow he had expected that Rule would stay as far away as possible from the law, and that no one on the Texas Star would come into town to report something as simple as having seen a man lurking in the pasture that morning. Yet they were walking toward the Last Chance Saloon, and it was obvious from their expressions that they weren't looking for a leisurely drink.

Bellamy studied Rule a moment longer. There was something about him, a determination in the line of his mouth and in the set of his shoulders. His stride was almost predatory, expectant, as if he was primed for a confrontation he did not intend to lose.

The three men pushed their way through the Last Chance's swinging doors and disappeared from sight.

They emerged minutes later and headed for the hotel.

Bellamy's jaw hardened. Nobody had to tell him what had happened. Somehow, they had identified him.

Waiting only until the three men disappeared through the hotel doorway, Bellamy stood up, placed a coin on the table, and headed for the street. He forced himself to maintain an unhurried pace as he crossed to the hitching post, mounted up, and turned his horse out of town. He glanced back casually at the bend of the road before he slipped out of sight. The three men had still not emerged from the hotel. They had probably gone upstairs to check if he had slipped past the desk clerk unnoticed.

Safely out of view of town, Bellamy kicked his mount into a gallop. He didn't know what had turned Rule and the sheriff in his direction, but he was sure of one thing. It would take them some time to get organized. They had no idea where he would go or what he had in mind. That gave him the advantage he needed—because now he knew exactly where he was heading and what he was going to do.

Honor paced nervously in the Texas Star kitchen. The house was silent. Buck's conversation with Jace had seemed to suck the strength out of him. He had gone to his room immediately after they left and had not yet emerged.

Madalane had not come out of her room at all that morning, and Honor didn't expect her to. Madalane was paying the price for ignoring Doc Maggie's warnings about using the wheelchair before her leg was sufficiently healed. Her ambitious efforts had left her in pain and temporarily immobile.

Celeste had kept out of the kitchen, for which Honor was grateful. She had no patience for that woman's contemptible duplicity. She was uncertain if she would be able to maintain the civility she would need in order to continue her employment there.

The cold knot of fear inside Honor clenched tighter. She had heard Jace's entire discussion with Buck in the parlor earlier. She had longed desperately to cast aside all pretense so she might stand supportively at his side, but she had known she dared not. The memory of the tragedy years earlier still haunted Jace. It was important to him that she remain safe from any intimate connection to him until he learned the reason behind the mysterious attacks. She couldn't afford to add to his stress, but keeping her distance was hard. The thought of the mysterious red-haired stranger frightened her. Jace was at that man's mercy. She could not see how the sheriff could possibly be of help as things presently stood.

Honor took a deep breath. Meeting Jace when she first came to Lowell had been unanticipated. Realizing that he was as instinctively drawn to her as she was to him had left her shaken. Discovering the full power of the emotion they'd eventually come to share had brought her matchless joy.

She could not lose Jace to the vague shadows that threatened him.

Finding the wait more than she could bear, Honor

succumbed to impulse and turned toward the storage room where her clothes were folded. She removed her gun belt from underneath the neat pile and strapped it on over her baggy blue dress. She was walking resolutely toward the kitchen doorway when she heard Celeste command, "Stop where you are!"

Honor turned slowly toward her. Meticulously attired in a dress of soft pink, Celeste presented an ethereal picture that contrasted sharply with her shrill tone as she said, "Where do you think you're going?"

"I'm going for a ride."

"No, you're not. You're needed here. It's time to start getting supper ready."

"I'm going for a ride."

"I said—"

Her patience snapping, Honor said sharply, "I don't care what you said, I'm going to ride out to the pasture to talk to the men. If you don't like it, you can report me to Buck and I'll settle it with him later."

"You'll settle it with me, now!"

Honor did not bother to reply. She was striding out the doorway as Celeste screeched behind her, "You'll be sorry for this!"

After quickly saddling a horse, Honor turned toward the pasture where the men were working. A short while later, Mitch was saying, "There's nothing else to tell you, Honor. We was eating and talking when Jace heard something. Jace turned around to look, and that red-haired fella jumped up and started running the second we spotted him."

"It was Randy's idea to go back to tell Buck everything after Jace told us about that wire being strung across—" Big John stopped talking abruptly.

"I know about the wire strung across the trail. Jace told me."

Mitch and Big John exchanged glances, and Honor said, "I'm afraid for Jace. I don't want anything to happen to him. He . . . I . . ." Honor paused, suddenly realizing from their expressions that no explanation was necessary.

Big John consoled, "We don't want nothing to happen to him neither."

Mitch added, "Truth is, we've gotten kinda fond of that big fella, and we sure as hell don't like somebody coming after him on Texas Star land. We'll watch out for him. Don't worry."

Touched, Honor flashed a smile. "Thanks." She unconsciously sighed. "I suppose I have to go back to the house now. Celeste had a fit when I left."

"Celeste . . ." Big John's expression turned hard. "She's the worst thing that ever happened to the Texas Star." He added unexpectedly, "Don't worry about her. The boss will stand up for you against her. He's got that much sense, at least."

Honor nodded, suddenly beyond further conversation as she turned her horse toward the ranch.

Honor was still examining her conflicting emotions as she rode back along the trail, so she was unprepared when a rider spurred his horse out of the brush in front of her. She was struggling to retain control of her startled mount when she glanced up and glimpsed the blazing red color of the rider's hair—the moment before his clenched fist exploded in a burst of pain against her jaw, and darkness overwhelmed her.

Jace's heart pounded as he emerged from the restaurant with Randy and Sheriff Carter beside him.

They had missed Bellamy, and Bellamy knew they were after him.

Trudy had confirmed that fact when she told them Bellamy had left his meal half eaten and had ridden off no more than a half hour earlier, about the time they had gone into the hotel. They had taken the time to search Bellamy's room and the other rooms along the hall with the thought that he might have seen them coming and hidden there. In doing so, they had inadvertently allowed Bellamy time to escape.

Sheriff Carter grumbled, "He's gone again! Now what?"

The sound of a heavy step turned Jace toward Cal Star, who was stepping up onto the boardwalk beside them. Cal's expression was tense as he addressed Jace directly.

"I want to know what's going on at the Texas Star. Doc Maggie told me about all the accidents that have been happening since you got there, and they don't sound like accidents to me. It looks like you're thinking the same thing, if you got the sheriff involved."

When Jace did not immediately reply, Cal prompted, "It has something to do with that Bellamy fella, doesn't it?" At Jace's startled expression, he

283

said, "Nothing stays a secret in Lowell very long. Everybody's talking about the way you were all after him this morning."

Speaking up in Jace's stead, Sheriff Carter responded, "We've got a problem with Bellamy, Cal, but we ain't exactly sure what it is."

A sudden instinct prickled along Jace's spine and he said abruptly, "I'm going back to the Texas Star."

Cal grasped his arm, his expression grim. "I need to know one thing. Does any of this trouble threaten Honor?"

"I'm not sure."

Cal's grip tightened. "I need to know."

Freeing himself, Jace responded tightly, "All I can tell you is that Bellamy is after me for some reason, and now that he knows we're on to him, the only way he has left to get to me is through Honor."

Cal went still. He searched Jace's expression.

Apparently reading the response to his unspoken question there, Cal joined them as they started for their horses.

Disoriented, her head pounding, Honor emerged slowly from the tunnel of darkness that had engulfed her. She raised a hand toward her aching jaw and looked around her. She was in a dank, roughly built cabin that had obviously suffered years of neglect. Limited light filtered through filthy, broken windows, and discarded trash and broken furniture littered the interior, leaving little of the dirt floor exposed. She realized abruptly that she was lying on a cot that was filthy and spotted. A shiver rolled down her spine at the scurry of tiny feet in a dark corner.

Honor swung her legs off the cot, then clasped her head as a wave of dizziness held her momentarily motionless.

"What's the matter? That cot ain't good enough for you?"

Honor jumped as a man stepped out of the shadows near the doorway. The sight of his shoulder-length red hair clenched her throat tight. She reached instinctively toward her hip to find her gun belt gone.

"You didn't scare me much with that gun of yours." The man walked closer, and Honor went still. He was average in height and build, had fair skin and pleasant features, and his curly hair was a blazing red. If not for the sinister twist of his lips as he approached, he would have appeared surprisingly harmless. He continued, "I figured you didn't know how to use that gun worth a damn, but I wasn't taking any chances, so I got rid of it."

Honor said stiffly, "What do you want? I don't even know you."

"I know you, though." The fellow's sneer grew meaningful. "You put yourself in the middle of my plans that morning Rule came back to the ranch unexpectedly, when he pushed that bunkhouse door closed behind the two of you."

Honor felt her face flush.

"You thought nobody knew about you and Rule, didn't you? You were wrong." His gaze drilled into her. "To be honest, I don't know what you see in Rule. If I was a woman like you, I'd be looking for somebody more like . . . like me."

It did not miss Honor's notice that the red-haired man had continued approaching as he spoke. The cold, lifeless look in his eyes sent a chill down her spine. She glanced around her for an avenue of escape, but there was no clear path amidst the debris surrounding her. Shrinking backwards, she said, "Whatever your reason is for going after Jace, you're making a mistake."

"Whatever my reason is?" The fellow loomed over her. "The reason is money."

"Money?"

The red-haired fellow sat on the cot unexpectedly. His tone softened. "And I'm going to have a lot of it when this is all over and done. If you're real nice to me, I might even fix things so we can spend some time enjoying it together afterwards."

"You're crazy."

"No, I'm not."

The fellow reached for her, and Honor slapped away his hand. His face distorted into a suddenly vicious mask. "You're making a mistake. I can make this real good for you if you cooperate—or I can make it bad. It's your choice," he said.

"Make what good for me?"

"Do I have to spell it out for you?"

"Yes, maybe you do." Struggling for a way to gain some time, Honor said, "Everything that's been happening since I arrived on the Texas Star is a mystery to me. I don't understand any of it."

"You don't have to. There's only one thing you have to understand now." Grabbing her, the red-haired man crushed her tight against him, seeking her mouth with his.

Punching and pounding, Honor struggled to escape him. She was twisting and turning, squirming in his grip when he warned, "Stay still, you witch!"

Managing to get her foot free, Honor kicked out with all her might. At his howl of pain, she pushed him away from her, then ran tripping and stumbling toward the door. She pulled it open and took a step outside, only to be yanked viciously backwards by the hair and thrown against the floor.

Looking up, she glimpsed the fury on her assailant's face the moment before he raised his fist to deliver a crashing blow that thrust her back into oblivion.

Jace drew up at the ranch house and jumped down from the saddle as the men dismounted behind him. On the porch in a few long strides, he came face to face with Celeste as she walked outside.

Ignoring Jace, Celeste trained her heated gaze on Cal as he approached. She said, "What are you doing here?"

Jace demanded, "Where's Honor?"

Fury flushed Celeste's delicate features as she turned toward him and snapped, "I have nothing to say to you. I'm speaking to Cal. I want him off this ranch!"

Stepping up, Sheriff Carter began appeasingly, "Wait a minute, ma'am. We're here for—"

"I don't care what you're here for. I want Cal Star off this land!"

"Listen to me." Jace's warning tone turned Celeste toward him as he continued, "I don't care what you said or what you want. I want to know where Honor is."

"You're referring to our *kitchen help*?" Celeste sneered. "She left more than an hour ago. She said she was riding out to talk to the men . . . and I couldn't care less if she never comes back."

Jace went suddenly cold. "We just talked to the men in the pasture. They said she started back for the house. She should've been here by now."

"Really? Then she's probably lolling away the time somewhere like she always does. She pretends to work so hard—"

Panic-stricken, Jace interrupted, "You're sure she's not here?"

"Look in the kitchen yourself if you don't believe me." Turning as Cal took a step toward the porch, she exclaimed, "Not you! I don't want you in the house. Buck said—"

The rest of Celeste's wrathful statement was forcibly halted when Jace pushed her aside and entered the house.

He checked the kitchen. Honor wasn't there.

Somehow knowing it was futile, he looked into the storage room where Honor was quartered, and found it empty.

Back out on the porch within minutes, he met Randy, who reported breathlessly, "She's not in the barn or anywhere else in the yard."

"Do you think I care?" Celeste was beginning to rave. "Get off this ranch, all of you!"

Ignoring Celeste's rantings, Jace turned to Cal and said, "Bellamy's got her somewhere. I know it."

Sheriff Carter offered, "She might've gone into town. We could've missed her."

Haunting images flashed before Jace's mind as he said with sudden certainty, "No. It's like the last time. Bellamy's got her."

His face drained of color, Cal said, "There's an abandoned cabin not too far from here. It's totally isolated. Taylor and I used to play there when we were kids, but I don't think anybody's been there in years. It's the only place close by where Bellamy could possibly find shelter until dark."

Jace's tone was emotionless as he said, "Lead the way."

She was cold. Her head ached and her jaw was numb.

Honor opened her eyes slowly, then gasped aloud at the sight of the red-haired man standing over her. She glanced down at herself to see she was lying on the littered floor. Her dress had been torn down the middle and her breasts were partially exposed. She clutched her dress closed as the red-haired man said viciously, "Don't bother. You've wasted enough of my time already. I ain't waiting any longer."

Honor snapped back, "Why did you bother to wait? I'd think a man like you would enjoy taking a woman while she's unable to fight back."

"That's what you think, huh?" The fellow leaned down over her, then grasped the front of her dress and yanked her to her feet as he said, "Well, you're wrong. I want you to appreciate what's going on when I take you. I want to make sure you don't miss even a minute of what I got ready for you." He moved his hand over the obvious bulge beneath his belt as he said, "Besides, I like my women feisty."

"Stay away from me." Honor took a backward step.

"Not a chance."

Unprepared when he thrust her suddenly backwards, Honor fell down against the cot, frozen as the red-haired man advanced toward her. She managed shakily, "You said you're doing this for money. Who's paying you?"

"Ain't you figured that out yet?" Pausing as he loomed over her, he said, "Rule made a big mistake when he killed Walter Coburn's only son."

"Coburn's son raped and killed Jace's wife!"

"Coburn don't give a damn about that. Rule killed his son. That's all that matters to him."

"Jace already paid for what he did with five years of his life."

"Coburn wants him to pay *in full*." The red-haired man snickered. "Your boyfriend would've been dead already if Coburn had let me do things my way, but he didn't want me to make it end too fast for Rule. He wanted Rule to suffer before I killed him—and at the price Coburn's paying, I aim to please. I figure your boyfriend will feel real bad when he gets here and finds you exactly the way he found his wife all those years ago."

Honor's blood ran cold.

"Still can't figure it all out, can you?" The red-headed man sneered. "When we get done together here, I'll leave, but I'll make sure your boyfriend can follow my trail. When I get to a spot where I have the advantage, I'll let him see me first. That'll be the perfect touch. Then I'll finish him off just like Coburn wants."

"You won't get away with this!"

"Won't I? Who's going to care for more than a day or two if a jailbird and his girlfriend end up dead on a ranch owned by a spiteful old man who probably won't live out the year?"

"You can't kill Jace that easily."

The red-haired man laughed. "I've had a lot of practice."

"Not this time! Jace will—"

Honor halted abruptly as the man's head snapped toward the sound of a whinny outside the cabin. Suddenly alert, he drew his gun from the holster and walked toward the window.

He turned back toward her to say, "It's your boyfriend." Surprising her, he grinned. "It looks like this is going to be more fun than I thought."

Honor started as the red-haired man fired a shot out the window and yelled, "Stay where you are, Rule. If anybody comes any closer, I'll put a bullet in your girlfriend."

The man fired again, then said, "Did you hear me, Rule?"

Honor glanced around her. Debris of all kinds, broken furniture . . . She spotted a chair leg and reached for it cautiously. The red-haired man was waiting for Rule's reply as she moved silently toward him. She raised the chair leg and was ready to swing when he turned in a flash and struck her with the butt of his gun.

"Honor's in there with him." Cal turned toward Jace. "We have to get her out."

Jace could not immediately respond. Cal suffered at the thought of again losing a sister, while a sense of impending loss raged inside Jace.

"Stop and think a minute, boys." Sheriff Carter spoke softly, his voice calm. "Bellamy, or whoever that fella is, came here with something specific in mind. Jace was his target, not Honor. I figure if we're smart, we can talk him into letting Honor go . . . maybe if we agree to let *him* go."

"That's crazy!" Randy was the first to speak up. "He won't go for it. He'll think it's a trick. Besides, Buck would have a fit if we let him go."

"I don't care what Buck wants right now." Cal was adamant. "I want Honor out of that cabin safely, and I'll listen to whatever Sheriff Carter has to say if he thinks he can do it."

Jace made no comment as Carter began, "I said we'd *agree* to let him go, but that doesn't mean he'd get away. Hell, nobody knows this territory better than we do. We'd be able to track him, no matter how big a head start he has."

Jace said tightly, "You're talking like we're in control here. We're not. Bellamy is in control as long as he has Honor, and he knows it."

"I don't agree." Sheriff Carter was adamant. "A

fella always thinks twice when he sees his life flashing before him. He'll talk to us—to me. I know he will."

Gunshots rang out unexpectedly from the cabin, striking the ground close by, and Jace turned to Cal, questioning, "Is there a back entrance to that cabin, Cal?"

"A door, but it was boarded up long ago."

"Any other way to sneak up on him?"

Cal shook his head. "That cabin may be old, but it's a fortress. Taylor and I tried a hundred ways to sneak up on each other there. It never worked."

Sheriff Carter said, "So it's my way or no way." Not waiting for a reply, he turned toward the cabin and called out, "Bellamy, we need to talk."

Bellamy's voice rebounded in immediate response, "I don't want to talk. I want a horse brought to the front door of this cabin so me and my lady friend can mount up and ride off nice and peaceful like."

Carter shouted back, "Let's talk about it. I'll come out without my gun, to show you I mean what I say. I'll come into the cabin to talk to you personally, if you want."

"Stay where you are! I told you what I want. There's only one way you'll get Jace's girlfriend out of here alive, and that's to bring me my horse."

Determined, Sheriff Carter said, "I'm coming out."

"I'm warning you."

Before anyone could stop him, Sheriff Carter stood up and stepped out into the open. His lined face sober, he tossed his gun onto the ground and said, "It's time to make a deal, Bellamy. We—"

A single gunshot dropped Sheriff Carter on the spot.

Jace surged instinctively forward. Dodging a hail of Bellamy's bullets, he dragged Carter's body back under cover. He was still struggling to catch his breath as Randy examined the sheriff's wound and Bellamy called out, "I warned you. Now, get my horse."

Jace stared at the bloody circle widening on Sheriff Carter's chest.

Suddenly coldly certain, Jace said, "Bellamy won't let Honor live even if we agree to his terms. There has to be another way, and we can't waste time finding it."

"Stay where you are." Bellamy's eyes were ice as Honor lay where she had fallen.

Still disoriented from his blow, Honor remained motionless as he glanced back out the window and said, "Your head had better clear up fast, because we're going out of here together in a few minutes."

At Honor's obvious confusion, Bellamy said, "That old boy sheriff did me a favor by making himself a perfect target. That's one less man to worry about out there."

"What did you do?"

"What do you think I did? He was a bullheaded old fool. I had to prove to him and to the others who was in charge. With the sheriff's body lying out there, they know I mean what I say."

"I won't go with you."

Bellamy's smile turned sinister. "Your boyfriend

will probably be the first one to try to save you if I appear without you. He'll be a perfect target."

"No!"

"There won't be no shooting if you come with me real easy like when they bring up my horse."

"They'll come after you."

"But the odds will be better for both of us. Think about it. You might even get away."

"I'm not that stupid. You'll kill me just like you killed the sheriff as soon as you don't need me anymore."

"Maybe. But like I said, there's always a chance you'll get away. You don't have a chance here."

"You're crazy!"

"That's the second time you said that." His expression suddenly vicious, he said, "Say it a third time and you'll never open your mouth again."

A voice outside the cabin shouted, "Bellamy, can you hear me?"

Honor recognized the voice. It was Cal, but Bellamy seemed to make no distinction as he responded, "I hear you."

"We're bringing up your horse. We're going to leave him by the cabin door, like you wanted. We'll hold our fire as long as you hold yours."

Bellamy snickered as he glanced at Honor and said, "Get yourself ready. We'll be on our way in a few minutes."

Bellamy looked back toward the window as Cal shouted again. "If you come out without Honor, we'll figure . . ." Cal hesitated, then said, "We'll shoot."

Bellamy smiled widely as he replied, "Just bring up my horse and everything will be fine."

The eerie silence that followed was broken by the sound of a horse's hooves against the hard-packed ground outside the cabin. His attention in that direction, Bellamy reported victoriously for Honor's benefit, "They're bringing up my horse. It looks like—wait a minute. . . . that ain't Rule. That's—"

Honor gasped as a sudden crashing in the rear of the cabin jerked Bellamy toward the sound.

She cried out at the sight of Jace standing with his gun drawn in a doorway that was still partially boarded.

She screamed as Jace and Bellamy fired simultaneously.

She gasped when the gunsmoke cleared and she saw Bellamy still standing.

She caught her breath on a sob when Jace forced his way through the remaining boards in the rear doorway at the same moment that Bellamy toppled motionless to the floor.

Honor sobbed breathlessly as Jace clasped his arms around her. She closed her eyes briefly at the joy of knowing he was alive. She was still struggling to catch her breath when he drew back from her, his eyes dark wells of emotion as he whispered, "I love you, Honor."

Precious words.

Honor was hardly aware of the approaching footsteps outside the cabin before the door burst open and Cal rushed to her side. She turned toward Cal as he said with relief hoarse in his voice, "Honor . . . you're all right."

Honor clasped the hand Cal extended toward her. Still trembling, she composed herself enough to draw back from Jace and say softly, "Jace, I want you to meet my brother, Cal Star."

She held Jace's dark-eyed gaze for silent, intimate moments before whispering tremulously words that came from the bottom of her heart.

"Cal, I want you to meet Jace Rule, the man I love."

Buck was weak and unsteady, but he stood determinedly on the ranch-house porch with Celeste a step behind him as the solemn entourage approached. Randy had returned to the house at a gallop a short time earlier. He had taken only a moment to report that Sheriff Carter was badly wounded, and that he was taking the wagon back to the cabin so he and Mitch could transport the old man to Doc Maggie in town.

He had also said that it was all over. Bellamy was dead.

Buck had then waited for the entourage that was now approaching. He saw Jace, Honor, Big John . . . and Cal. He commanded as they reached the porch, "Stop there, all of you." Looking at Big John, he demanded, "Tell me what happened."

Big John shrugged. "I can't rightly say, boss. Me and Mitch got there when the shooting was all done. Sheriff Carter was lying on the ground, and Bellamy was dead inside the cabin. You'll have to ask somebody else to get the whole story."

Buck turned toward Jace. "What happened out there?"

Jace responded, "Maybe you should ask Honor."

Buck's temper erupted in a sudden flash. "What in hell's going on here? You all want a woman to speak for you?"

Honor started up the porch steps, and Celeste ordered, "You heard Buck. You weren't invited up onto this porch. You'd be better off if you kept in mind that you're temporary kitchen help, and that's all."

Ignoring her, Honor continued up the stairs. She halted to stare levelly into Buck's eyes as she said, "You want to know what happened, so I'll tell you. Bellamy was paid to kill Jace by the man whose son raped and killed Jace's wife. None of the accidents that happened here were accidents. Bellamy failed to kill Jace because Jace, Cal, and Randy made sure he'd fail."

Buck's lined face pulled into a sneer. "Don't try to tell me they're heroes, if that's what you're intending. Jace was only saving his own life, Randy gets paid for what he does, and Cal . . . Cal ain't worth a damn."

"How dare you say that!" Honor was suddenly irate. "Cal came to help the minute he knew something was wrong on the Texas Star. He has *always* wanted to help, but you're too damned filled with hate to let him! He risked his life out there today, and you don't even appreciate it!"

Celeste stepped forward hotly. "Is that so? Why don't you tell Buck the truth—why Cal rushed here to help, and why you're standing up for him now? It's because Cal Star's your *lover!* You thought nobody knew. You thought nobody saw you alone with Cal in Doc Maggie's office that day. You thought nobody would figure out that Cal is already tired of that plain widow woman he married and is starting to wander. You thought nobody would find out the truth—that you're Cal Star's *whore!*"

Honor took a step toward Celeste. Standing her ground, Celeste said, "Deny it if you can."

Honor turned toward Buck, her eyes sparking fire as she said, "What do you have to say about all this, Buck? Do you believe her? Do you think I'm Cal's whore?"

When Buck did not immediately reply, Honor demanded, "Well, do you?"

Buck's piercing stare pinned her, but Honor did not flinch. She saw his lips move wordlessly before he replied, "Celeste is upset."

"That's not an answer."

Buck snapped, "That's the only answer you're going to get."

"Why, Buck?"

"What do you mean, why?"

"Why don't you think I'm Cal's whore? Because there's something about me that holds you back from agreeing with Celeste? What is it about me that stops you? My coloring, maybe the way I speak, or the way I walk?"

"What in hell are you talking about?"

"Do I remind you of somebody, Buck?" Honor's throat choked tight. "Cal saw it right away."

"Cal saw what?"

"He knew right away that there was something special between him and me."

"So you admit it." There was a victorious ring in Celeste's voice. "She admits it, Buck!"

299

Honor took a step closer to the man her mother had loved, the man whose name her mother had protected to her death. She said, "Look into my eyes, Buck. Who do you see?" She whispered, "Do you see Bonnie?"

Buck gasped. He swayed momentarily. "Bonnie's dead."

"That's right, she's dead . . . but I look like her, don't I? Cal saw the resemblance, and it nagged at him. Others saw the resemblance but couldn't put their finger on it so they dismissed it. *You* saw it, and you refused to believe it."

"What are you talking about?"

"Do you remember Betty Montgomery?"

Buck went still.

"You never gave her a thought after that day she gave herself to you with love. I now believe that you probably forgot she even existed, but Betty didn't forget you."

Her voice taking on the sting of painful years, Honor continued, "Betty raised your child. She loved that child until her dying day, so much so that her daughter became determined to make the man Betty loved acknowledge her once and for all."

Buck said breathlessly, "You—"

"I'm Betty's daughter, Buck. I'm also *your* daughter."

"It can't be!"

"I have my mother's written word for it in dozens of letters she wrote to you over the years, but never mailed."

"I never loved Betty. I loved Emma."

Honor winced at the harsh cruelty of Buck's reply. She remained silent as Buck said, "Emma was the only woman I loved. I loved her until the day she died."

Honor rasped, "Just like my mother loved you."

"Don't listen to her, Buck." Suddenly frantic, Celeste rasped, "She's lying. She can't prove she's your daughter. She can't, because it isn't true."

Buck looked at Celeste. "Yes, it is. It's all true. Honor doesn't have to prove anything to me, because she's right. There was something about her from the first, and now I know what it was. Bonnie . . ." Buck's voice choked off before he forced himself to continue, "She looks like Bonnie."

Honor waited. She had dreamed of a moment when her father would acknowledge her, when he would accept her and love her. Yet—

Holding himself rigidly upright, Buck turned back to face Honor and said, "You're my daughter. I know that's true."

"And Cal's your son."

"No, he isn't!" A familiar flush returned to Buck's hollowed cheeks. "I don't have any sons."

Honor took a quaking breath. "Cal risked his life for me."

"He risked his life for himself . . . so I'd take him back, but he wasted his time. I'll never forgive him for being responsible for Bonnie's death."

Honor stared at Buck incredulously, then started back down the steps. She halted when Buck demanded, "Where are you going?"

"I don't know." Honor looked back at him as the trembling deep inside her expanded, "I only know that if Cal isn't your son, I'm not your daughter. It's as simple as that."

"You're making a mistake."

"Am I? Think about it, Buck." Honor continued in a rasping whisper, "On one side of me stands a man who claims he accepts me as his daughter while saying I was the result of a physical union that meant nothing to him. On the other side are two men who love me and have risked their lives for me. Which would you choose?"

"You're making a mistake, I tell you!"

Buck was shuddering, but Honor felt no sympathy for a heartless man upset because he could not get his way. She responded simply, "The only mistake made here today, Buck, is yours."

Her throat tight, Honor continued down the steps into Jace's arms. She heard the loving consolation he whispered in her ear. She felt her brother's palm stroke her back consolingly—and she knew, despite her tears, she would never be more truly loved.

Epilogue

Seething, Celeste forced herself to sustain a loving pretense as she slid into bed beside her husband. His bony hand stroked her, and she struggled against her distaste. An unexpected Star daughter had added a complexity to her plans that she had not anticipated. Buck had disowned Honor, yet the need to continue her adoring charade had never been stronger.

Celeste moved closer to her husband's emaciated body, steeling herself against her revulsion. Despite these new complexities, Buck was still under her control. Life at the Texas Star was returning to the norm she had so carefully cultivated.

Celeste assessed her situation coolly: Derek, unclean fool that he was, continued to entertain her while remaining as malleable as clay in her hands; Madalane had begun moving around the kitchen with less difficulty, and her cunning would soon return to its full potential; Honor, like Cal, had lost all favor in Buck's eyes; and she, Celeste, grew stronger in her sense of purpose every day.

Celeste allowed her husband's seeking hands the intimacy he sought with a mewling sigh and silent, inner conviction.

She would destroy Buck Star.

She would crush his entire family.

She would bring the Texas Star and everything Buck had accomplished at the price of her mother's blood to ruin.

Yes . . . she would accomplish that end, one way or another.

Honor moved restlessly in her sleep. She turned over and looked at her husband lying beside her. A heavy shock of dark hair had fallen forward on his forehead, and his compelling features were relaxed. Her gaze lingered. Jace's shoulders were so broad. They had carried a deadening weight for so many years, but he had emerged stronger and more loving for the adversity he had faced.

She smiled at the thick, stubby lashes lying against his angular cheeks, recalling the caress of his dark-eyed gaze. She sobered at the curve of his lips, remembering their warmth upon hers. Jace made love to her in so many ways. She felt it in his glance, in his touch, and in a tone of voice that spoke his love for her without the need for words. She recalled a time when she believed she had lost the only person who would ever truly love her, but she knew she would never feel that way again.

Moonlight shone through the bedroom window blind in the small house Jace and she now shared. It glinted on the plain gold band she wore, and the memory of the day Jace placed it there engulfed her. Family had surrounded them both on that special day: dear Cal, who treasured the sister still new to him and the new brother she had given him; Pru and Jeremy, who had welcomed them with love; Doc Maggie, whose eyes were filled with tears of joy; Randy, Big John, and Mitch, whose loyalty was firm and true; Cal's wranglers, whose devotion to the Star family now included Jace and her; and a smiling, recuperating Sheriff Carter.

Buck and Celeste were conspicuously absent, but she had not expected anything else. She had told herself Buck would never change, but although he had spoken the hard truth about his feelings for her mother without a twinge of regret, she was somehow unable to summon the same intensity of feeling against him that had previously consumed her. Buck was so infirm. She didn't expect he'd have much time. She wished with all her heart that he would come to see the error of his ways, most especially in denying Cal, because she knew it hurt both of them so badly. Yet she did not deceive herself that that would happen while Buck remained a loving slave to his young wife.

Honor had so many new blessings, but in her heart she knew that the anguish of having gained and lost a father in the space of a few short minutes would always be with her.

Despite Buck's absence, however, her wedding day

remained one of the most beautiful days of her life. The memory was a treasure she would always cherish, despite moments that still wrenched at her heart.

The ceremony, celebrated at Cal and Pru's ranch, had been everything she had dreamed it could be. She was still enveloped in its afterglow of love when Cal took her aside and hugged her tight. She sensed the pain that tinged the happiness in that hug, and she saw it in his eyes when he drew back and said tentatively, "There's something I need to ask you—something I need to know."

She had waited, expectant.

She was momentarily at a loss when Cal asked, "Did you send me the letter, Honor?"

She responded, "What letter?"

"About Bonnie."

When she did not reply, Cal withdrew a wrinkled sheet from his pocket and showed it to her.

Have you forgotten Bonnie?

It is time to go home.

The heat of tears had filled her eyes as she said, "No, I didn't send it, Cal. I'm so sorry."

He had explained then how those brief lines had caused him to return to Lowell after many years, bringing him to the place where he now stood. She had hugged him, sharing his pain as they returned to the parlor arm-in-arm, with the nagging mystery of the letter remaining.

Brought back to the present as the flickering moonlight touched the metal star lying on the dresser a few feet away, Honor recalled the day a short time after Sheriff Carter was shot, when Jace and she visited the old fellow as he recuperated in Doc Maggie's spare room. Jace had been stunned when Sheriff Carter placed the badge in his hand, saying the citizens of Lowell and he were agreed that Jace should carry on the proud tradition of wearing it now that he was retiring. Jace had protested, saying Lowell deserved a sheriff free of the stain of prison.

Sheriff Carter's response had touched her heart when he said, "You're a man of courage, Jace. You proved that to me and to everybody else in town when you risked your life for an old man who should have known better than to think a badge made him invincible. Lowell needs a man of courage who faces reality with a dream for the future. That's the kind of man you are, Jace. I know it. Lowell agrees. We want you to wear this badge proudly."

Jace had promised he always would.

But a lingering menace had continued to cast a shadow over their lives. She remembered when the wire from New York City was delivered. Jace had read it and gone silent. She took it from his hands to read that Jace's report on the circumstances surrounding Bellamy's death had dispatched two New York detectives to Walter Coburn's office to investigate the claims Bellamy had made before he was killed. Coburn had been incensed at the indignity. He had vigorously denied any part in hiring Bellamy. He was ranting his innocence when the first pain struck his chest and he sank to the floor. When the second pain struck, it ended Coburn's life and terminated the threat against theirs.

Honor moved closer to her husband and fit herself into the curve of his strong body. Her contentment soared when he tightened his arms around her.

Jace's brief kiss was sweet with a yearning he restrained as he whispered, "I remember thinking the first day I saw you that you were a woman whose mind was set on a course that wouldn't be changed regardless of what anybody thought about it. I told myself you were trouble, and that I'd had enough trouble in my life to last a lifetime. What I didn't know was that it didn't make any difference what my mind said once my heart had decided otherwise."

Jace's voice dropped a note softer as he said, "Love was a risk to me then, Honor, but when all was said and done, I realized the only true risk was that I might lose you."

Jace's eyes were dark pools of emotion as he said, "You brought purpose and meaning back into my life when I believed I had lost it forever. I loved you then, before that reality was clear to me, Honor, and I love you now that it's a part of me."

Jace's mouth touched hers and Honor separated her lips to deepen their kiss, aware that their love was a gift that neither of them had expected or intended.

Yet it was the gift that had brought them *home*.

* * *

The second letter was delivered. It had traveled far, but it lay still unopened.

The wording was concise:

"Have you forgotten Bonnie?
It is time to go home."
The question was deliberately and accusingly phrased.
. . . And the writer waited.

Turn the page for a special sneak
preview of the exciting conclusion
to the TEXAS TRILOGY:

TEXAS
TRIUMPH

Coming in April 2005!

Prologue

New Orleans, Louisiana—1869

The glittering New Orleans ballroom came alive with the lilting strains of a waltz. Fashionably dressed couples danced, laughing and conversing as they circled the polished floor to the gradually accelerating swell of music. No one appeared to notice as a handsome couple swept through a nearby doorway, then slipped into the seclusion of a darkened room.

Taylor Star closed the door behind him, not bothering to turn on the light as he released his beautiful partner and began removing his clothes. He stripped off his evening jacket and tie as his partner loosened the neckline of her crimson gown. They conversed in soft, tense tones.

"Did you get the information you were looking for?"

She whispered, "Of course, I did. Did you doubt me?"

"I never doubt you, Vida."

"It's Lisette this time, remember?"

"How could I forget?"

"We don't have much time. Pierre doesn't take lightly to having someone steal the woman of his choice out from under him. He'll be on my tail like a hawk."

Stripping down to her undergarments, Vida lay down on the couch. She groaned when Taylor flopped on top of her.

Not a moment too soon.

There was a sound at the door.

Taylor covered Vida's mouth with a passionate kiss as she mumbled, "You're crushing me, dammit!"

The door opened to reveal Pierre Maison standing in the opening. His lean, aristocratic figure stiff with subdued anger, he deliberately ignored Taylor as he addressed Vida haughtily.

"I thought you had better sense, Lisette. I assumed a young woman of your breeding would be impervious to the attentions of an infamous rake like Taylor Star, but it appears I was wrong. However, you will soon learn that you were the one who was made a fool of tonight, not I."

Allowing a moment for the import of his words to register, Pierre continued, "You will both leave immediately. Neither of you are welcome in my home any longer. You may be assured that I will personally see to it that from this evening on, you will no longer be welcome anywhere else in New Orleans where polite society meets."

Not waiting for a response, Pierre snapped the door closed behind him.

Taylor scrambled immediately to his feet. He pulled Vida up behind him, noting that she disregarded her partial nakedness as she reached for her clothes. Unable to resist an appreciative, purely male glance at the white swells of her breasts, he urged, "Make it quick, Vida. Our carriage is waiting."

Stepping out into the hallway minutes later, he guided Vida politely as they walked with heads high, ignoring the shocked whispers following them as they made their way toward the doorway.

Taylor returned Vida's amused glance as their carriage pulled away. Vida Malone. His smile lingered as he silently scrutinized the gleaming black of Vida's upswept hair, her flawlessly fine features, her dark, fathomless eyes, and the womanly proportions that turned men's heads—all inherited from a Spanish mother who had impulsively married a fast-talking Irish lad. That volatile combination had produced a woman of unusual beauty, sharp intelligence, keen sensitivity, and an adventurous spirit that was a match for any man.

A match for any man . . .

Impulsively brushing her warm lips with his, Taylor whispered, "You're beautiful, Vida. There wasn't a woman at the ball tonight who was your equal. It's no wonder poor Pierre was smitten."

"Yes, poor Pierre." Vida's smile dimmed. "Poor Pierre who grew wealthy on the blood of innocent seamen."

Withdrawing a sheaf of papers from the lining of her dress, she continued, "But poor Pierre will have much more than our perceived dalliance on his mind when we deliver this information to Allan Pinkerton and it becomes known that Pierre is responsible for the criminal activities that have almost brought New Orleans shipping to its knees."

"Another job well done, my dear partner."

Vida replied with a faint air of caustic acceptance, "And since Pierre will never learn how the authorities became aware of his criminal involvement, you'll escape our scandalous episode tonight completely unscathed—*as usual.*"

The clear blue of Taylor's eyes sparkled with amusement. "Actually, tonight added another layer of polish to my already sterling reputation as a womanizer. After a few days, I'll be more in demand at these society soirees than ever before."

"Of course, while I—"

"While you, my poor, unfortunate dear, will probably be banned from polite New Orleans society forever."

"It's a man's world!"

"Yes, it is."

Her expression suddenly tight with irritation, Vida exclaimed, "I believe you're actually enjoying this, damn you!"

"I am, to an extent."

"Taylor!"

"Vida, you know my reputation in New Orleans is valuable to the agency."

Vida's caustic smile returned. "What would Allan do without you?"

"Or without you?"

Halted by his unexpected response, Vida stared at Taylor for a silent moment, then said, "You mean that, don't you?"

"Of course, I do. I've never had a more competent partner." He added more softly, "Or a more appealing one."

Vida replied instinctively, "Your reputation is going to your head, Taylor."

"I meant every word!"

After hesitating a moment, Vida responded, "You probably did, considering that I'm the only female partner Allan ever assigned to you."

"That's true, too, but—"

"And don't think you'll be getting rid of me so easily. With a change of hair color, dress and demeanor, I'll be able to slip back into New Orleans without anyone giving me a second look."

"I'm counting on it. I'd miss you sorely."

"Taylor . . ."

The slowing of the carriage at his lodgings averted Taylor's gaze from the unexpected softening of Vida's expression. When he turned back, all trace of familiarity was dismissed from his tone as he instructed, "I'll pack up my things and leave New Orleans tonight for our meeting with Allan. Make sure you wait at least a day before following. We can't chance anyone becoming suspicious of collaboration."

Resignation heavy in her tone, Vida responded, "I'll endure the hypocritical whispers, properly chastised—*as usual.* Then I'll leave the city humiliated, never to return—*as usual.*"

"Vida . . ." Hesitating, Taylor linked Vida's gaze with his. Then appearing to think better of his intended response, he pushed open the door and whispered in farewell, "Allan and I will be waiting for you."

Taylor stepped down onto the sidewalk, then turned when the concierge stepped unexpectedly into view. The balding fellow handed him an envelope as he said anxiously, "This arrived for you a little while ago, Mr. Star. It's marked urgent."

Apprehension moved instinctively up Taylor's spine as he opened the envelope. He unfolded the single sheet.

It read:

"Have you forgotten Bonnie? It is time to go home."

Taylor went still as a melange of vivid, painful memories flashed across his mind. He was still staring at the letter when Vida asked, "Is it from Allan? What does it say?"

Volatile emotions suddenly overwhelming him, Taylor crushed the sheet in his hand.

Uncertainty rang in Vida's voice as she inquired, "What's wrong, Taylor?"

Taylor responded enigmatically, "Tell Allan not to expect me in Baton Rouge. I won't be coming."

Taylor did not wait for Vida's response as he tossed

the coachman a few coins and ordered, "Take the lady home."

"Taylor!"

Vida's exclamation trailed away as the coach jerked into motion and Taylor walked into his quarters without a backward glance.

Chapter 1

Lowell, Texas—1869

The bi-weekly stagecoach rolled to a halt on Lowell's deeply rutted main street. The door snapped open and a well dressed, middle-aged gentlemen exited the conveyance, muttering under his breath as he turned to assist an overweight matron down the steps behind him.

Deliberately waiting for the driver to finish tossing down the baggage, the fellow approached the gray-haired, heavily mustached fellow and said irately, "You may rest assured, my dear fellow, that neither my wife nor I will ever use this stageline again if drunken degenerates continue to be allowed to travel with decent passengers."

A veteran of countless years at the reins, the driver eyed the gentleman, then replied as politely as he could manage, "I ain't your 'dear fellow,' mister. My name's Pete Sloan, and I'm sorry to tell you this, but as long as a man pays his fare and don't cause me no trouble, he can ride in my stage."

The gentleman continued speaking angrily as Pete strode toward the open door of the coach and looked inside at the unkempt, unshaven passenger snoring noisily with an empty bottle of red-eye tucked in the corner of the seat beside him. Shaking his head, Pete said loudly, "Wake up, fella! Lowell is the destination you paid for, and that's where we are. It's time to get up and on your feet."

The man barely stirred.

Taking the two steps up into the coach with the spring of a man years his junior, Pete grasped the fellow by the shoulder and shook him hard. The drunk's eyes opened into slits of brilliant blue.

"You heard me, fella. Get up!"

The drunk unfolded his tall, spare frame slowly and glanced around him as he said, "We're in Lowell?"

"That's right."

"Well, I guess it's time for me to get out."

Hardly waiting for Pete to touch down on the dusty surface of the street, the drunk staggered down the steps behind him. He stood, swaying unsteadily as he looked around him.

Pete stared at the fellow, noting his unexpected height and breadth of shoulder and the brilliant, presently bloodshot blue eyes under dark brows. He studied the thick, unruly dark hair that hung against the fellow's shirt collar and searched the even features hidden underneath the unshaven stubble of a week-long beard. He said, "Seems to me I've seen you someplace before, fella."

"Maybe." The drunk turned to stare back at him. "What's your name?"

"My name's Pete Sloan. What's yours?"

"Hell, now that would be telling, wouldn't it?" The drunk laughed, then spotting the saloon at the end of the street, he said, "There it is, the Last Chance Saloon—just like I remembered it."

The drunk staggered away as the gentleman and his wife walked toward the hotel in disgusted silence.

Pete stared after the drunk. He raised his hand to scratch his head, then froze midmotion with eyes widening before turning in the direction of a storefront halfway down the street.

Bursting through the doorway minutes later, he stopped still when the buxom, middle-aged woman inside gave a start and said, "Dammit, Pete, you just about scared the life out of me!"

"I didn't mean to scare you, Doc, but . . ." Pete lowered his voice as he said with a touch of incredulity in his tone, ". . . but I'm thinking I just brought an old friend of yours back into town."

"An old friend?" Doc questioned impatiently, "What are you talking about?"

Pointing out onto the street at the tall drunk staggering toward the saloon, Pete responded, "Unless I'm mistaken, and I don't think I am, that big fella is . . . *Taylor Star.*"

* * *

Taylor paused at the swinging doors of the Last Chance Saloon. His slow, unsteady approach had allowed him time to covertly scrutinize the changes the years had wrought on the small Texas town that had once been his home. It hadn't taken him long to realize that the changes were few. The necessary businesses still lined the street behind false-fronted facades worn by time, and the most prominent establishment of all was still the saloon that occupied the greater portion of the street at the far end. He wondered if Miss Ida's fancy house was still located around the corner—a place he had come to know early on when searching out his pa after his mother's unexpected death.

Harsh memories of the past returned as the saloon's inevitable aroma of stale beer met his nostrils. His mother, dead at the age of thirty-six from an unexpected heart attack; his father whoring away his sorrow; his beloved little sister, Bonnie, killed in an accident only weeks later; his brother's departure from the ranch in the middle of the night. The tragic progression of events had come to a stunning climax when his father married a widow young enough to be his daughter only months later.

Have you forgotten Bonnie? It is time to go home.

No, he hadn't forgotten Bonnie. He hadn't forgotten any of it. His outrage still haunted him in the dark hours of the night, burning a hole inside him that he had never been able to fill.

Finally able to achieve enough distance from the emotion that the letter had induced, he had studied it as the Pinkerton professional that he had become.

The message had been cryptic and the note unsigned. That fact had made him wary. He had questioned the how and the why of it too; he'd had no contact with anyone in Lowell in recent years.

Professionalism had taught him caution, and a warning flag had gone up in his mind that he had been unable to ignore. Realizing he could shrug aside neither the letter nor the nagging images it had stirred to life, Taylor had known he needed to find out who had sent it and exactly what was intended. He suspected that discovering the answer to those questions would not be easy; and to his mind, there was only one safe course he could take.

No one watched his tongue in the presence of a drunk.

Suppressing the angst within, Taylor pushed open the swinging doors and staggered up to the bar. He was not surprised when the graying bartender failed to recognize him. He had been too young to be a customer years earlier, although his father was not. The bartender's summons to take his father home became familiar to him in the early days after Bonnie's death. Pa's drinking had stopped after he remarried; but, strangely, Taylor truly believed he would have preferred to see his pa still sagging against the bar, rather than married to Celeste DuClair, the woman who had so quickly turned Buck Star against his remaining son.

Taylor downed his drink, then tapped the bar for another as he glanced casually around the room. It was early in the day and the saloon had few customers. In addition to three weary saloon women lounging in the rear, he saw two wiry cattle-punchers seated at a table in the corner in laughing conversation. He didn't recognize them, but they appeared harmless. The dark, hairy fellow with coarse features at the end of the bar was also a stranger to him. The fellow also appeared harmless at the moment, but Taylor reserved opinion on that one. Then there was Jake Colt and Barney Wiggs, both engaged in emptying their glasses a few feet away. They did not give him a second glance, and he was glad.

Taylor noted that the bartender assessed him silently before saying, "You've had enough to drink, fella. It's time for you to move on."

Taylor smiled. Same old Bart, a saloonkeeper with a wary eye.

Emerging onto the street a few minutes later, Taylor continued his affected, wavering stance as he scrutinized the town. He turned toward the familiar voice when a robust, middle-aged woman appeared unexpectedly beside him and said, "I'll be damned. It's true. It is you, Taylor Star!"

Suddenly enveloped in an enthusiastic hug, Taylor felt his throat tighten as Doc Maggie released him just as abruptly, and with an uncharacteristic display of emotion, brushed away a tear and said, "Welcome home." Her smile faded when she added soberly, "You look like hell, boy. What happened to you?"

Regretting the deception he felt forced to maintain, Taylor affected a lopsided smile as he replied, "I'm glad to see you, too, Doc." He added with a wink, "So, where do we go from here?"

"I'll tell you where we're going . . ."

Back in Doc's office with a third cup of steaming black coffee half consumed in front of him, Taylor eyed the frowning, motherly woman in front of him. Apple-cheeked and full-figured, she still wore her graying hair in a tight bun and obviously still dismissed the importance of fashion, but Taylor felt a swell of warmth at the sight of her. His mother's friend and confidant, Doc had delivered all three of the Star children into the world. She had remained as close to the family as a blood relative. He had kept up an erratic correspondence with her during the lonely years spent back East in the military school where his father had banished him after marrying Celeste. With Cal gone and his father so wrapped up in his new wife that he seemed to have dismissed all attachment to the life he had led before Celeste entered it, Doc had been his only contact with home. She had been his lifeline, the only warmth remaining when other memories were too painful to recall. He loved her dearly, but even so, he couldn't afford to reveal the way he made his livelihood.

Interrupting his thoughts, Doc asked abruptly, "Are you ready to talk to me now, Taylor?"

"I'm always ready to talk to you, Doc."

A smile flickered briefly on Doc's lips. "Still the same silver-tongued devil, aren't you?" Sobering abruptly, she added, "But you're not going to wangle your way around me this time. I want to know what in hell you've been doing to get yourself in the condition you're in!"

"Doc . . ."

"Don't 'Doc' me! The last thing I expected was to

see you like this. The Taylor I remember was handsome, smart, headed for a future that would make us all stand up and take notice." Her voice thickened as she asked simply, "What happened to you, darlin'?"

"Nothing happened, Doc. I graduated school back East and I've been finding my way ever since."

"Finding your way . . ."

Taylor took Doc's callused hand in his. Seeking to provide her some kind of consolation, he said, "Maybe coming back to Lowell like this wasn't the best way for you to see me again after so many years, but—" Taylor took a chance and continued soberly, "But I got an unsigned letter a while back that mentioned Bonnie. It shook me up pretty badly. It forced me to come home, and coming home wasn't easy."

"A letter?" Doc's rosy cheeks paled. "You got a letter about Bonnie, too?"

Taylor's attention sharpened. "Too?"

"Cal came home a few months ago. A note about Bonnie also brought him back."

Silent at the mention of his brother's name, Taylor remembered the closeness Cal and he had shared while growing up. The memory of their harsh parting twisted tight inside him.

He asked bluntly, "Did you send those letters, Doc?"

"No."

"Do you know who did?"

"No. Cal doesn't know, either."

Taylor remained silent as Doc continued hesitantly, "Cal has married a fine woman he met here in town a few months back."

Cal . . . married.

Doc frowned and Taylor was suddenly wary. The years had not dulled his memory of that expression. She had something else to say that she was reluctant to add.

He prompted, "And . . . ?"

"And . . . you've got a sister."

Standing up abruptly, Taylor responded, "Bonnie's dead."

"You're right. Bonnie is dead."

Taylor waited for Doc to continue.

"Your sister's name is Honor. Her ma was your mother's friend, Betty Montgomery."

The knot inside Taylor twisted tight as he muttered, "That damned old man!"

"Honor's a fine young woman."

Taylor would not reply.

"She lives in town. You can meet her anytime you want."

"I don't want to meet her."

Doc shrugged. "That might be best, considering the way you look right now."

"I don't ever want to meet her."

"Don't talk like that, Taylor. Your ma wouldn't want—"

"Don't tell me what Ma would or wouldn't want, Doc. I know what she'd want, and she wouldn't want the proof of Pa's infidelity parading around the streets, reminding everyone of her shame."

"It isn't *her* shame, Taylor. It's your pa's."

"I don't want to talk about it."

Doc continued determinedly, "Buck's sick, you

know . . . damned sick, but the truth is it hasn't changed him none. He's still the same, hardheaded, stubborn old man—"

Doc halted abruptly when Taylor turned toward the door. She said as he reached for the knob, "Are you going to see Buck now?"

Taylor did not respond.

"Don't go off half-cocked, Taylor."

"Don't worry about me, Doc."

Taking the few steps to his side, Doc grasped Taylor's arm and whispered, "You were always such a bright young fella. I figured you could do anything you wanted to do with your life."

"Are you trying to tell me something?"

"I'm trying to tell you that the saloon isn't the right place for you to be. You're better than that."

Taylor's voice softened as he whispered, "I told you, don't worry about me. I'm fine."

Her eyes moist, Doc replied, "And damned handsome underneath all that dust and scratchy beard, I'm guessin'."

"Right."

"Don't waste all you got going for you, you hear? And don't go too far before we have more time to talk."

Unable to reply, Taylor turned and walked out the doorway.

The sunny knoll was achingly familiar. Feeling driven after his conversation with Doc, Taylor had approached it steadily, while unwilling to admit where he was going even to himself until his destination came into view.

Dismounting in a shaded spot, Taylor tied up his horse and turned toward the small, fenced-in graveyard. He halted beside the two gravestones, the ache inside him deepening as he read the inscriptions:

EMMA ELIZABETH STAR	BONNIE EMMA STAR
Beloved Wife and Mother	Beloved Daughter
Born January 10, 1824	Born May 3, 1853
Died June 12, 1860	Died June 29, 1860

The inscriptions were sadly inadequate.

The text on his mother's stone did not speak of her endless capacity for love, of her patience, understanding, or the gentle guidance she had extended to her children. Nor did it express the agony her passing caused for those she left behind.

Bonnie's inscription did not describe the laughter or the celebration of life the dear child had brought to each day. It did not speak of the laughter and joy she shared so easily, nor of the aching gap she left in the hearts of those who loved her when her brief life ended so tragically.

Taylor surveyed the small, carefully tended plots more closely. Freshly cultivated and raked, they were free of the weeds and undergrowth that covered the surrounding area. Freshly planted flowers bloomed in the fenced plot, a glorious burst of color that would surely have warmed the hearts of the two buried there, while a bouquet that had long since faded rested between the twin stones.

Doc's hesitant revelation a short time earlier returned to his mind, and Taylor felt again a wrench of pain. He whispered, "I've been away too long, and I'm sorry, Ma. A lot has changed in the time since I was here last. The living proof of Pa's infidelity now walks the streets of Lowell for all to see—another thoughtless cruelty dealt to you by Pa. But you always forgave him, although I never could. I was young when everything happened so unexpectedly all those years ago. I handled things poorly. In the time since, I've settled longstanding accounts for others, while I still wasn't able to face the unfinished business in my own past. I suppose that's part of the reason why that unsigned letter made me so angry, why it made me so determined to find out who sent it. But now that I'm here, it looks like learning who sent it is even more important than I realized."

After a moment Taylor continued, "The truth is, I never forgot either you or Bonnie. I never will, but I've come to realize that I can't avoid the past any longer. I don't know who sent those letters to Cal and me, or why, but I'll find out. And I promise you this— when I leave, you and Bonnie will rest peacefully."

Taylor's husky whisper faded into silence, but he was somehow reluctant to leave as he stared down at the weathered gravestones. The aching void inside remained, but a peacefulness and calm that had long escaped him now seemed to fill his soul. He wished that he—

Taylor turned abruptly at the sound of footsteps behind him. He did his best not to react to the sight of the tall man striding toward him.

"Hello Cal," Taylor said. "I don't have to ask how

you knew I was back. Doc sent somebody out to tell you, didn't she?"

Halting close enough so that Taylor could see the dark flecks in his brother's honey-colored eyes, Cal replied in a voice deep with maturity, "Yeah, she did. I suppose she thought I should know."

"How did you know where to find me?"

Cal shrugged. "Where else would you be?"

Yes . . . where else?

Taylor remarked, "You look more like Ma than ever."

"And you look like hell."

A smile touched Taylor's lips at his older brother's comment.

Cal scrutinized him more intently. He said abruptly, "Why the act, Taylor?"

"The act?"

"Others might be taken in, but you can't fool me. You're not the drunk you're pretending to be. What's going on?"

"I don't know what you're talking about."

"You forget, I know you. You may not smell right or seem to be in good shape right now, but I've seen that look in your eyes before. You've got something going on inside your head that you don't want anybody to know about."

Taylor inwardly smiled. Yes, he *had* forgotten.

Suddenly solemn, Taylor replied, "The truth is, there's only one thing I'm thinking about right now, and what I have to say has waited too long already." Taylor took a breath before continuing slowly, "I need to apologize to you, Cal. I'm sorry. I was wrong that last day when I said it was your fault Bonnie was killed. It was an accident. Nobody could've seen it coming, not even you."

The impact of Taylor's words registered hard in Cal's expression. Taylor saw the difficulty with which his brother swallowed before he responded, "I'm not so sure about that."

"Dammit it, Cal . . ." Taylor took an aggressive step. "I've spent countless sleepless nights going over that last day in my mind, and the answer is always the same. We both know Bonnie had gotten water from that well many times before. However the accident happened, however she lost her balance and fell in, you couldn't have anticipated it."

"I was supposed to be watching her."

"But Pa got in the way—him and that floozy he was easing his 'grief' with."

"Yeah . . ." Cal frowned. "Speaking of Pa—"

"He's sick. I know. Doc told me."

"He's not the man you remember."

"Is that supposed to be good or bad?"

Cal replied simply, "He's dying, Taylor."

Cal's statement sucked the wind out of Taylor, leaving him suddenly wordless as Cal continued, "But you need to know, he's still the same bastard he always was . . . maybe more so, now."

His breath returning in a caustic laugh, Taylor shook his head. "Somehow I wouldn't expect anything different." He asked, "How are things going with Celeste?"

"She's got him wrapped around her little finger."

"So that hasn't changed either, but she must have some good in her the way she's been taking care of Ma's and Bonnie's graves."

Responding with unexpected heat, Cal snapped, "Celeste couldn't care less about these graves. My wife's been taking care of them."

"Your wife . . ."

"Pru says the graves are her responsibility now that Ma and Bonnie are her family, too."

Silent for long seconds, Taylor commented, "Pru . . . your wife's name is Prudence, huh? That's one helluva moniker."

Truly smiling for the first time, Cal replied, "Yeah, but she does it proud. You have to meet her. We have Old Man Simmons's place now. It was left to Pru when the old man died."

"Settled in, are you?"

"In some ways."

Attuned to the note in his brother's tone, Taylor said abruptly, "Doc told you what brought me home. I need to know . . . truthfully. Do you know who sent the letters?"

"No."

"Pa?"

"He didn't send them. He still blames me for Bonnie's death. If he never had to see me again, it would be too soon. I expect your reception won't be much different."

"Doc?"

"She didn't send them, either. She'd own up to it if she did. And it wasn't Honor." He added cautiously, "Doc told you about her, didn't she?"

"I don't want to talk about her."

"Taylor, she—"

"I said, I don't want to talk about her!"

Cal shook his head. "Same old Taylor . . . won't give an inch."

"That's right, 'same old Taylor,' so I'm going to be honest with you and tell you exactly why I came home." Realizing he was defining his reasons for the first time, Taylor said, "The first reason was to find a way to apologize to you. I shouldn't have said what I did and I've regretted it. It was my fault that you turned your back on all of us at the Texas Star."

"No, it wasn't."

Not bothering to argue the point, Taylor continued, "My second reason was to find out who sent me the letter. I have the feeling someone wants both of us back here, Cal. I need to know why."

"So do I."

The realization that they were united in that cause kept Taylor and Cal briefly silent as they stood eye to eye. Taylor severed the silence to say, "So we know where we stand—but I need to warn you—from this moment on, believe only a quarter of what you hear about me, and even less of what you see."

"Taylor, what are you . . . ?"

"That's all I've got to say right now."

Cal studied Taylor's expression. He said abruptly, "Take care, brother."

Taylor shook the hand Cal extended toward him. He was unsure who took the first step when they embraced suddenly and heartily, and Cal whispered, "Let me know if you need me."

Taylor was mounted when Cal's horse disappeared back through the trees.

About to leave, Taylor glanced back at the two, solitary headstones, somehow suddenly certain that Ma was smiling.

From the Author:

I'm happy to hear so many of my readers are anxiously following my Texas Star series.

As you know, *Texas Star* (Book I, January 2004) relates the way the life of Cal Star, the eldest of the Star progeny, is impacted by the treacherous love-'em-and-leave-'em past of his father, Buck Star. How Cal's meeting with a stubborn young widow gives him the strength to face the demons of the past and accept the love that will heal his wounded soul, both thrills and warms the heart as it sets the stage for the second book in the series.

Texas Glory (Book II, September 2004) is the story of Honor Gannon, the illegitimate daughter of Buck Star, who journeys through the intrigues surrounding the Texas Star ranch, to find true love in the arms of Jace Rule, a man whose life is as filled with danger and unexpected turns as her own.

Texas Triumph, Book III in the Texas Star series, will reach the bookstores in April 2005. The third and final book in the series, it relates the story of two exciting, unconventional protagonists: Vida Malone, the Pinkerton Detective Agency partner of Taylor Star, the youngest of the Star progeny. Working both together and apart, Taylor and Vida are a formidable force that brings to a final, startling conclusion the mysteries of the Texas Star past, and the love that two powerful personalities can no longer deny.

The Texas Star series has been exciting for me to write. The characters remain in my mind as I hope they will remain in yours long after you read the final text of *Texas Triumph*. It has been my pleasure to bring the Texas Star series to life for you.

—Elaine Barbieri

TEXAS STAR
ELAINE BARBIERI

Buck Star is a handsome cad with a love-'em-and-leave-'em attitude that broke more than one heart. But when he walks out on a beautiful New Orleans socialite, he sets into motion a chain of treachery and deceit that threatens to destroy the ranching empire he'd built and even the children he'd once hoped would inherit it. . . .

A mysterious message compells Caldwell Star to return to Lowell, Texas, after a nine-year absence. Back in Lowell, he meets a stubborn young widow who refuses his help, but needs it more than she can know. Her gentle touch and proud spirit give Cal strength to face the demons of the past, to reach out for a love that would heal his wounded soul.

Half-Moon Ranch

Somewhere in the lush grasslands of the Texas hill country is a place where the sun once shone on love and prosperity, while the night hid murder and mistrust. There, three brothers and a sister fight to hold their family together, struggle to keep their ranch solvent, while they await the return of the one person who can shed light on the secrets of the past.

From the bestselling authors
who brought you the *Secret Fires* series comes . . .

Crosswinds
CINDY HOLBY

Ty – He is honor-bound to defend the land of his fathers, even if battle takes him from the arms of the woman he pledged himself to protect.

Cole – A Texas Ranger, he thinks the conflict will pass him by until he has the chance to capture the fugitive who'd sold so many innocent girls into prostitution.

Jenny – She vows she will no longer run from the demons of the past, and if that means confronting Wade Bishop in a New York prisoner-of-war camp, so be it. No matter how far she must travel from those she holds dear, she will draw courage from the legacy of love her parents had begun so long ago.

CHASE THE WIND
CINDY HOLBY

From the moment he sets eyes on Faith, Ian Duncan knows she is the only girl for him. But her unbreakable betrothal to his employer's vicious son forces him to steal his love away on the very eve of her marriage. Faith and Ian are married clandestinely, their only possessions a magnificent horse, a family Bible, a wedding-ring quilt and their unshakable belief in each other. While their homestead waits to be carved out of the Iowa wilderness, Faith presents Ian with the most precious gift of all: a son and a daughter, born of the winter snows into the spring of their lives. The golden years are still ahead, their dream is coming true, but this is just the beginning. . . .

Dorchester Publishing Co., Inc.
P.O. Box 6640
Wayne, PA 19087-8640

_5114-1
$6.99 US/$8.99 CAN

I Do

MIMI RISER

"Florrie or Dorie—'tis such a wee dif'rence. Dinna ye fear, lassie, Alan'll still wed ye," declares Angus MacAllister, chief of the Texas branch of the Clan MacAllister. And with these words, the mixed-up mayhem begins. When Dorcas Jeffries offers to temporarily stand in for the bride in a ridiculously archaic arranged marriage, she never imagines she will find herself imprisoned in an adobe castle or being rescued by the very man she is trying to escape. She is sure her intended bridegroom will be the worst of an incorrigible lot. But what do you say to a part Comanche Highlander whose strong arms and dark eyes make you too breathless to argue? What else but "I do"?